THE DRIVE-IN

THE
— DRIVE-IN —

A Double-Feature Omnibus

by
Joe R. Lansdale

CARROLL & GRAF PUBLISHERS, INC.
NEW YORK

Contents

THE
DRIVE-IN

This novel is dedicated to my very good friend David Webb, and to our nocturnal gatherings at the famous (famous to us, anyway) TRASH THEATER. I'll bring the nacho chips, Dave, you make the dip.

Acknowledgments are hereby given to all the drive-ins that have influenced this book. Among them The Lumber Jack, The River Road and The Apache, as well as a little sleaze drive-in that showed bad porno movies (perhaps a redundancy in terms, but these were *really* bad) across from the Baptist church in Turnertown, Texas.

Also, all the movies I've seen at drive-ins, good or bad: horror movies, motorcycle flicks, women in chains, the whole nine yards. And though many of the incidents in this book are influenced by things that happened at these drive-ins, the influence only goes so far, and it should go without saying that nothing here is meant to represent any individual or specific drive-in theater. The Orbit is a creature of this writing creature's imagination.

Fade-in/Prologue

I'm writing now about the time before things got weird and there was high school to kiss off, college to plan, girls, parties and the All-Night Horror Show come Friday night at The Orbit Drive-in off I-45, the largest drive-in in Texas. The world, for that matter, though I doubt there are that many of them in, say, Yugoslavia.

Think about it for a moment. Set your mind clear and see if you can imagine a drive-in so big it can hold four thousand automobiles. I mean, really think about it.

Four thousand.

On the way to The Orbit we often passed through little towns with fewer people listed on the population sign than that.

And consider that each of those cars generally contained at least two people, often more—not counting the ones hiding in the trunks—and you're talking a lot of cars and people.

And once inside, can you imagine six monstrous drive-in screens, six stories high, with six different movies running simultaneously?

Even if you can imagine all that, there's no way, unless you've been there, that you can imagine what goes on inside come Friday night and the tickets are two bucks each and the cars file in for The All-Night Horror Show to witness six screens leaking buckets of blood and decibels of screams from dusk to dawn.

Picture this, brethren:

1

A cool, crisp summer night, the Texas stars shining down like rattlesnake eyes glowing in a deep, dark wood. A line of cars like a tacky necklace trailing from the paybooth to the highway, stretching alongside it for a mile or better.

Horns are honking.

Children are shouting.

Mosquitoes are buzzing.

Willie Nelson is singing about blue eyes crying in the rain from a tape deck, competing with Hank Williams, Jr., Johnny Cash, ZZ Top, The Big Boys, The Cars and Country Bob and The Blood Farmers, groups and singers you can't identify. And it all rolls together into a metal-velvet haze until it's its own kind of music; the drive-in anthem, a chorus of cultural confusion.

And say your car is about midway in line, and clear as your first good wet dream, standing tall, you can see The Orbit's symbol—a big silver globe with a Saturn ring around it, spinning on a gradually tapering concrete pole jutting up to over a hundred feet above the concession stand; little blue and white fairy lights flittering out of it, alternating colors across your windshield. Blue. White. Blue. White.

God Almighty, it's a sight. Like being in the presence of The Lord of Razzle-Dazzle, The Dark Crown Prince of Blood and Mayhem and Cheap, Bad Popcorn. The All-Night Horror Show God, his own sweet self.

You drive on into this Friday-night extravaganza, this Texas institution of higher partying, sex education and madness, and you see people dressed out in costume like it's Halloween night (and it is Halloween night every Friday night at The Orbit), yelling, talking, cussing and generally raising hell.

You park your car, go to the concession stand. Inside it's decorated with old horror-movie posters, plastic skulls, rubber bats and false cobwebs. And there's this thing called bloody corn that you can buy for a quarter more than the regular stuff, and it's just popcorn with a little red food coloring poured over it. You buy some and a king-size Coke to go with it, maybe some peanuts and enough candy to send a hypoglycemic to the stars.

Now you're ready. The movies begin. B-string and basement-budget pictures. A lot of them made with little more than a Kodak, some spit and a prayer. And if you've watched enough of this stuff, you develop a taste for it, sort of like learning to like sauerkraut.

Drooping mikes, bad acting and the rutting of rubber-suited monsters who want women, not for food, but to mate with, become a genuine pleasure. You can simultaneously hoot and cringe when a monster attacks a screaming female on the beach or in the woods and you see the zipper on the back of the monster's suit winking at you like the quick, drunk smile of a Cheshire cat.

So there you have it. A sort of rundown of The All-Night Horror Show at The Orbit. It drew me and the gang in there every Friday night like martyrs to the sacrifice; providing popcorn and Coke instead of wine and wafer.

Yes, sir, brethren, there was something special about The Orbit all right. It was romantic. It was outlaw. It was crazy.

And in the end, it was deadly.

PART
ONE

THE ALL-NIGHT HORROR
SHOW
(With Popcorn and Comet)

1

I suppose, ultimately, this will read like a diseased version of those stupid essays you're asked to write in school each fall after summer break. You know, "How I Spent My Summer Vacation."

Guess that can't be helped.

This is where I think it begins.

It was Saturday morning, the morning after a night at The Orbit. We drove back to Mud Creek smelling of beer, popcorn and chocolate bars.

Our eyes were cloudy, our minds more so. But we were too wired, or maybe just too stupid, to go home. So we did what we usually did. We drove over to the pool hall.

The pool hall, or Dan's Place, as it's called, is an ugly joint in an ugly section of an overall pretty nice-looking town. It's the area where you hear about knifings and the lowlife congregating, twenty-dollar women, bootleg whisky and Mud Creek's drug deals.

Dan's was a beer drinker's pool hall, had a bar along with the tables. Theoretically the place didn't serve beer until after noon, but Dan and the guys who came there were real short on theory.

There were a few men in there when we went in that morning. Most of them were in their forties or older, and they were sipping long necks, their hats on their heads or on the bar or the stools beside them. Those without cowboy hats and boots wore blue and

7

gray work clothes with worn work boots, and it seemed that no matter how quietly you came in, they always heard you and turned to look with disapproval.

The place was supposed to be off limits to minors, but who were we to tell, and Dan wasn't telling either. Not that he liked us, but he did like our money for the pool games, and once in a small while, when he felt brave and we did too, he'd let us buy a beer, just like he didn't know we were under age.

But there was this: he always had a look about him that let us know he'd take our money, but for little or no reason wouldn't mind killing us for the fun of it. And he looked quite capable of killing us without breaking a sweat. He was kind of fat, but it was hard-looking fat, like there was a great iron washpot under his too-tight T-shirt. And his arms were big and meaty. Not body-builder arms, but workingman's arms; arms that had done real work: bounced drunks, and, from what I'd heard, slapped wives. He also had funny-looking knuckles; knuckles that had remolded facial flesh as if it were silly putty, and, in turn, had been remolded themselves.

Still, we'd go in there like men born for a suicide mission. There were things we wanted out of the place. Attractions. It was forbidden, for one, and that was appealing. Gave us a sense of manhood. Danger hung in the air like a sword on a hair, and as long as the hair didn't snap and the blade didn't fall, it was stimulating.

Dan's was where we met Willard. Saw him there the first time we went inside, which was about the time we started going to the drive-in. I guess we felt if we had permission to stay out all night, we could go over to the tough section of town and shoot pool. Maybe talk some about the twenty-dollar women we didn't dare actually speak to (we weren't even sure we'd seen any) for fear we'd have to shell out money and perform. Something none of us was sure we wanted. We had heard vague stories about viruses and carnivorous insects that grew like sourdough starter in the pubic

8

thatches of twenty-dollar women, and we felt that they would know so many tricks, and we'd know so few, that the cheap little hotel rooms where we planned to consummate our financial arrangements would ring of feminine laughter instead of the satisfying squeaks of bedsprings.

But the pool room and the possibility of violent death didn't worry us as much as sexual embarrassment, so we went there Saturdays to play pool and to watch Willard do the same.

First look at Willard, and he seemed downright skinny. But closer examination proved him long, lean and muscular. When he bunched over the table for a shot, let the cue glide over the top of his thumb, you could see the muscles roll beneath his hide, and the tattoos on his biceps popped forward and back so fast they were like billboards viewed on the highway at top speed. The left tattoo read KICK ASS and the right read EAT PUSSY. It was understood that he could do either, and probably quite well.

But Willard was a nice guy in an odd sort of way. Smart, too, if, shall we say, not classically educated. He was three years older than us physically, and about ten years older in experience.

That was one of the reasons we liked to be around him. He gave us a glimpse of a world we didn't normally see. Not one we wanted to live in, but one we wanted to investigate.

And I think Willard liked us for the reverse reason. We could talk about something besides beer, women and the plant where he worked all week and Saturday afternoons making aluminum lawn furniture.

None of us had to work. Our parents provided, and we were all college material. Had dreams and a good chance of seeing them come true, and I guess Willard wanted some of that hope to rub off on him.

We didn't really know much about him. Story was his father didn't think the kid looked like him at all, and had been told by some Louisiana Mojo man that the boy had a curse on him, and since Willard's mother, Marjory, was into weird business, like believing in old gods and voodoo-type stuff, this made him even more suspicious. Bottom line was the father left before the baby could crawl. Baptists around town called Willard and his mother sorry as part of their entertainment, and truth was, his mother was no prize. She later took up with a man who had a bad back and a regular check of some sort, and when he went away she took up with another with ailing posture and a steady government income.

This initiated a pattern. Men with bad backs and checks, and it kept Marjory in cigarettes and Willard in throwaway diapers. But when Willard turned sixteen, his birthday present was good-bye and the street—a place he spent a lot of time anyway. Marjory went away to who knows where—probably a fresh town full of bad backs and welfare checks—and Willard did the best he could. Dropped out of school when he was old enough and got some odd jobs here and there, the best of them being a projectionist at one of the movie houses. When he turned eighteen, he went to work at the aluminum-chair factory.

It seemed obvious to me, in the short time that I had known him, that he was hungry for something beyond that, something more substantial, something that would give him respect in the eyes of the Uptown folks, though I doubt he would have admitted that—even to himself.

But to get back to it, we came into the pool hall this Saturday I'm telling you about, and there was Willard in his familiar pose, pool cue in hand, leaning over the table, eyeing a ball.

Shooting against him was a guy we'd seen a couple of times before but avoided talking to. His name was Bear, and you didn't ponder why he was called that. He was six-five, ugly as disease, had red-brown hair and a beard that mercifully consumed most of his face. All that was clearly visible were some nasty blue eyes and a snout that was garage to some troublesome nose hairs thick enough to use for piano wire. The same gruesome down as in his nose also covered his arms and curled out of the neck of his T-shirt to confuse itself with his beard. What could be seen of his lips reminded me of those rubber worms fishermen use, and I wouldn't have been surprised to see shiny silver hooks poking out of them, or to discover that the whole of Bear had been made from decaying meat, wire and the contents of a tackle box and a Crisco can.

There was something rock 'n' roll playing on the jukebox—a rarity for Dan's, which mostly catered to country and western—and Randy went over to lean on it. Wasn't just because he liked what was playing, it put him closer to the door.

Being black, Randy was a bit uncomfortable about bopping around a redneck pool hall. Even if he was with Bob, who wore a toothpick-laden cowboy hat, dipped snuff and wore snakeskin boots. And me, Mr. Average and All-Around Natural Blender.

Wasn't that Randy was the only black that came into the place (though just about), but he was the only one that was skinny, five-five, with headlamp glasses and an inferiority complex. And, most importantly, he was the only black in there this morning I'm telling you about.

I guess if Bob and I had really thought about what we were putting him through as a member of our "gang," we probably wouldn't have gone in there in the first place.

This is not to say Bob and I weren't nervous. We were. We felt like weenies compared to these guys. But there were those attractions I told you about, and there was also our onrushing manhood we were trying to deal with, attempting to define.

When Willard raised up from his shot he nodded at

us, and we nodded back, found places to lean and watch.

Bear wasn't playing well. He had a mild temper on, and you could tell it even though he hadn't said a word. He didn't have a poker face.

Bending over the table, Bear took a shot and missed.

"Damn," he said.

Willard winked at us, shot again, talked as he did. He wasn't a temperamental player. He liked to joke and ask us about the movies we'd seen, as he knew our schedule.

He was also interested in special effects, or professed to be, and he liked to talk to Randy about that. Randy was the resident expert; he wanted to do movie makeup and special effects when he got out of college. And there was something between those two from the start. A sort of bond. I think Willard saw in Randy the intellectual side he wanted, and Randy saw in Willard street savvy and strength. When they were together, I had the feeling they considered themselves whole, and there was a yearning to know more about one another.

Willard shot for a long time before missing.

Bear missed.

"Damn."

Willard continued to talk to Randy, shot three more times before missing, and that one was close. He went around and got his beer off the edge of the pool table and took a long pull on it.

"Do your worst, Bear," he said.

Bear showed a few ugly teeth at one corner of his mouth, took his shot.

He missed.

"Damn."

Willard put the beer down, went around and took his shot, chattering all the while to Randy about some blood-squirting technique he'd seen in some cheap low-budget film on television, and Randy explained how it was done. And when those two were talking, no one else existed. You would have thought the yin and yang had come together, that two destined lovers had at long last met and fulfilled the will of the gods.

Willard made one ball, missed another.

Bear grunted, took his shot.

And missed.

"Damn." He turned his head slowly toward Willard as he straightened up. "Hey, Willard. Take your pet nigger somewhere else. I'm trying to shoot a game here and he's talking through it."

There was a long pause in which it seemed the seasons changed, and Willard stood where he was, expressionless, staring at Bear.

Bear wasn't looking at Willard. He was glaring at Randy. Randy's right foot kept turning out and in, like he was considering running for it, but he was too scared to make the break. He was pinned there, melting like soft chocolate under Bear's gaze.

"Maybe I'll rub your head for luck," Bear said. "You know, with my knuckles. Or maybe that ain't enough. Maybe I'll pull it off and wear it on a chain around my neck for luck. How's that sound, nigger? You like that?"

Randy didn't say a word. His lips trembled like he wanted to say something, but nothing would come out. His right foot was flopping back and forth, not quite able to lead him away.

"Kid didn't do anything," Willard said.

"Talked while I was shooting."

"So did I."

"I ain't forgot that. You want me to, best be quiet."

He and Willard looked at each other awhile, then Bear turned back to Randy. "This won't hurt long," he said, and he stepped in Randy's direction.

"Let him be," Willard said, and he was almost polite about it.

"Warning you, Willard. Don't make this your business. Step aside."

The seasons were changing again as they stared at one another, and it was the right time for us to run, but we didn't. Couldn't. We were frozen.

I glanced about for help. Dan was in the back. And though I doubted he would take our side, he was damn sure one to protect his property if he thought it was about to get smashed. I'd heard he broke a guy's jaw once for accidentally shattering an ashtray.

But Dan didn't come out of the back, and the other guys at the bar and at the pool tables looked mildly curious, not helpful. They were hoping for a little blood, and weren't willing to let any of it be theirs. Some of them got out cigarettes and lit them, just in case what Bear was going to do might take a while.

Bear doubled up his fists and snarled at Willard. "Well, what's it going to be?"

We held our breath.

Willard smiled. "All right, Bear. He's all yours."

2

Bear showed his ugly teeth and moved forward, said, "Let's see how you bounce, little nigger."

I was going to move. I swear I was. Bear or no Bear, I was going to try something, even if I got my head torn off for the effort. So was Bob. I could feel him tense beside me, about to move. Kamikaze attack.

But we never got the chance to get ripped apart and dribbled out the door.

Willard's pool cue whizzed out and the thin end of it caught Bear across the back of the neck. There was a cracking noise like the report of small-arms fire, then the pool cue splintered, went in all directions.

Bear turned his head toward Willard and smiled. He had kind of a nice smile.

"Oh, hell," Willard said softly, and his face went sad and ash-colored.

"Stepped in it, didn't you, bro?" Bear said.

But Willard brought the rest of the cue around—the thick end—hit Bear a solid lick on the nose. Bear staggered a little. Nothing to brag about, but a little.

Willard swung again, and this time it had plenty of hip in it, and when it met the side of Bear's head it was like Reggie Jackson connecting the good wood on a clean fast ball. The blow actually brought Bear up on his toes and leaned him starboard.

But the bastard didn't go down.

Willard let what was left of the cue drop from his

hands, shot out a left jab, hit Bear on the point of his two-car garage, again and again.

A tributary of blood flowed out of Bear's nostrils and made thin creeks through his mustache and beard. Bear tried to hit back, but Willard sidestepped a sloppy right, left-hooked one into him, knocked him into the pool table. Bear's big ass worked as a kind of spring-board, bounced him back into Willard, and Willard gave him another combination.

When Bear's minuscule brain realized his face was being made into red grits, he tried to unleash a wild right, but it didn't even come close.

Willard ducked that baby and the wind from the swing lifted his hair. He went into Bear then with an overhand right that connected on Bear's already destructed nose, and he followed it with a hooking left to the kidneys that made the front of the monster's pants go wet.

Then came the right again, an uppercut this time, and this one was backed with powder and a fifty-caliber load. It caught Bear on the point of his chin, lifted him onto the pool table.

Bear's feet came up high, then flopped down over the edge of the table as if his pant legs were stuffed with straw. The echo of Willard's punch reverberated through the pool hall even as Bear's chin and half his jaw turned the color of bad fruit. A thick trickle of blood fled out of his nose, over his beard and onto the green-ery of the pool table.

Willard thrust his fist into his mouth and hopped around a little. "Damn, that hurt."

Dan had wandered out of the back room about the time Willard threw his first punch, but he hadn't made a move to stop the fight. He'd just stood there frowning with his arms crossed. But now that the fun was over and there was a broken pool stick and a bloodstained table to complain about, he was furious.

"That was a brand-new pool stick," he said, coming over.

"Not now it ain't," Willard said.

"And that big bastard is bleeding all over my god-damn pool table."

"Fix that." Willard reached out, grabbed Bear by a boot and jerked him onto the floor. Bear made a grunting noise when he hit the tile, but that was it.

"Blood'll mop off the floor easy," Willard said. "I'll pay you for the pool stick."

"Damn sure will. Twenty dollars."

Willard took twenty out of his billfold and gave it to Dan. "There."

"Get out," Dan said. "You hadn't brought them boys in here wouldn't have been no trouble."

"We came in on our own two legs," Bob said.

"You shut up, boy," Dan said, and he cast an eye at Randy. "And this ain't no colored hangout. Ain't no good idea to come here, you hear me, son?"

"Yes, sir."

"Don't 'sir' that line of crap," Willard said. "This is a free country, ain't it?"

Dan studied Willard. "If you're big enough, you're free to do most anything. Now you've paid for the cue, what about the table?"

"What about it?"

"Blood'll stain."

"Use cold water on it."

"Go on, you little smart-mouth sonofabitch. Get on out of here and don't come back. Take these jerks with you, and don't none of you darken this door again."

"No problem," Willard said. "I ain't gonna miss this class joint none."

"And it ain't gonna miss you," Dan said, and kicked Bear in the ribs a couple of times. "You too. Get up from there and get out." Bear didn't move. "Sorry trash."

We went out with Dan still kicking Bear and Bear still not moving.

* * *

Out on the sidewalk, Bob said, "Sorry we got you thrown out of there, Willard."

"No sweat. I was tired of it anyway. This whole town, for that matter. It stinks. Don't reckon I'll be staying around much longer. I got laid off at the plant yesterday, and I figure that now is as good a time as any to get out of this one-horse town. In fact, I'm glad I don't have that damn job anymore. It was like working in hell. Always felt like I was making lawn furniture for Satan. I'm free now to go somewhere better and find a good job, something with a future. I got a feeling that me losing that job was just a turning point, and that from here on out, things are going to start looking up."

We stood there, not knowing what to say. Willard watched some cars go by, got out a cigarette and put fire to it. He took a couple of drags before he spoke again.

"Before I leave for good, thought maybe I'd take in that drive-in you guys go to. What do you say? Can I go with y'all over there Friday?"

"Yeah," I said. "Sure. Why not? We leave at five. Where can we pick you up?"

"Larry's Garage. He lets me keep my bike there."

"Sounds good," Bob said. "We'll pick you up in my truck." He pointed to it in the lot.

"I know it," Willard said. "I'll be watching for you guys."

"Good," Bob said.

"Willard?" Randy said.

"Yeah, kid."

"Thanks for not letting me get killed, or otherwise mutilated in a hideous manner."

Willard almost laughed. "Sure, kid. Nothing to it. Saw your buddies were about to step into it, and I didn't want them to have all the fun."

"Generous of you," I said, "considering Bear breathes harder than we hit."

"Hell with it," Willard said. "Always figured I could take him. Now I know."

We walked Willard to his bike. He climbed on and flipped his cigarette in the gutter. Randy stuck out his hand and Willard shook it for a long time. Then he nodded at us, cranked his machine and rode off.

Randy stood there with his hand out, as if he were still shaking with Willard.

Willard didn't look back to see if we were watching him. Hell, he knew he was cool.

3

Friday morning I awoke and was attacked by the glare off the garish paperbacks in the little space for books at the head of my bed. The sun was shining through the window and making the red and yellow spines on the astrology and numerology books seem brighter yet. This wasn't the first morning I had awakened to see them there and hated them because they had let me down. I had tried to believe in the little bastards, but life and reality kept coming up against them, and pretty soon I had to decide the planets didn't give a frog jump about me and that numbers were just numbers, and when you got right down to it, pretty boring.

It was like I was punishing myself, leaving them there, and it was like my body knew to get twisted to the edge of the bed so I'd wake up with my head turned toward them so I could see their bright spines shining at me, reminding me that I had spent money on them and that some jackass writer was spending the royalties he got off them, partly provided by me, to drink beer and chase women while I read his books and made charts and tried to figure out how to use them to find the right gal and divine the secrets of the universe.

I figured as long as I was punishing myself, I might as well sit up in bed and get so I could see all the spines and really feel rotten. There were also books on Eastern religions that mainly had to do with holding your thumb next to your forefinger, wrapping a leg around your neck and making with some damn-fool chants. There was even one of those hip modern books that told me I just thought I was a schmuck, but wasn't really. It was everyone else, and I was a pretty neat fella. I liked this one best until I realized that anyone with the price of a paperback was a pretty neat fella. That sort of let the air out of my tires.

Only book I didn't have up there on my shelf was one on divining the future through chicken guts, and I'd have had it had it been for sale.

I couldn't figure why I was such a sucker for that stuff. I wasn't unhappy, but the idea of everything just being random didn't suit me, and didn't seem right. And I didn't like the big bang theory. It was kind of disappointing, came across like a lab experiment that had gone wrong and made something. I wanted things to be by design, for there to be some great controlling force with a sense of order. Someone or something up there keeping files and notes.

I figured I just hadn't found the right book.

I got out of bed, got a trash sack out of my closet and took all those little dudes off the shelf and put them in the sack. I went downstairs and threw them in the main garbage in the washroom, then went into the kitchen.

Mom was in there running that crap she has for breakfast through a blender. It smelled like wet dog hair and mildewed newspapers to me.

"Want some eggs and bacon?" she asked, and smiled.

She was standing there in her tennis outfit, her long blond hair pulled back and bound with a rubber band. I'm sure some backyard psychiatrist will make an Oedipal thing out of this, but to heck with it. My mom is damn fine-looking.

She started pouring the smelly mess from the blender into a glass.

"Well, I don't want that," I said. "And if I were you,

I'd see if a nest of roaches, or maybe a rat died in that blender overnight."

She grimaced. "Does smell bad, doesn't it?"

"Oh yeah. How's it taste?"

"Like shit."

I got some cinnamon rolls out of the fridge. "Let's have these."

She patted her flat stomach. "Nah. Got to keep my girlish figure. Otherwise, I'll die while I'm out playing tennis. Bad form to die on the court."

"You couldn't gain a pound if you were wearing galoshes."

"For that, you may have two bone-building, nutritious cinnamon rolls. And though I wouldn't normally eat that garbage, pollute my body with those foul chemicals and sugars, I will, on this occasion, knowing how you hate to eat alone, make an exception."

"If you ever finish your speech, that is."

"Precisely."

She sat down and ate four rolls and drank three cups of coffee. When she was through she smacked her lips. "God, but I hated every horrible minute of that. Each bite was agony, acid to my lips. The sacrifices mothers make for their children."

Dad came down. He was wearing an old brown bathrobe that Mom hated. She had tried to throw it away once, but he'd found it in the garbage, rescued it and slinked upstairs with it under his arm. Mom had laughed after him and he had looked down at her, hurt.

She had also given it to Goodwill, thinking they'd turn it into rags, but they'd washed it, put it on the racks. And Dad, looking for used paperbacks, saw it, bought it and came home mad. He told Mom never to say his robe had come apart in the washing again.

That robe *is* an ugly thing, tattered and threadbare. He had at least three good ones in a drawer upstairs, but as far as I knew, he had never so much as tried them on. Wearing that old brown one, his feet in house sandals and his hair thinning on top, he always reminded me of Friar Tuck.

He wobbled in sleepily, weaved over to the counter and came suddenly awake when he got a whiff of what was in the blender.

"Goddamn, woman," he said. "There's something dead in that blender."

"That's what I said, Dad."

"Funny," Mom said. "It's just that old robe you guys smell."

"Ah," Dad said. "The melodious voice of the serving wench. Make me some ham and eggs."

"Poof!" Mom said. "You are some ham and eggs. Any more requests?"

"None I can think of," Dad said. He got a bowl, spoon, milk and cereal, arranged them at the table and pulled up a chair.

"What happened to the ham and eggs, Your Majesty?" Mom asked.

"Too lazy to fix them myself."

"And I won't feel sorry for you, will I, snookums?"

"Looks that way," Dad said. He looked at me and grinned. "Up early, aren't you?"

"Friday," I said.

"Ah. No school and tonight is the big night. A trip to The Orbit with the boys. You should try going out with girls, son. They're a lot more fun."

"I go with girls," I said. "It's just that The Orbit is special . . . something I prefer to do with the guys."

"I always liked drive-ins with girls." He looked at Mom. "A purely puritan adventure, of course."

"That's not the way I remember you," Mom said. "Aren't you running late this morning, Mr. Big Shot?"

"I own the company, my dear. I can do damn well as I please. Outside of this house anyway."

"Ha," Mom said. She got up and started for the cabinet. Dad slapped her on the butt. She whirled. "Harold . . . could you do that again?"

I laughed. Dad stood up, grabbed her, bent her back like they do in those old movies. "Woman, my little dove. You are the love of my life. Patting your ass is a pleasure unmatched by gold and video . . . And remember, serving wench, no TV dinners tonight or I sell you to the Arab traders."

He kissed her.

"Thank you, Harold. Now will you lift me up. My back hurts."

"When the going gets rough, when it looks like we're not going to make it, I'll save the last two bullets for us."

"Harold, you're crazy. Now pull me up, will you? My back hurts."

He pulled her up. "That's what happens when you get old. Back trouble. And no sense of romance."

"Go shower and shave . . . and for heaven's sake brush that hair off your teeth," Mom said.

"My breath is sweet. I go to bed with sugar breath, and I awake with it even sweeter. I—"

"Go!"

"Yessuh, Massuh," he said, and shuffled off.

When he was gone Mom gave me an exasperated look.."He's crazy, you know?"

"I know," I said.

A little later on, Mom went to play tennis and Dad went to work and I never saw them again.

4

Before we started going to the drive-in, come summer mornings you couldn't get me up if you fired a bazooka under the covers. But now Friday meant The Orbit, and I was usually up early. And there was also The Early Morning Monster Show that I had acquired a taste for. It showed on Channel 6 at eight and Randy came over every Friday to watch. Bob would have, but he worked half a day at his dad's feed store. As I said, none of us had to work, but Bob was more willing, and he liked having plenty of pocket change.

So Randy came over and the movie was *The Crawling Eye,* and it wasn't bad until the monsters showed up. The wind kind of went out of its sails after that. It was hard to feel threatened by things that looked like large rubber mops. Still, I enjoyed it, and it gave Randy a chance to make fun of the special effects.

He got what I thought was a sort of strange, even perverse, pleasure out of that, considering most of those movies had been made on a rubber-band budget. But I think it was important for him to have something to look down on, considering he felt pretty much low man on life's totem pole. He had brains and he was nice, but there was some invisible thing about him that led others to direct their hatred toward him, the incident with Bear being a case in point. In fact, I sometimes felt that behind that mousy, quiet exterior was a tyrant without courage, someone looking for his edge on humanity.

He was good in school, but he didn't take any particular pride in that because no one gave a damn. He was knowledgeable about film, makeup and special effects particularly, but again, no competition. Bob and I loved that stuff too, but we weren't wrapped up in it like Randy. So the only thing he could measure his knowledge and skills against were low-budget films, mentally playing out in his mind that he could do better if given a chance.

But the thing I remember best about that morning was Randy turning to me while all hell was breaking loose in the movie (admittedly the hell in the movie wasn't as intense as it ought to have been), and saying, "Do you think Willard has a steady girl?"

"Hell, Randy, I don't know. I'm sure he has girls, but I don't think he's the wear-my-ring kind. I think the tattoo on his arm, EAT PUSSY, is sort of a statement on romance, don't you?"

"Yeah," Randy said. "I suppose so."

After that he just watched the movie, but I could tell his mind wasn't on it. He had a sort of dreamy look in his eyes, like he was thinking about something that lived way down deep in his brain.

About noon we ate some ham sandwiches and drove over to Safeway and bought some supplies for the night: Cracker Jacks, chocolate-covered almonds, potato chips, some Cokes and a few bags of cookies. Bob was supposed to get a case of beer; he had connections. Connections that bought it cheap and sold it dear, and didn't give a damn if you were a minor or a warthog. In spite of that, Bob could deal with them better than we could. He dressed the way they did, could talk their line of talk, and the bottom line was he was so damn tight, when he blinked the skin on his dick rolled back. Just the man for hard money dealings.

He had also promised Randy and me that he would bring us some jerky from his dad, who had made it himself from last season's deer. He'd given us some of it before, and it was fine. In fact, last time he'd given us enough to feed an army. Well, mine mostly fed my dad, even if it did give his teeth a workout. He loved the stuff, tried to convince everyone who came by the house they should too. My dad and Bob's dad should have gone into business together. Bob's dad could make it and my dad could hawk it.

I remember passing the kitchen once, and Dad was sitting in there at the table with one of his business partners, and he had pushed a strip of the meat off on him, and I heard the guy say, "I'm not so hot on this stuff, Harold. It's kind of like chewing on a dead woman's tit."

From then on when I ate the stuff, I had to chew it in an absentminded sort of way, not thinking too much about the texture so I could enjoy it.

We took the goodies home, read some *Fangoria* magazines Randy had brought over, and Bob arrived an hour later than usual for our ventures.

Two things were noticeable right off. One was that the fool was fresh from the shower and hadn't bothered to dry off; his shirt was stuck to his back and the hair that hung out from beneath his hat was wet and shaggy. The second thing was that he had been in a fight; he had a black doughnut around his left eye.

"You know that girlfriend I used to have?" he said.

"Used to have?" Randy asked.

"Yep, used to have. Caught her with Wendle Benbaker."

Wendle was about the size of a small camper trailer. He had played tackle for Mud Creek High until graduation, and his hobby, when he wasn't drinking beer and talking about girls, was talking about girls and drinking beer. He was the only guy I knew who moved his lips over the *Playboy* foldout as well as the magazine's text. I think it was the staples that confused him.

And to be honest, Bob's girlfriend, Leona of the Big Tits, didn't strike me as any great loss. Her nickname was how she was known by the staunchest anti-male

27

chauvinist, both male and female. She invited being called that, even liked it, thought it was an honor; she wore those monstrous boobs like war medals on a proud general's chest.

"Reckon this discovery," I said, "caused you and Wendle to fight."

Bob rubbed his sore eye. "Good, Sherlock. You're right. Jeke was supposed to meet me out back of the Dairy Queen with the beer, and he did. But after I loaded it up, I saw Leona and Wendle sitting in his car around front. She was sitting so close she might as well have been wearing his pants with him. Burned my ass up. She told me she didn't do nothing on Fridays but watch TV. Told me I could go with the guys, no sweat. Now I know the hell why. She's been letting Wendle check her oil."

"What did you do?" Randy asked.

"Went over there, yanked the door open and called him a sonofabitch, I think. I was a bit under stress right then and don't remember so good."

I nodded at the black eye. "And I take it he wasn't scared none?"

"Not that I could see. And he can move fast for a big guy. Sucker popped out of that Dodge like a ripe zit and hit me in the eye before I could shag it."

"Looks bad," I said.

"You oughta see him."

"You hit him?" Randy said, amazed. "You hit Wendle the tank?"

"No, but I damn sure got some oil stains on his pants. I mean I ruined them little buddies."

Randy and I let that hang, trying to work it into the scheme of things.

"Oil stains?" I finally asked, as if I were delivering the cryptic line "Rosebud" in *Citizen Kane*.

"When he knocked me down, I crawled under his car and he crawled after me. Some car had been leaking oil there—Wendle's, I hope—and he got his white pants all nastied up. Covered both knees. Won't wash out. Them boogers are ruined."

"That's showing him," I said.

"He was so big I got over beneath the muffler and he couldn't get under there after me . . . remember that if he starts for you. You get under his car by the muffler and you're safe. He can't get there."

"Good tip," I said. "Go for the muffler."

"He did kick me, though. He can get his legs under there after you pretty good, so it ain't completely safe. He jammed my little finger some, but he finally gave up, got back in the car and tried to back it over me."

"Looks to me you escaped," I said.

"Rolled out from under there like a dung bug. You remember how fast I could roll in gym when we was doing that tumbling exercise, don't you?"

"You were an ace roller, as I recall," I said.

"Damn right."

"What was Leona doing?" Randy asked.

"She got out of the car, started screaming and cussing—which was a thing that hurt me. She told me a couple of times she was a lady and didn't say them kind of words. Swore she wouldn't say 'shit' if she had a mouthful. But she was out there yelling at Wendle to pull my head off and to kick a turd down my throat.

"When I rolled out from under the car and started running, her and ole Wendle yelling at my back, I knew right then and there that things between us were over."

"Does sound kind of past the patching stage," I said.

"Well . . . I ruined that sucker's pants."

We put the goodies in Bob's truck, drove over to Buddy's Fill-up to get gas and some ice for our beer chest.

While we were there, I went to the bathroom to take a leak and Bob joined me at the urinal. The two caballeros.

The place was really nasty, smelled awful. The urinal was stopped up with candy wrappers and some things I didn't want to examine too closely, lest I identify them. Over in one corner was a mashed item I hoped was a Baby Ruth.

Most of the graffiti were illiterate and the artist who had drawn naked women on the walls seemed to lack acquaintance with human anatomy. My dad told me his generation learned a lot about sex from writings and drawings on bathroom walls. I hoped to goodness our generation was getting its information from better sources.

"Nice place, ain't it?" Bob said.

"Maybe we ought to bring us some dates in here."

"We could sit on the commodes and talk."

"Bring in some dip and stuff."

"Have some of them little sausages wrapped in bread with toothpicks through them."

"Serious now," I said. "How are you making it?"

"Good enough. Splashed a little on my boots is all. But I ain't having a good enough time to stick around when I finish. Kind of stinks. How about you? What are your plans?"

"That's funny, Bob."

"Okay, I'm doing fine. She was just some ole gal. You worry about other people too much. Me included."

"Yeah, I'm a regular bleeding heart."

"Well, you are . . . but, yeah, I'm okay. I'm going to miss her some."

"There's nothing to miss, Bob."

"I don't know. Them tits were sure nice and warm."

Randy was leaning on the truck when we came out.

"I was about to organize a search party," he said.

"Well," Bob said, "we got to talking, you know, and damn if we don't have all kinds of things in common."

"Yeah," I said. "You just wouldn't believe."

Randy rolled his eyes. "How about we get in the truck?"

We drove over to Larry's Garage, got there fifteen minutes early, but Willard was out front, smoking a cigarette, the damn thing hanging off his lip like a leech. His long hair was clean and combed back and he wore a black T-shirt with a cigarette pack stuck under one short sleeve. He had a faded blue-jean jacket tossed over one shoulder. He looked like he was waiting for someone to come along so he could mug them.

He strolled over to the truck. "Ready?"

"We're always ready," Bob said.

"You look ready," Willard said. "What happened to your eye?"

"A truck named Wendle Benbaker."

"Get in," I said, "and he'll tell you how he ruined Wendle's pants, and how to hide from him under a muffler."

Randy got out of the truck and made Willard take his place at shotgun. He went around to ride in the back, carrying a *Fangoria* with him to read.

"He's a nice little guy," Willard said when he was seated, his arm hanging out the window.

"That's the truth," Bob said, cranked the truck and drove on out of town. As we went, I took the whole place in, noticed for the first time some houses and stores I had looked at before, but hadn't really seen. We drove down the main drag, past the university that I planned to attend, past the big pines that were slowly being thinned by idiots with no concept of city planning but a firm grasp on the concept of greed; drove past the stinking chicken plant and the plywood plant and the aluminum-chair factory, which Willard saluted with an upward push of his middle finger; drove on out of there with me photographing it all in my mind, perhaps sensing somehow it was for the last time.

31

5

It didn't seem like a night for horrors. Least not the real kind.

It was cool and pleasant. We got there a little later than usual, due to some bad traffic. Quite a line had formed. You could see The Orbit's Saturn symbol spinning blue and silver against the night.

"I'll be damned," Willard said.

"We'll all be if we don't change our ways," Bob said.

"Wait until you see the inside," I said.

We moved up in line, finally drove by the outdoor marquee. It listed *I Dismember Mama, The Evil Dead, Night of the Living Dead, The Toolbox Murders* and *The Texas Chainsaw Massacre*.

Inside, the big party had already started. There were lawn chairs planted in the backs of pickups, and folks planted in the chairs. There were people on the hoods and tops of their cars. Punkers. Aging hippies. Conservative types. Fraternity and sorority kids. Families. Cowboys and cowgirls with beer cans growing out of their fists. Barbecue grills sputtered away, lifting sweet smoke into the fine Texas sky. Tape decks whined in conflict of one another. A few lovers on blankets were so hot at it, Willard suggested that they should charge admission. Cars rocked in spastic rhythm to the sexual gyrations of unbridled youth. Someone somewhere called someone a sonofabitch. Other people yelled things we couldn't understand. Bikini-clad women walked by. People in monster suits walked by. Some-

32

times young men in monster suits chased the bikini-clad women by. Dogs, let out of their owners' cars to do their business, pissed on tires or left deposits of another nature in the vicinity.

And, most important, of course, *there was the screen.*

One of six, it stood stark-white against a jet-black sky, a six-story portal into another dimension.

We tried to get as close as we could, but most of the front rows were taken. We ended up in the middle of a rear row.

We got the lawn chairs out, the goodies. Bob and I went to the concession stand and bought some bloody corn for all of us, and by the time we got back with it, the sleaze classic *I Dismember Mama* had started.

We rolled through that one, drinking, eating, laughing, shouting at the gory spots, and finally *The Toolbox Murders* came on, and it was halfway through that one that it happened.

I don't remember any great change in the atmosphere, anything like that. Everything was normal—for The Orbit. Sights, sounds and smells as they ought to be. The bloody corn was gone, so were several Cokes, and Bob and Willard had made good work of the beers. We were about a third of the way through a bag of chocolate cookies. Cameron Mitchell had just opened his ominous box of tools to take out an industrial nailer, as he had designs to use the wicked instrument on a young lady he'd been spying on in the shower, and we were ready, hoping as much for blatant nudity as celluloid gore, when—

—there was light.

It was a light so bright and crimson, the images on the screen paled, then faded.

We looked up.

The source of the light was a monstrous red comet, or meteor, hurtling directly toward us. The night sky and stars around it were consumed by its light, and the thing filled our vision. The rays from the object felt soft and liquid, like being bathed in warm milk and honey.

Collision with the drive-in seemed imminent. My life didn't pass before my eyes, but I thought suddenly of things I hadn't done, thought of Mom and Dad, then, abruptly, *the comet smiled*.

Split down the middle to show us a mouthful of jagged saw-blade teeth. Instead of going out of life with a bang, it appeared we were going out with a crunch.

The mouth opened wider, and I was turning my head away from the inevitable, thinking in a fleeting second that I would be swallowed by it, like Pinocchio by the whale, when—

—*it whipped up and away*, dragging its fiery tail behind it, leaving us awash in flickering red sparks and an even more intense feeling of being engulfed in warm liquid.

When the red pupil paint peeled away from my eyes and I could see again, the sky had gone from blood-red to pink, and now that was slowly fading. The comet was racing faster and faster, ever upward, seemingly dragging the moon and stars after it, like glitter swirling down a sewerish drain. Finally the comet was nothing more than a hot-pink pinprick surrounded by black turbulence that sparked with blue twists of lightning; then the dark sky went still, the lightning died out, and the comet was memory.

At first, it looked as if nothing had changed, except for a loss of the moon and the stars. But the exterior of the drive-in was different. Beyond that seven-foot, moon-shimmering tin fence that surrounded it was . . . *nothing*. Well, to be more exact, blackness. Complete blackness, the ultimate fudge pudding. A moment before the tops of the houses, trees and buildings had been visible beyond the drive-in, but now they were not. There was not even a dot of light.

The only illumination came from the drive-in itself:

from open car doors, the concession-stand lights, the red neon tubes that said ENTRANCE (ƎƆИAЯTИƎ from our angle) and EXIT, the projector beams, and, most brilliantly, the marquee and the tall Orbit symbol, the last two sources being oddly located on a spur of concrete jutting into the blackness like a pier over night ocean. I found myself drawn to that great symbol, its blue and white lights alternating like overhead fan slats across the concession, making the Halloweenish decorations against the window glass seem oddly alive and far too appropriate.

Then I glanced at the screen. *The Toolbox Murders* was visible again, but there was no fun in it. It seemed horribly silly and out of place, like someone dancing at a funeral.

Voices began to rumble across the lot, voices touched with surprise and confusion. I saw a rubber-suited monster take the head off his suit and tuck it under his arm and look around, hoping he hadn't seen what he thought he saw, and that it would be some kind of trick due to bad lighting through the eyes of his mask. A bikini-clad girl let her stomach sag, having lost the ambition to suck it in.

I realized suddenly I was walking toward the exit, and that the gang was with me, and Bob was chattering like an idiot, not making any sense. The din of voices across the lot had grown, and people were out of their cars, walking in the same direction we were, like lemmings being willed to the sea.

One man fired up his car. It was a new Ford station wagon and it was full of fat. Fat driver in a Hawaiian shirt with a fat wife beside him, two fat kids in the back. He jerked the car around a speaker post with surprising deftness, pulled on the lights and raced for the exit.

People scattered before the wagon, and I got a glimpse of the driver's face as he raced past. It looked like a mask made of paste with painted golf balls for eyes.

The headlights hit the darkness, but didn't penetrate. The car pushed down the tire-buster spears with a clack and was swallowed foot by foot by the pudding. It was as if there had never been a car. There was not even the sound of the motor retreating into the distance.

A tall cowboy in a Stetson full of toothpicks and feathers sauntered over to the opening, flexed his shoulders and said, "Let's find out what the hell gives here."

He put a boot on the tire-buster spears to hold them down, stuck his arm into the fudge, up to the elbow.

And the cowboy screamed. Never in my personal history of real life or movie experiences have I heard such a sound. It was like a depth charge to the soul, and its impact blew up my spine and rocked my skull.

The cowboy staggered back, flopped to the ground and turned himself around and around like a dog with its guts dragging. His arm was gone from hand to elbow.

We ran over to help him, but before we could lay a hand on him, he yelled, "Back, goddammit. Don't touch me! It runs."

He started screaming again, but it sounded as if his vocal cords were filling with mud. And I saw then what he meant by "It runs." Slowly his arm was dissolving, the sleeve going limp at the shoulder, then the shoulder folded and he tried to scream again. But whatever was eating him from the outside seemed to be working inside him even faster.

His forehead wobbled forward as bone and tissue went to Jell-O, caved in on the rest of his collapsing face. His cowboy hat came to settle on top of the mess, floated in it. His entire body went liquid, ran out of his clothes in nauseating streams. The stink was awful.

Carefully, holding my breath, I reached out and took hold of one of his boots and upended it. A loathsome goop, like vomit, poured out of it and splattered to the ground.

Beside me, Bob let out with a curse, and Willard

said something I didn't understand. I dropped the boot and looked at the darkness beyond the tin fence and the strange truth of it struck me.

We were trapped in the drive-in.

6

That we were trapped in the drive-in was realized immediately by most, but accepted slowly by all of us. And there were some who didn't know right off, like the couple in the Buick parked near where a bunch of us had gathered, looking at the hat, boots and empty clothes of the dissolved cowboy. Neither comet nor screams had reached them. They were too wrapped up in their lovemaking. They were in the back seat of the Buick, and the girl had one ankle draped across the seat and the other on the package shelf. We were all watching the car rock, watching it threaten the shock absorbers and test the strength of four-ply tires. And as the car was at a slant, dipping its rear end toward us, we could see a pale butt rising to view, vanishing, rising, vanishing, all with a regular rhythm, like an invisible man dribbling a basketball. It was something we kept our eyes on, something that tied us to our old reality, and I really hated for it to end and for the girl's ankles to come down, and a little later for them to come out of the car with their clothes rumpled, looking mad at first, then confused. It was our faces that did that to them, the way we were bunched up, the rumble of our voices, the fact that more people were walking our way, and, of course, there was the absolute blackness all around.

Someone tried to tell the couple about the comet, the fat folks in the Ford and the brave (or stupid) cowboy who got dissolved, and they just grinned. The guy said, "No way."

"Well," Bob said, waving a hand at the fudge surrounding the drive-in, "I guess we just dreamed all this crap. You think we're giving you a bill of goods, why don't you two just take you a little stroll out in that shit —but don't expect to come back."

The guy looked at the girl; she looked at him; he looked at us and shook his head.

People tried radios, CBs, and some clustered to the concession to make a stab at the phones. But nothing was in order. Just a little static on the radios.

The crowd grew. Must have been over a hundred of us standing around, and more people were coming. They were starting to congregate over in Lot B too, in little spots here and there. Some were driving cars around and around, honking horns, maybe not scared yet, but certainly bewildered. But that didn't go on long. Pretty soon no cars were moving about, just groups of people, talking or looking lost.

A story came to us from Lot B about a motorcycle gang that was over there, about how one of their members panicked and drove his bike off into the stuff, with the same result as our fat man and his calorie-laden family in the Ford station wagon.

The theories started then, those by the loudest and most persistent ones among us being the ones heard. The man with the beer gut wearing a T-shirt a size too small with a mustard blossom on the neck of it, for instance.

"Well, I think it's them men from outer space, whatever color they are. They've done this to us. With us shooting our rockets and stuff up there, they were bound to get sore with us. So they've come down with some of them sophisticated weapons they've got, and they've done this. I don't see how it could be anything else."

"I don't think so," said a guy in a sports coat, his hair neat and stiff as a J.C. Penney model. "I suspect the Communists. They're a lot stronger in this country than most people imagine. And I don't want to open any old wounds here, but maybe McCarthy wasn't as far off as some people thought. These Communists are into everything, and they've said all along that they planned to take us over."

"Why in the hell would they want some Texas drive-in picture show?" Bob said. "They like horror movies, or what? That don't make no damn sense. I like the one about the guys from outer space, whatever color they are, better than that, and that's dumb."

"Hey," said the man with the mustard-colored T-shirt.

"Call 'em like I see 'em," Bob said.

"It's the will of God," said a girl in a long blue cotton dress. "There was so much sinning going on here, God has sent a blight."

The couple who had been practicing the rites of the three-toed salamander in the back of the Buick started shuffling their feet and looking over the heads of the crowd as if they were expecting someone.

"It wasn't God," said somebody at the rear of the crowd, "it was Satan done it. God doesn't punish. Man and Satan punish."

"We're uptight for nothing," said another voice. "Tomorrow the sun will come up and shine through this mess. It's just a freak of nature, that's all."

"No," said a punker girl with orange spiked hair. "It's dimensional invaders."

No one bought that one.

A pretty girl in a pink bathing suit suggested, "Maybe we're all dead, and, like, hanging in limbo or something."

Some consideration on that. A couple of maybes from the crowd; I think it might have edged out the Commie threat a bit in popularity.

"Ain't none of them things," said a fat lady with a nose like a red pickle. She was wearing a pink-and-green housecoat that could have served as a visual emetic and yellow bunny slippers. She had her arm around her skinny husband's waist and two small ankle biters (a girl and a boy) were at her feet. "It's the ghost of Elvis Presley. I read about something like this in *The Weekly World News*, and Elvis was involved in that. His ghost came down and did some things to some sinners. He said to them that he wasn't happy with the way people were living on Earth."

"Hell," Bob said. "He's got to be a self-righteous sonofabitch now that he's dead. He wasn't nothing but a fat doper."

"He was the King," the woman said, as if she were talking about Jesus.

"King of what?" Bob said. "Constipation? I heard he died on the floor of his toilet with a turd hanging out of his ass. Report said he died 'straining at stool.' He wasn't any more than the rest of us, except he could sing. And even then, he wasn't any Hank Williams."

"Hank Williams!" said the fat lady, taking her arm from around her husband's waist and looking as if she were about to leap. "Now there was a drunk and a doper. And he wasn't near as good-looking as Elvis."

"That may be," Bob said, "but you don't hear of his ghost coming down to bother nobody. He knew to mind his own business."

This went on for a time, not really solving anything, but it was entertaining. I got to thinking about how much time had elapsed, and looked at my watch. It had stopped.

Bob and the lady with the red pickle nose had finally quit going at it, and a black guy wearing a straw hat and a worn-out gray sweatshirt with "Dallas Cowboys" on it spoke up then. "We could be here a time. What about food? We're gonna need that."

I thought about the cookies and junk back at the truck and wished we'd brought something more substantial, but then maybe that was carrying worry too far, projecting this strange situation too distantly in the future.

The manager of the main concession joined us then. "Look, it isn't going to come to that, worrying about food, I mean. This will pass. Whatever it is, it can't last long. But to ease your minds, let me tell you that if we're here awhile, if food becomes a problem, we've got enough back there in that concession, and over on Lot B, to last a long time."

"How long is a long time?" Willard said.

"A long, long time," the manager said. "But let's don't jump the gun here. This'll pass. Maybe some sort of industrial accident put this mess around us."

"And the comet?" Randy said.

"I don't know, but I'm sure there's a logical explanation to it all, and I don't see any need to get worked up over starving to death. We haven't been in this mess but a few minutes, and I can tell you now, it won't last."

"God has spoken," Bob said, and the manager glared at him.

"I think we all ought to hold tight," the manager said. "Go on back to your cars, try to forget all this, get your mind on the movies. Pretty soon someone will come to get us out of this. Some kind of accident happened out there, someone knows about it. Hell, they'll have the National Guard in here pretty soon."

"That makes me feel comfy all over," Bob said. "My uncle is in the National Guard and he don't know dick about nothing, has a belly that hangs down to his knees. Great, the National Guard."

"You boys think like you want," the manager said. "Me, I'm going back to the concession, try the phones again, see if they've got to working. Tomorrow we'll all have something to tell our families about."

"Right," Randy said. "A comet smiled at us, put us in Limbo Land, and the edge of Limbo Land ate a station wagon full of fat people and dissolved a cowboy."

The manager tried to smile. "I'm not saying this isn't a dangerous situation, but I am saying we have to make the best of it. Keep our spirits up, stay away from that gas . . . jell, whatever it is . . . and you'll see. We'll be fine. Now I'm going on back to the concession to try the phones."

The manager went away and Randy said, "Yeah, fine."

"He's right, though," a tall guy said. "We can't do much else. We've got to make the best of it . . . unless someone here has a great idea."

No one did.

One guy went out to the trunk of his car, came back with an old box and a shovel. He scooped up the cowboy and put him in the box. The mess had lost its acidic quality and was congealing. The box remained intact. He used the point of the shovel to scoop up the clothes and the boots, dropped the hat on top of it all.

"I'll just . . . keep him in my trunk," he said. "Wife said she didn't mind . . . seems like the decent thing to do. Maybe we can figure out who he is . . . get his folks to bury him when we get out . . . Anybody here know him?"

No one said they did.

"Guess he came by himself," the guy said, and carried the shovel and the cowboy in the cardboard box away.

"What a way to end up," Bob said. "In the trunk of a car next to a spare tire."

"In a dirty box, no less," Randy said.

Now to make a long story short, or at least this part of it, this went on, this standing around and talking, this looking at the black mess and waiting for the National Guard, but no one showed up to rescue us.

"We've talked and talked about it," Willard said, "but nothing's gotten any better."

"I'm gonna get me a Baby Ruth," Bob said. "It's good for my skin."

"Not much else to do, is there," I said.

"Let's just do like the manager suggested," said the black guy in the straw hat.

We drifted away from the crowd, and the crowd started to break apart, wandering back to their cars with a stunned look on their faces. The immediate drama was over and nothing had changed. We were still trapped in the drive-in, and the adventure of it was old already.

We all went back to the truck, and I took up my position in the chair and recovered my bag of popcorn. I even found I could get interested in the movies again.

Bob came back with his Baby Ruth and smacked his lips over it enough to make me look through our stuff for some cookies. I had eaten so much I was beginning to feel queasy.

We watched the movies, but after they had run through and started over again, I began to lose interest and really worry. With that many movies shown, and them starting a second run, it ought to be getting toward dawn. There wasn't a ray of sunlight, however. Just the same artificial lights. I was getting sick of movies, the drive-in, even the goofballs who were wandering around in monster suits. I couldn't even feel any warmth for the gals in their bikinis. I felt like a roach in a toilet bowl with someone's hand on the handle, ready to flush. I wanted to go home to my nice warm bed, with Mom and Dad down the hall.

The concession manager we had talked to spoke over the speakers. "The phones still aren't on, folks, and we haven't been able to pick up anything on the radio, but I'm sure the National Guard is on this, and we'll be out of here soon—"

"Guy has a hard-on for the National Guard," Bob said.

"—until then, we're going to keep right on showing

the movies, and if there's no help by the time of the third one, we'll be serving breakfast here at the concession—on the house. No eggs and bacon, I'm afraid. But we've got hot dogs, fresh hot popcorn, plenty of candy and soft drinks, plus some real good orange drink we got in just for tonight."

The manager went off then, and Bob said, "Here we are surrounded by acidic goo, and all this guy can think about is the National Guard, free hot dogs and good orange drink."

"The odd thing to me," Randy said, "is how come the electricity works here in the drive-in, but radios, things that connect us to the outside world, don't? Hell, my watch has even stopped."

"Mine too," I said.

Bob took out his pocket watch. "This one's dead too. First time ever."

"Bet they're all dead," Willard said. It was the first time he had said a word in some time. He had just been sitting, watching the movies, eating popcorn. "Time is an outside connection too."

"You getting at something, Willard?" I asked.

"Not really. I don't know any better what's going on than anyone else. But this all has a kind of artificial feel to it . . . like, hell, I don't know—"

"A B science-fiction movie," Randy said.

"Yeah," Willard said. "I guess so."

"Personally," Bob said, "I think the lady in the blanket and bunnies was right. It's the ghost of Elvis."

"I just hope the damn bulbs and such in the projectors don't burn out," Willard said. "Or in the Orbit sign. They do, and it's going to be some kind of dark in here."

Willard got out his cigarettes, passed them around. We all took one, just as if we smoked, and Willard put his lighter to them, and we leaned against the truck and puffed them until we coughed.

"That poor cowboy," Randy said. "It melted him like salt melts a slug. Looked like cheap special effects.

Like in that movie *The Hydrogen Man,* or maybe *The Blob.*"

"And that fat family and their car," Bob said. "Rendered right down, I figure."

So we smoked our cigarettes and the movies rolled on.

7

After a time, I gave it up and crawled in the back of the truck, found one of the bedrolls we kept back there for camping trips, got in it and fell asleep. Kind of sleep you get from depression and absolute exhaustion.

I dreamed about what Randy had said, about this being like a B science-fiction movie, and the dream was very real. It was like I was tapped into some truth somewhere. There was this B-string god and he was making a movie. He didn't have the power to make the Big Movie, so he just borrowed some people (us) and a setting (the drive-in) and made do with that. Real shoestring stuff. There was a bunch of other creatures with him, maybe they were gods too—hell, maybe none of them were gods—and they were like technicians and the like. They were real ugly hombres. They were speaking in a language I had never heard before, but I could understand it. The main ugly was telling them that it all had to be under budget. If it wasn't, it was all over. He wanted them to do it cheap but be proud. Mostly, he wanted it quick. The technicians were very much in agreement. In fact, they seemed agreeable to most anything the main critter wanted.

It all seemed very real.

Then it was like someone was calling me, my dad yelling at me to come eat breakfast, but the voice didn't sound quite right. It sounded far away, filtered. And when I woke up and ran my hand through my hair I was in the bedroll in the camper, and the voice was coming from the outside, and it was Bob's.

I got out of the bedroll and came out of the back of the camper, still groggy.

"I was about to come in there and drag your ass out," Bob said. "Breakfast, such as it is, is being served."

I sat on the tailgate of the truck and looked at a line forming at the concession. People were talking in a friendly, if not happy, way, but you could feel the tension in the air, like some sort of invisible mesh. Seeing all those folks thinking about what the line must be like over at Lot B, I realized that big as The Orbit was, it wasn't *that* large, and there were a lot of hungry people here, and when it came to living here awhile, it could get pretty crowded. And fast.

But at this point, things were still not bad. This was the time between hot dogs and horrors. When people were still trying to pull together, stiff upper lip, like all those old science-fiction movies where an alien menace makes them cooperate to thwart it, and in the end earth overcomes and learns to live as one, and Moscow opens some McDonald's and Disneyland puts in a branch over there.

We got in a breakfast line and went through. There were three people operating the concession stand, plus the manager. I noticed the girl giving out the candy right off, and in time I would come to think of her as the Candy Girl. She was blond and very pretty. She had cheekbones so sharp you could have picked your teeth with them. It looked fine on her. If she hadn't been so short she would have looked like a model instead of a doll.

"There's plenty of food here," the manager said loudly, trying to keep everyone's spirits up. "Everything's going to be all right. It might take a little time, but it'll all work out in the wash."

I felt sorry for the manager. He was really trying. But Bob didn't give a damn.

"National Guard show up yet?" Bob asked.

The manager gritted his teeth. "Not yet."

I got my hot dog, drink and candy, and up close the Candy Girl was no disappointment. The dark brown uniform dress she wore set her skin and hair off nicely. She had dark brown eyes, pale, clear skin. Her legs looked nice. I wouldn't have minded being strangled between them. She was as delicious as the sweets she was passing out.

I said hi to her and she gave me a quizzical look and said it back.

So our ritual started. We would eat our meals, go back and watch the movies, visit with folks who came by and wanted to talk, mostly speculating on what was happening. Nobody had an idea any better than Willard's and Randy's about it all being a B movie, and nothing as loony as Elvis Presley's ghost, which made all the other ideas a little less loony in comparison.

One guy from Lot B came by regularly. He was tall and lean and probably thirty. He carried all the information from one lot to the other, sort of a town crier. Because of that, we got so we simply called him Crier, and he liked it and adopted the name.

"I used to drive a beer truck for Budweiser," Crier said. "Only Friday, whenever the hell that was, I got in the samples, if you know what I mean, and turned me a corner a little quick and I didn't have the door closed tight, and I slung Bud all over the highway. Bunch of cars behind me had blowouts on the glass, and some other folks grabbed up the crates that weren't broken before I could get the truck braked and run the hell off with them. Budweiser frowned on this and canned me. I got good and drunk and come to the drive-in. I wish now I'd stayed home and watched the Friday-night movie on television. It looked like it was gonna be a good one. One of them Godzilla-versus-another-guy-in-a-monster-suit movies. Before my wife left me for a Miller Lite driver, me and her and our dog Boscoe, he's dead now on account of I backed the beer truck over him, used to sit up on the couch and watch them Jap movies every chance we got. There ain't a comedy good as a Jap monster movie."

"How are things all about?" Willard asked.

"I guess it's better than heart disease at the moment, but it's about to turn real nasty. There are signs. I always had a knack for signs. I could watch the news or read in *People* magazine about something, and I could always project, you know. Meaning I could look at a thing and see where it was really going. It's a gift."

"Well, where's it going then?" Willard asked, shaking us all out a cigarette.

"As I was saying," Crier said, taking a smoke and putting it in his mouth and producing his own lighter, "there are signs. Over in Lot B a man and a woman pulled their car up close to the tin fence, got on the roof of the car and climbed over the fence into that black crap. So long, sweeties. Suckers went out like June bugs on a hot griddle. It was quick, though. I seen a fella fall under one of them rollers they use to flatten out tar on the highway once, now that was tough. And it didn't kill him right away. Can you believe that?"

"Yeah?" Willard said.

"Yeah," Crier said, and he gave details, then went away.

Without clocks, the sun and the moon to measure time by, it was up to the projectionists to mark the hours. They did this by counting the number of movies they changed. They kept them running constantly. Six of them. Three from our concession stand and film house, another three from the concession in Lot B. When one film was finished, they would measure by its reel time. Usually about an hour and a half per flick. That way, when enough films had been changed, they could compute time for meals. The manager would then announce over the speaker: "Snack bar will be serving breakfast now." Or whatever meal was on the roster. Not that it mattered, since it was the same stuff every time.

"Hot damn," Bob would say, "popcorn. They make a mean bag here, don't they? Regular four-star restaurant." And he would always ask the manager about the National Guard.

That Bob. What a kidder.

For a while I tried using one of Bob's old history composition notebooks and a Bic pen to keep time by the number of movies seen, like the projectionists. But I could never remember if the mark on paper was for the previous movie or the one I had just seen. Things ran together kind of rapid like.

I don't think I was the only one having trouble with time. I think the projectionists were missing it now and then too. Certainly, I was pretty hungry a few times, and I think they missed calling us for meals. But mistakes were expected. I could attest to the fact that keeping time by the number of movies shown wasn't an exact science. And I was sick of the movies. I knew them by heart. You could hear people across the drive-in chanting the dialogue ahead of the actors. Sometimes I dozed when the zombies were eating guts, or when Mitchell was using the industrial nailer on the pretty woman from the shower.

People continued to be patient. Or most. There were a few fights. I saw a guy slug a guy in front of us once, but I don't know what started it. It was fast and explosive. But mostly, people were doing pretty good. It was still like what I was talking about earlier, about those old science-fiction movies where we all pull together against the menace. Only our menace was silent and surrounded us, and we didn't have any bombs to throw at it, and the damned old National Guard didn't seem likely to show up.

When we were tired, we slept in the camper using the bedrolls, giving Willard spare blankets and an old backpack for a pillow. Sometimes one of us would sleep in the cab, or lie down on our bedroll under the truck. We didn't always sleep at the same time. Bob especially seemed to have a different body clock. He would usually climb into the camper for a nap when we were waking up. There seemed to be something furtive about this, but I couldn't figure what it was, unless he wanted to masturbate.

We used the bathroom at the concession, but I could see that wasn't going to last. It didn't work well. It was getting so bad I longed for the toilet at Buddy's Fill-up.

My highlights were saying hi to the Candy Girl and eating. It got so I was getting kind of fat. I took up exercising, but I couldn't stay with it. Just too damn tired. Nothing seemed real or important. The idea of being trapped in the drive-in, though depressing, began to seem normal, as if we had always been there. I wondered why ants in ant farms didn't commit suicide.

The weather in the drive-in was fairly consistent. Not too warm, not too cold. Yet it did change occasionally. Wild winds would twist up out of nowhere and tear across the lots, blowing paper cups and popcorn bags before them like frightened coveys of quail. The paper would fly against the wind-rattled tin fences or over them and into the blackness to be consumed. Sometimes the wind was so strong it shook the truck like a mechanical pony ride.

There was also a now-and-then movement in the blackness overhead. It bulged down, made lumps. Fuzzy blue lightning leaped out of it, produced crackling stick figures that danced across the strange sky to the rhythm of metallic thunder and ran together like idiots to explode in dazzling displays of fireworks.

It never rained, however, and it got so the electrical storms were welcome. They were a break from the monotony. They gave more light. People would lie on the ground, or on top of their cars, hands behind heads, looking up, entranced.

And when there wasn't the lightning, there were the meals at the concession, and the movies. The movies, ever rolling: chainsaws and zombies, drills and screams, common as spit.

With all of us so close together, it got so sex was super casual, damn near a spectator sport. There had always been this element at The Orbit, but it was more blatant than ever, and the romance had gone out of it. To the front of us a group formed that participated in orgies. We were hurt no one invited us over. We used to sit in lawn chairs and watch them wallow on the asphalt. Bob would cheer them on and call out points, and I would wonder where they got their energy. Watching them made me tired.

I remember this little girl who used to walk her poodle between the fornicating bodies. She must have been about eleven. The bodies could have been hedges for all she and the mutt cared. The dog had a pink bow, the girl a red one. The dog was too small in its white fur, the girl too small in her dress. The red ribbon against her oily blond hair looked like a wound.

There were fights. People got mad over very little. Over to our right a fellow wearing a welder's cap got into some kind of shindig with a hatless fella over the quality of the chainsaw Leatherface was using in yet another viewing of *The Texas Chainsaw Massacre*. They did some excellent name-calling. Even Willard and Bob were impressed, and they were well versed in tongue-lashing. Willard had been raised on the streets, and Bob had a dad who thought most of humanity was a sonofabitch, and that the word "sonofabitch" itself was the period to a sentence. "I'll be a sonofabitch. There goes that sonofabitch. You got to watch them sonofabitches. Remember now, boys, folks are just sonofabitches."

The guy with the hat was the sharper of the two, as he had a three-foot length of two-by-four, while the hatless fella had only a popcorn sack, and that mostly empty. Even as Leatherface chased an intended victim

53

across the screen, Hat laid a lick on Hatless's noggin that would have made a sadist wince. Hatless, wobbling a little from the blow, flapped his popcorn bag at Hat, and the bag burst open and sent popcorn bouncing into the night.

It got better than championship wrestling. Folks nearby, maybe friends or relatives, or just interested parties, got in the act, chose up sides, started kicking and slugging. After a while, sides didn't matter. It was getting the good blow in that counted. One guy got crazy, ripped a speaker off a post, went at everyone and anyone with it. He was good, too. Way he whipped that baby around on that wire made Bruce Lee and his nanchukkas look like a third-grade carnival act.

He started coming our way, whirling the speaker fast as a propeller, yelling. He smashed the windshield out of the car next to us.

From my lawn chair I could see him coming straight for me. Bob had already vacated his seat and beat a hasty retreat. He called for me to do the same, but I couldn't move. I was excited and wanted to move, but couldn't quite find the energy to get up. Lately everything was a major chore, even fleeing before a madman. I waited for my destiny. Death by drive-in speaker.

Willard calmly got the baseball bat out of the truck and stepped smoothly over and swatted a home run with the guy's head before he could reach me. The best part of me feared the fella was dead, the worst part of me hoped he was.

"Thanks, Willard," I said. I could have been thanking him for a cigarette the way it came out.

"Hell," he said. "I was going to do that anyway."

The fight was still going on, though it was now moving in the other direction. There was a guy in the car that had gotten its windshield knocked out, and he was sitting there behind the windshield with glass in his hair and on his shoulders. He looked as if he'd tried to ram his head through a block of ice and made it. "Who's gonna pay for all this?" he said. "That's what I want to know."

No one came forward with an answer.

The fight was so far down the lot now, encased in shadow, the grapplers looked like frogs jumping together. After a while, you could just hear cussing, but it was losing some of its originality.

I finally shifted my chair and started watching the next movie, *Night of the Living Dead.* Out of the corner of my eye, I saw the guy Willard had swatted wake up. The side of his head looked dark and pregnant. He had one eye open and he was moving it from left to right, scoping things out.

He rolled smoothly and gently onto his stomach, started to crawl off, dragging the speaker behind him by the wire. He didn't seem to notice it was clattering on the asphalt like a bad transmission. He crawled a great distance down the row of cars and disappeared under a Cadillac festooned with so many curb feelers it might be mistaken for a giant centipede. He stayed there through most of *Night,* and by the time of the next movie, he was brave enough to crawl out from under it, go on his hands and knees for a few yards, rise up to a squatting run and weave off into a maze of parked automobiles, the speaker following him like a tail.

I looked around for Bob, Randy and Willard. They were not in sight. Perhaps they had gone to sleep, or gone off to look around the lots for girls, for action. Me, I didn't want to get out of my chair. I didn't know what was wrong with me, and couldn't seem to concern myself with it. I closed my eyes and thought again of B-string gods. In the dream these gods were made of big eyes and bladders and tentacles. They had a cobbled look, as if a good special-effects man was doing the best he could with leftover parts. They were the same creatures as in the dream before, but they were clearer this time, as if my brain had been focused.

They were up there behind the blackness, and when they writhed across it, it made those bumps we saw from time to time. They had great machines with great cogs and wheels and gears and gauges. They pulled switches that made lightning. They even had lightning that came out of the tips of their tentacles. They took clubs and beat large sheets of metal for thunder. They talked in that strange language, a noise like a rat with its tail in a fan. Like before, it made no sense, yet I understood it. They were talking about motivation of scene, drama, needing something ugly and special. One wanted some cuts. Another thought there was too much sitting around and it wasn't funny enough. He said something about humor making horror better. The gods argued. Finally they put their misshapen heads together and agreed on something, but whatever it was wouldn't stay with me. I felt as if I had tuned in on them, and was now being tuned out.

Then I wasn't thinking of that anymore. The dream had gone to steak and potatoes, country gravy and toast, a big glass of ice tea. In the background of this dream the speaker coughed out screams from *The Toolbox Murders*, or maybe it was *I Dismember Mama*. It didn't matter. I fell into a deep, deep sleep, the screams my lullaby.

8

Dingo City.

Everything started getting fuzzy around the edges. Sometimes my lawn chair moved through time and space. (Spin me around, Jesus, save me stars, get Scorpio in line with my moon, Lord Almighty, let my good number come up, put some beefsteak on the table and wish me luck.)

It got so about all I could do was eat and sit in that chair. And take care of my bodily functions, and that had become quite a chore. Not only was I weak, but the restroom had gotten so bad I didn't want to use it. The odor waited there for me like a mugger, and inside the concrete bunker the floor had gone so stale and tacky with overflowing toilets and urinals, my shoes stuck to it like cat hairs to honey. I damn near needed skis to get to the john, which was now doorless, the hinges hanging like frayed tendons. And once I made it that far, I would find the commode even more stuffed with cigarette butts, candy wrappers, used prophylactics and the stuff that was supposed to be there. What the toilet wouldn't hold was on the floor. So going into that stinking pit was rather pointless. I was terrified at the idea of standing over one of those malodorous urinals or johns (this item of wisdom crayoned above the latter: REMEMBER, CRABS CAN POLE-VAULT) and having something ugly, fuzzy, multilegged and ravenous leap out at me.

I took to using large popcorn tubs to do my business in, carried them to the tin fence and used a flat board I

57

had found to catapult tub and contents into the blackness to be devoured.

Take that, B-string gods.

Sometimes I was so dizzy I couldn't even carry the tubs to the fence to launch them, and then Bob would do it for me. He was the only one of us who seemed firm, relatively unchanged. I wondered what his secret was, or if he had any. I kept wanting to ask, but the words hung in my throat like phlegm. What if there wasn't a secret and there was no knowledge that could help me.

I took to sitting in the lawn chair for longer and longer periods, watching the movies. They were familiar and they made me comfortable. I liked the movies better than people. They were so damned dependable. The same ghosts were revived and slaughtered again and again. Leatherface became adorable. He seemed like an action kind of guy. Knew what he wanted and went after it. Didn't sit around in a lawn chair feeling dizzy. He ate good, too.

Bob leaned over the chair and put his face down close to mine. "You know," he said, "you need to get you some focus. Quit looking at them movies, you're starting to drift." He gave me a pat on the shoulder and went away. I fell into the well of film for a time and came out when I heard voices, some laughter.

"What did you think about that?" Willard's voice. I was too weak to turn and look at him.

"Great." Randy's voice. "I hit him right where you said, the way you showed me, right on the button. Did it kill him?"

"Naw," Willard said. "You just decked him. You get a guy on the chin like that, especially when he's not expecting it, and most of the time he'll go down."

The camaraderie in their voices was strange. Like Siamese twins rediscovering each other after a lengthy separation at birth. Maybe meeting at a dogfight, or something bloody.

Randy had gone from quiet and shy to swaggering,

and Willard had become content, like an empty cup that had been filled.

And me, I was out in Bozo Land, flying about in a lawn chair, watching stars and planets and hamburgers fly by. Something about that bothered me, but I couldn't nail down exactly what it was. I watched Leatherface for a time, then I heard:

"Let's look for trouble," Randy said.

Willard laughed. "We are trouble."

"Maybe you boys are getting a mite out of hand." It was Bob's voice. Calm and in control. "You're not eating good, none of us are, and it's changing us. We're not thinking right. We've got to—"

"Mind your own business." It was Willard's voice, and it was a snarl. "You just take care of the basket case over there and leave us alone."

"Have it your way," Bob said.

I think I flew away in my lawn chair then. I don't know how long I was gone, but when I came back to earth, my chair had been turned around so that I was facing the truck. I think Bob had done that, to keep me from watching the movies.

Randy and Willard were on the hood of the truck. Willard was stripped down to his underwear. Randy had a gallon-sized popcorn tub on his head for a hat. He had poked holes in either side of it and run a piece of leather (probably from his belt) through it so he could fasten it under his chin. He was leaning over Willard, who was lying on his stomach, and he had Willard's knife, and he was using it to cut designs in his back. He'd cut, then use a popcorn bag to sop up the blood. He'd put the bag in his mouth and suck on it while he used the black asphalt from the lot (he had it collected in a large Coke cup) to rub into the wounds he was making. From where I sat I could make out animal designs, words, a bandolier of bullets even. All of the tattoos had the slick look of crude oil by moonlight.

Bob floated into view. "Ya'll ought to quit that. End

up getting an infection and ain't a thing can be done about it here."

"I've told you to mind your own business," Willard snapped.

"Yeah," Bob said, "and I said I'd mind it too. So carve away, Randy. It's his skin. But don't screw up the hood of my truck. Blood'll rust it."

Willard, who had raised up on his elbows, relaxed again. Randy looked at Bob for a moment, then looked at me, smiled like a cannibal watching the pot, then bent to his work.

And so it went.

Movies and tattoos.

I got so weak that Bob would have to help me to the concession for my meals. The Candy Girl had lost her smile and a lot of flesh, the sharp bones in her face were like tent poles pushing at old canvas, her hair was as listless as a dead horse's tail. She didn't put the candy in your hand now; she slapped it down on the counter and let you pick it up. She seldom stood anymore, preferred to roost in a chair behind the counter, just the top of her head showing. I quit saying hi. She didn't miss it.

The manager and the counter boy argued with patrons and with each other. Bob still asked the manager about the National Guard, but now the manager would cry. Finally, even Bob felt sorry for him and didn't mention it again.

When we got our food, Bob would help me back to the truck and feed me by hand. I couldn't make my fingers work, couldn't always keep the food down. It was too sweet. My teeth felt loose and my gums hurt.

And the drive-in changed. People were not so good now. Nobody said "please" and "thank you" anymore. Patience was as hard to find as steak. The fight I'd seen with the welding-cap fella and the others had been just a preview. It was going a step beyond that. There was lots of yelling and fighting now. We heard gunfire frequently over in Lot B and from the west screen in Lot

A. When Crier came by he would talk about murder. He had developed a sense of humor about it and was able to mix it in with his telling. It had gotten so nothing was real to me.

I remember seeing the father of the little girl with the poodle come out of their car, butt naked, climb on the roof and hop around yelling, "I feel better now, I surely do, yes, sir." Then he hopped down, ran across the lot, leaped onto the hood of a car, leaped off, repeated the process down the row until, in mid-leap from a Toyota, he was shot out of the air by a big fat guy brandishing a pump shotgun.

The little girl had come out of the car to watch her father's run, and when he was shot, she yelled, "Two points," at the top of her lungs. I thought it was more like four, and something inside me told me I should be concerned about that kind of attitude, but the voice was small and tired.

Later I saw the little girl wearing a ratty white cape held to her neck by a dog collar. The cape had a pink ribbon on it. The little girl was dragging the empty leash around the lot talking to it. Her mother, who looked like a death-camp survivor, was telling her, "Don't tug on it."

All this scared Bob enough to get his shotgun down, and he kept it close by him for a while. Eventually he returned it to the rack in the truck, chained and locked it.

I remember some of Crier's visits. He came by often. He had found a hoe handle somewhere, and he used it for a walking stick. His hair was almost to his shoulders. He said there had been murders again.

"There were these two brothers over in Lot B," he said, "and they got into it over a popcorn kernel that rolled under their truck. The fastest brother dove under after it, and the slower brother cut the quick one's throat, pried his mouth open, got the bloody kernel and ate it. Afterward, he cut his own throat."

"That ain't good," Bob said.

"I'll say. And the brothers' bodies disappeared, and a short time thereafter there were some well-fed folks over there stepping pretty lively, and I reckon what happened with the brothers was what got this couple fired up to eat their baby *raw*."

Crier had emphasized "raw" as if that were the crime. Smoked, barbecued or plain fried baby was probably all right with him, but *raw*?

Personally, I couldn't see a thing wrong with a raw baby. The idea of eating a baby had certainly not become acceptable to me, but I was beginning to think ahead to the time when it would, and I was quite certain I wouldn't mind my baby raw. Oh, I'm like anyone else, I prefer my meat cooked, but if raw was the only way my baby would come, then raw it was.

"They were out there eating this kid on the hood of their car," Crier continued. "Each one had a leg and was going at it, and the motorcycle gang over there, Banditos, I think they call themselves, seen this and they got some upset, brothers."

" 'Cause the baby was raw?" I asked.

"I don't think so," Crier said. "The cycle guys have taken over in B Lot. They run the concession and keep the movies showing. They've appointed themselves the police officers for over there, and I figure this side of the lot is next when they get around to it.

"Anyway, they got this wrecker from somebody over there, took that couple of baby-eaters and hung them one at a time from the wrecker's wench. When that was done, they tore the couple's car apart looking for food. Found some popcorn kernels and a chocolate almond under the back seat. The corker is someone stole what was left of the kid when the bikers weren't looking, and one of their own men got up there on the hood and started licking the spot where the baby had been. The bikers had to take him over to the wrecker and hang him too. Afterward, the bodies of the executed disappeared faster than a horny man's conscience. Oh, they found the clothes, but not the stiffs that went in them. They watched for charcoal smoke around and about from those who brought barbecue grills, but no smoke was detected. You might say Lot B's law enforcement was thwarted."

"When you get some more cheerful news like that, Crier," Bob said, "you be sure and come share it with us."

"I will," Crier said, winking, and he moved on.

"I think he's a little too cheery about things," Bob said. "Then again, maybe my sense of humor is on the blink."

Moment by moment I felt worse. Got so bad Bob had to decide when it was time for me to sleep. He'd come get me from my chair and guide me over to the truck and put me inside to lie down. Randy and Willard had gotten even chummier, and they didn't have anything to do with us anymore. They took to sleeping under the truck.

Willard had given up his underwear and now went around naked. Randy had tattooed Willard's buttocks so that it looked as if black dahlias were blooming out of the crack of his ass. When he walked, the flower arrangement wiggled as if moved by the wind.

Black blooms on a white-marble ass. I should have seen it as some kind of omen.

The last time the concession was open, I almost didn't make it. We were having one of those electrical storms, and it was the wildest ever; blue fuzz-bolts slamming across the sky (what served as our sky anyway), colliding, blowing patterns like neon quilt designs against the blackness.

Bob got me out of my chair, said something to me that I don't remember, and started leading me. All I recall was that there was lots of light from overhead and I was as crazy as a blind mouse in a paint shaker. I leaned against him and walked, tilted my head up to watch the raging electricity. I remembered my dreams about the B-string gods and thought if they were real, they were pretty worked up this time.

Close as we were to the concession, when we got there, a line had formed, and a long one. There were a lot of naked people. It seemed to be the fashion. Not far up in line was Willard, naked, of course, his knife on a strip of cloth around his neck. His black tattoos were flat and dull in the bad light. He had Randy on his shoulders, and Randy was naked too, except for that silly popcorn container on his head.

Since no one was bathing, it stunk there in line and it was hard to breathe. It made me feel worse than I already felt, and I hadn't thought that possible. A moment later, when we actually entered the concession and the stink of bodies was intensified, mingled with body heat, it was even more intense. I kept wondering in an absent sort of way if the air in the drive-in was limited, if, like rats under glass, we could use it all up.

"Breathe through your mouth," Bob said.

I was leaning against him, and he was holding me up. I turned and noticed for the first time that he had a light beard. There was a band of sweat between the brim and the crown of his hat. All the toothpicks and feathers were gone. His face was hard and there was something different about his eyes. I wondered idly what I looked like.

The Candy Girl looked worse than ever, her movements were automatic. Her mouth hung open and there was chocolate drool running out of the corners and a spot of it was beaded between her teeth. She slapped the candy onto the counter with ill humor.

The counter boy seemed to be having a hard time getting the hot dogs on the buns, and he kept squirting mustard on the outside of the bread. After dropping his third weenie, he threw the bread and mustard squirter down, walked toward the back. The manager yelled at him, "You're fired. You hear? That's it. Fired!"

"That's good," said the counter boy. "I won't have to quit. I was looking for a job when I found this one, so it's no big deal." He disappeared into the storage room.

The manager was wild-eyed and his hair looked spiked from having gone greasy and uncombed for so long. His lips were purple, and there was something on his shirt that might have been dried vomit. He was mumbling under his breath about "freeloaders and sorry no-goods."

Willard was next in line with the manager, who was doling out the popcorn, and when he got his little sack handed to him, he said, "Hell, that ain't half what you're supposed to give."

"Think not?" the manager said.

"No, it ain't half."

"That right?"

"Yeah, that's right."

"Yeah," Randy said.

"Who asked you, you four-eyed nigger?"

And then the chili hit the fan.

Willard may have lost some pounds off his frame, but unlike me, he still had some stamina. His right hand flicked out and hit the manager in the nose, flicked out again, grabbed the manager by the throat. Willard applied both hands then, and the bag of popcorn went flying. A woman dropped to her knees and scuttled after it, chased the bag across the floor. A man stepped on her hand, hard, and she screamed. A kid grabbed for the bag, but his foot was ahead of his hand, and he accidentally kicked it, and it was like a hockey puck going into play. The line broke, folks went after the bag. It sailed past us, then sailed back our way. No one could quite lay a hand on it until the girl with the poodle cape nabbed it with "I got it, I got it," but a man behind her slammed a fist into the back of her head and knocked her to the ground. "No you don't," he said triumphantly.

The bag and the little girl both were now in play, getting kicked up and down the length of the aisle. The bag burst and pops of corn rolled every which way. People scuttled after them on their hands and knees, shoving what they could grab into their mouths. I wanted that corn too, but I was too weak to let go of Bob.

Meanwhile, back to Willard, who was choking the manager.

Willard had the guy pulled across the counter, and he quit choking him long enough to grab him by the back of the hair and slam his face into the glass display case. The manager's face went through with a crack of glass and skull, and a shard of glass went through his throat, spraying the candy boxes and wrappers below with blood. The Candy Girl said, "Oh wow."

Randy, who was still miraculously on Willard's shoulders, was yelling, "Four-eyed nigger, my ass. That'll show him, that'll show him."

The little girl with the poodle cape had become open season. She was surrounded by people who were kicking her, including her mother, who was screeching, "I told you not to jerk on that leash."

"Time to shake out of here," Bob said. He grabbed me and steered me away from the line, headed me toward the door. A fist caught me in the side of the head, and it hurt, but I was already so dizzy and messed up, it didn't make much difference.

A woman with a nail file tried to stab Bob, and Bob kicked her kneecap with the toe of his boot. She went yipping and hopping along the wall, past the rows of horror-movie posters. She clutched at a strand of black-and-orange confetti strung across the window and pulled it down, along with some paper bats and skulls. Finally she tripped over a foot and fell down. The crowd that had been kicking the little girl moved in mass over to the woman and went at it. I could see the shape of the little girl beneath her dog cape. Her body was the color of the red ribbon in her hair, but the ribbon didn't flow.

Then I saw Willard. He had his knife out. He was spinning around and around with Randy on his shoulders, slashing out at anyone in reach. For a moment Randy's eyes caught mine, held recognition, then went savage.

Bob pulled me out of there, outside into the storm.

9

Bob sat me on the tailgate of the truck and went away. He came back with the shotgun, pushed me inside, pulled up the tailgate and locked it. He sat me over by one of the camper windows, then hunkered down by me. From there we could see the concession and the lightning that was sparking across the sky. The truck rocked against the wind, paper bags and cups fluttered across the lot. It was the strongest wind yet.

People were fleeing out of the concession, jamming in the door. There were fights out front of the place. Lots of biting and kicking.

Bob moved over to the trap that held the spare tire and pulled it up. There was a cardboard box next to the spare. He took it out, opened it. It was full of homemade jerky wrapped in cellophane. I had forgotten about that. Something tried to click together in the back of my mind, but it wouldn't. All I could do was say "But—"

"Not right now," Bob said. "Take this and eat it. You're hypoglycemic, pal. Bad. You eat this. Chew it slowly and swallow the juice."

I took it and began to chew. It hurt my gums at first, but it was like new blood was being pumped into me. I wanted to gobble it, but Bob kept warning me to suck it, to make it last.

"If Willard and Randy come back to the truck," Bob said, "I'm not going to let them in. No matter what. Understand?"

"Randy's our friend."

"Not anymore. Eat."

I looked at him holding the shotgun. He looked like a young Clint Eastwood, only shorter, ready to step out of a spaghetti Western.

"I've had the jerky all along," Bob said. "I forgot about it at first—all that was happening and it out of sight. I brought it for you and Randy to split and take home, enough there so your folks could have some. I've been slipping in here and eating it from time to time."

It was as if my head were clearing, cotton stuffing was being pulled out. "You should have told us," I said.

"I can tell you're feeling good already. You're starting to get self-righteous again. First thing you've said in a while that makes any sense. You been out in Bozo Land, pal. All you needed was a rubber nose and some flappy shoes."

"You could have told us," I said again.

"Naw. Randy and Willard were out there in orbit, man. If I'd told them about the jerky, it would have been all she wrote. Willard would have taken it from us, and if we'd given him any trouble, he'd have killed us. No, wasn't nothing friendly about it. And telling him about it and keeping him at shotgun point all the time didn't appeal to me none neither."

"It was needing protein that made them goofy," I said. I closed my eyes and chewed the last of the jerky. I had never tasted anything better in my life.

"That may be, but I ain't no hero, Jack. I was watching after me. What can I say? I knew we had us a ticklish situation here, and I wanted to have my strength for as long as I could. More meat I had, longer I could last. I took it easy on the soft drinks and the candy, tried to drink enough to keep liquid in my body, but to balance the sugar out with the meat. I figured if I could stay alive long enough, all this might go back to the way it was."

"So how come you're telling me?"

"I don't know. Worse you got, worse I felt. Hell, we

been partners a long time . . . Look at you. You look like crap. It was tough to look at."

"But you managed."

"For a time. My dad always said when it got right down to it, people were sonofabitches. If it was a difference between honor and no food, he said they'd take the food every time. Looks like he was right about that. We get home, I'll tell him so."

"Well, you don't look so good neither," I said. "And to hell with your old man."

"I ain't feeling up to snuff, Jack, but with this jerky in me I could kind of figure which was my left hand and my right, know my pecker from my leg, know what was going on in here wasn't just something to look at . . . Man, this is humanity shredding."

"Randy's been a friend a long time," I said.

"Yeah. I care about him. But you and I been friends a long damn time—since kindergarten. And Randy has gotten real weird, partner. Him and Willard are . . . well, they didn't just get that way from lack of groceries. Those two and this drive-in and the things that have happened go together like bourbon and Coke . . . I think they're happy with the way things are. Hell, I don't know, maybe they're queer and in love and it's all this making them find it out. And maybe it isn't that; maybe they're just super fucked up and this is the straw that broke the camel's back, so to speak."

"It still doesn't strike me as the way you should have handled it," I said.

"No? Here, take another piece."

I took it without argument. In fact, I took it a little too fast. I almost ate it with the cellophane on it.

"You're a nice guy, Jack. Kind of a bleeding heart, but a nice guy. I wanted to tell you about the meat, but I knew you'd tell Randy and Willard. A bite of jerky meat wasn't gonna help them none, so I couldn't have that. Finally, though, I figured, hell, I ain't gonna make this nohow, no matter how much meat I hold back. So, I thought, me and Jack, we'll split it, last as long as we can. I mean . . . well, guess I still got some kind of hope in me, just like that manager. Maybe down deep I think the National Guard is going to come through too . . . You see, I had to choose between Willard and Randy and you. And I took you."

"Am I supposed to feel flattered?"

"Be nice if you were. You been fucked up so long, you ain't really got a grip on your thinking. Look out there."

He slapped his hand against the camper window and I looked. People were fighting. They were on their hands and knees going at it. They sounded like rabid dogs.

"It's like I was saying, Jack, you're kind of a bleeding heart. If I'd told you about that jerky a time back, when you were feeling good and full of all that social-morality shit, you'd have wanted to share with Randy and Willard . . . maybe even invite Crier, some of the others over for lunch. Make a picnic out of it. Sing a few songs. We'd have been out of that stuff faster than a whore's out of pride. And I'll tell you again: Willard would have killed us."

"He seemed all right to me."

"He was. He was good to us because he needed friends. In spite of that tough-guy stuff, he was lonely. I've thought on this some, had time to. But he's a survivor, and Randy's a needer. Them two are together now and they ain't two people no more, they're one."

"So what if I want to share with them now?"

"I don't know."

"Would you shoot me?"

"I might. I could eat you then. That seems to be the trend around here. But I don't think so. But I might. Just look at it this way, Jack. Randy and Willard are out there —way out there. Twilight Zone theme time. You can forget them two boys unless the manager is right and the National Guard comes in here and rescues us and we all get turkey sandwiches and some rest. Otherwise, you ain't seen nothing yet. People ain't nothing but animals, Jack. You and me too. Things get bad enough, like animals, folks are gonna eat what they can, do what they have to."

I thought about those books I'd garbaged. All of them were junk, but the basic theme to most had been that man was better than the animals, had something inside him that blossomed like a rose and never died, even when the physical body decayed.

I looked out at the fighters in the lot. A guy in a werewolf costume with the mask missing was rolling around on the ground with a fraternity-type guy whose pants had lost their razor crease sometime back.

"And you're saying we'll end up like that too?"

"Could. We last as long as we can, though. Build up some hope. Get's too bad . . . there's always the shotgun."

I thought about Dad kidding Mom about the last two bullets back . . . when? Christ, who could know? Yesterday? Today? A century ago? What exactly was it he told her . . . ? "When the going gets rough, and it looks like we're not going to make it, I'll save the last two bullets for us."

I looked out the window again. There were people lying on the ground, not moving. A naked man was taking a swift kick in the nuts from a near-naked girl with a punk haircut. There were other people on the ground, on their hands and knees, grabbing for spilled popcorn and candy. One woman was lapping a spilled soft drink like a dog. She had her rear end to me and her dress was hiked up and she didn't have on any underpants. It was far from sexy. She looked like a desperate, dying animal. I felt sorry for her. For them. For us.

72

"Maybe you're thinking about going out there and giving a speech on the unity of mankind?" Bob asked.

"No," I said. "Guess not."

"That's wise. Now take one more piece of meat, chew it slowly, and be a happy animal."

10

We sat there for a time, not talking. I was thinking, watching the storm out there, and the people. I didn't want to watch them fight and kill one another, but I couldn't take my eyes off them. It was sort of like watching the Dallas Cowboys play when they were bad. You hated looking at it, but you had to see it through.

Physically, I felt better. Not ready to do any hurdles or anything, but it seemed my senses had floated to the top once more. A lot of things I'd seen while lost in the ozone clicked together now, and I could see them in a truer light. The little girl with the cape getting kicked to death, for one. Seemed to me I had wanted to kick her too. I could remember thinking that, but for the life of me couldn't remember why. Had I really watched her father get shotgunned out of the air and thought it funny? And hadn't there been something about eating a baby? (Raw as opposed to grilled.)

I thought about the jerky I had eaten and remembered what my father's friend had said about it, how it was like chewing on a dead woman's tit. The thought of that and what was happening out there, people eating one another now and then, made me feel weak and dizzy.

Maybe Bob was right. Animals. That's what we were. No different from the animals except for an opposable thumb and a desire to make popcorn and hit each other over the head with rocks, or whatever instrument was available.

Outside, it looked as if things had calmed down. No one was fighting and there were only gawkers. Standing and looking at the bodies on the ground (there were a few of those) and maybe considering them as steaks, but not quite ready to make the move.

But the calm didn't last long. A guy came walking up, and he had a revolver in his hand, a .357 Magnum. He had a big, loud voice and he was using it.

"Can't do this crap to Merve Kinsman. Merve Kinsman don't take this off anybody. I come here to get my food, real polite like, and I'll be damned if a punk without any drawers with a nigger on his back is gonna tell me dip. I don't take that crap, nosireebob. I'll blow their heads off, is what I'll do. Knife or no knife. I'll not have it, I tell you."

Merve didn't seem to be speaking to anyone in particular, but he was turning his head from side to side as he talked, as if those who were still milling about were hanging on his every word.

I looked at the concession itself. There wasn't any more activity there, and I hadn't seen Willard or Randy come out. It seemed pretty obvious that they were the "punk without any drawers" and the "nigger."

Merve Who - Didn't - Take - That - Off - Anybody stopped outside the concession and waved the revolver and talked to the air some more. "Ain't nobody gonna talk to my ass like that, you hear. I'll pull their damn head off and piss an ocean down their throat is what I'm trying to tell you."

Merve looked at one of the closest bystanders, an aging hippie dressed in old blue jeans and high-top tennis shoes and no shirt. The hippie tried to look casual. He tried a friendly smile.

"Don't you be looking at me like that, you weird little fart." Merve grabbed the hippie and gave him a rapid pistol-whipping about the head and ears and threw him down on the ground. The hippie lay on his side and tried to look dead, but I could see he was

75

blinking. Blood was dribbling down his face. This was a long ways from sixties flower power. I imagined he was trying to figure exactly how he had looked at Merve, so if the situation came up again he could play his cards differently.

Merve pulled open the concession door and put a foot in there quick as a door-to-door salesman. He threw his chest out and stepped inside, saying, "Got some bullets here with your names on them, assholes. Come and get 'em."

Then he moved to the right inside the concession, out of view. Patrons who had been hanging around, and still had enough functioning gray matter, sauntered briskly off. A few lay down on the ground like whipped dogs. The aging hippie remained stone-still.

A shot was fired inside the concession.

More patrons scrambled. More briskly this time.

When no more shots followed, the hippie rolled quickly to his right, came to his feet and darted off. He looked to have been taking lessons from the guy Willard had hit with the baseball bat.

The moments moved by slower than dental work, then Merve Kinsman made his appearance. He came out of the concession walking like a drunk trying to look sober. He had Willard's knife in his right eye. It was buried halfway to the hilt. Merve Kinsman Who-Didn't-Take-That-Off-Anybody was complaining, though not as loud as before. He was now Merve Kinsman Who-Would-Not-Be-Messed-With, By-God, and he wanted every damn one of us to know it. He said something about hell to pay when he found his gun, then he went face down on the lot, the knife point punching up through the back of his head.

Willard came out then. Randy was still on his shoulders, wearing the popcorn container. Willard had to duck to let Randy through the door. Willard had the .357. He looked real happy. He smiled. There was blood on his teeth (or maybe chocolate). Maybe he had been hit in the mouth or had bitten somebody. (Or had eaten an Almond Joy.)

"The concession is ours, you sapsuckers," Willard screamed. "Hear me? Ours!"

Nobody made with an argument. A few people who had been too dull to run shuffled their feet.

Merve Kinsman Who-Didn't-Take-That-Off-Anybody, alias Merve Kinsman Who-Would-Not-Be-Messed-With, By-God, didn't come back from the dead to debate the point, and I figured if anybody could, or would, it would be that guy.

Willard stepped forward a couple more steps, waved the .357 around. Randy beat his chest and let out with an anemic Tarzan yell. Away from the direct light of the concession, shadows falling across them, it was hard to see where one body quit and the other began, especially with Willard covered in those asphalt-black tattoos.

"We're in charge now," Randy screamed.

Willard waved the .357 around some more, turned, ducked back through the concession door and closed it. He pressed his nose against the glass door and looked out. You could only see Randy's legs. The rest of him was above the door, behind solid wall, that popcorn-cup hat damn near scraping the ceiling, I imagined.

Willard went away; the smudge circle of his nose remained to mark his passing.

"Reckon that concession is theirs," Bob said, "until someone with more firepower shows up."

"You got intentions?" I asked.

"Not me, but you can bet someone does."

The blackness above grew cluttered with electric-blue veins, and pretty soon there was more blue than black, and the thunder and the snake-hiss of lightning was tough on the ears, even inside the camper.

Bob got brave enough to open up the back and look out. He said, "Will you look at this?"

I did. The Orbit symbol and the marquee were drawing lightning like decay draws germs. The lightning was hopping through the symbol, kicking out dark blue lights that mingled with the fairy blue and white. The marquee's red letters looked like bright blood blisters about to pop.

We watched as the electric bolts from the symbol expanded, reached out toward the concession and touched it (like God giving the spark to Adam). The concession glowed blue and white, and those bat and skull symbols in the windows looked almost alive.

"Look at that," Bob said.

He was referring to the symbol again, or rather what was above it. Sticking out of the black was what looked like a green-black tentacle, though it could have been a trick of the lightning, a dipping rent in the blackness like a tornado tail. Out of the tentacle (I preferred to think of it that way as it went along with my dreams of *something* up there, something in control) the lightning was flowing faster than ever, zeroing in on the Orbit symbol, jetting from that to the strained marquee. The word "Massacre" exploded in a flutter of glass, fizzled. The rest of it looked ready to go, but held.

Now another tentacle shape dropped down, twisted in the air and gave lightning from its tip, and this lightning went through the symbol and the marquee, and it made the marquee blow the word "Dismember." And that damn symbol began to spin, rapidly, kicking out more and more bolts of energy, all of it going straight to the concession.

One of the black bats in the window flapped its wings and flew away into the depths of the concession. A paper skull twisted and fell to the floor, out of sight. The lights in there were blinking like a strobe show. They went out. But there was still plenty of light from the energy bolts, and it was a strange light, and it lit the concession up inside and out, bright and garish as a cheap nightclub act.

Then I saw Willard and Randy on the roof of the concession. Willard was still carrying Randy and Randy still had that damn container on his head. Willard had the .357 in his hand. They were spinning around up there in the blue glow, raising their hands, cussing, most likely, though there was too much thunder and hissing lightning to hear.

"Must be a trapdoor up there," Bob said.

"Yeah, but what the hell are they doing up there?"

"Believe me, they don't know."

Willard raised his pistol and shot at The Orbit symbol, and, almost as if in answer, a thicker strand of lightning leaped out of it like a hot, bony finger with too many joints and hit Randy on top of his popcorn container hat, turned him and Willard the color of the bolt, and made them smoke. Willard did a kind of funky-chicken dance across the length of the roof and back again. The lightning made him look like he was moving very fast. Randy stayed in place, didn't even wobble.

Willard heel-toed it over to the trapdoor, and with the two of them glowing like a nuclear accident, they dropped through the hole.

The concession was lit up like blue neon. The original lights did not come back on. The movies, defying electrical logic, continued to churn.

I looked to see if there were still any paper bats and skulls decorating the window.

Nope.

11

Things went from sho' is bad to sho' is rotten.

The lightning continued to shoot out of the blackness overhead (though the greenish-black tentacles were no longer visible), strike The Orbit symbol, and in turn strike the concession, and shower blueness over it.

Word of what had happened spread pretty fast through the drive-in, and in less time than it took for a messy dismemberment, the bikers showed.

They spun their bikes around in front of the concession and yelled some things. They roared around Bob's truck a few times.

Most of them had guns: shotguns, revolvers of all kinds. A few had knives, chains and tire irons. They looked nasty. There were twelve of them, and I couldn't figure exactly what had prompted them to show up, unless it was the idea of some guy with a gun and another guy on his shoulders taking over the concession that warmed their blood. Or maybe they had planned to take the concession over themselves and were just now getting around to it, mad because some chump had beaten them to it.

I tried to compute when they had taken over B concession, but couldn't. Time was just too screwed up. It could have been yesterday, last week, a month ago, a year back. No idea.

Whatever, they were here now, riding their bikes and yelling, shouting for the "sumbitches" inside to come on out and take their hanging like men.

To accommodate the hanging, one of the bikers showed up in a wrecker, which I'm sure didn't belong to him. He was more the wind and bugs-in-the-teeth type. There was a noose made of barbed wire fastened to the wrecker hook, and it looked ready for occupancy; one size fits all. I wondered where they had gotten the barbed wire, but not much. People carried everything in their pickups, wreckers and car trunks; all the tools of Texas trades.

There were also a barbecue grill and a bag of charcoal on the back of the wrecker. Not standard equipment. That made me think cannibalism wasn't a crime in the biker book anymore.

The biggest and ugliest of the bikers pulled up in front of the concession door, lifted one hip, farted, and yelled for whoever was in there to come out. Everyone else had quit yelling, and now he was giving it the "I'm the boss" tone. The others stopped their bikes, just sat on them and watched.

The one talking, calling out for Willard and Randy to give it up, was three hundred pounds if he was an ounce. A lot of that poundage was stomach, and it stretched his yellow T-shirt (I think the coloring was due to sweat, not dye) to the point of bursting. He, unlike most of us in the drive-in, didn't seem to be missing any meals. I wondered how big he had been before all of this. For that matter, all the bikers looked pretty good.

But this guy wasn't just a fat boy. He had arms big around as my head, a head a little bigger around than my arms. His hair was long and greasy, tied back with a piece of black cloth. He was wearing leather pants, chain-strapped boots, and an open leather jacket with BANDITOS on the back of it. Part of the jacket had been cut away, and it gave the impression of being too small; it was about halfway up between his waist and armpits.

I noticed the other bikers had done a similar thing to their jackets, or, if they had leather pants, to the legs of those. It hit me that they were cutting the leather off to eat. Maybe boiling it down in Coke so it wouldn't be so tough; making their own kind of jerky.

Though, after looking at the wrecker with the barbecue grill, I assumed they were willing to try more exotic fare. And that being the case, I sat real still in the camper, looking out of those windows that were blacked on the outside so you couldn't see in. I sat there glad that Bob had the shotgun. I had gone duck and squirrel hunting with him, and he knew how to use it.

I fretted over Willard and Randy. Knew they didn't have a chance against these guys, even if Willard was a bad ass and had a gun. There were just too many men out there with weapons and a bad attitude.

For that matter, I didn't even know if Randy and Willard were alive. We had seen them take lightning, lots of it, and walk away, but that didn't mean they were okay. They might have died from it; lying in there now on the floor, Randy's popcorn-container hat still on his head, Willard still gripping the gun.

The fat guy used his feet to push his bike forward, but when he reached the blue aurora around the concession, he backpedaled. It gave him such a shock that the handlebars and his hands smoked. He shook his hands rapidly and frowned.

"Damn you, in there, come on out and take it like a man. That 'lectricity ain't gonna keep you safe. Ain't nothing gonna keep you safe from the Banditos."

"That's right," one of the lackeys behind him said, and the big guy turned to look, as if the agreement had been unnecessary and off-key. The guy who had chimed out smiled wistfully. The big leader didn't smile back. "Shut up, Cooter," he yelled. "I'm the president of this here club, and I'll do the—"

But he cut short when he saw the look on Cooter's face, realized Cooter was looking at the concession.

The leader turned his head forward again, and there were Randy and Willard. They had come out of

82

the concession, and Randy was still on Willard's shoulders and he was still wearing the popcorn-container hat. But the lightning had melted the edges of the container, dripped it down over his head. His features had run together in such a way that one of his eyes was gone and the other had shifted to the center of his forehead. His legs had fused to Willard's shoulders, his knees sticking up like pathetic knots on a charcoaled stick.

Willard's tattoos were crawling all over his body like worms, in and out of his empty, blackened eye sockets. His nostrils had become two large round holes in his face, and his lips were gone, showing a wide mouth with smoldering teeth. Willard still had the gun, but there in the blue lightning you could see that it had fused to his hand, become one with flesh and bone. The tiger Randy had tattooed so lovingly on Willard's stomach was poking a three-dimensional head out and was growling; flesh-colored whiskers twitched against its dark face.

"Man," said the Bandito leader, "you are one geeked-out sucker. But we can fix you."

With that, the biker reached inside his jacket, under his armpit, and pulled out a pistol (also a .357) and snapped off a professional shot that hit Willard between the ears of the tiger tattoo on his stomach.

When the load hit, Willard flinched—a bit. The shot went into a rare pink space on his skin, and the flesh puckered up like a roughed mouth, spat the projectile out with a sputter. An ooze the color of Coke syrup boiled out of the hole momentarily, then the wound closed up.

"That's different," Bob said, his nose pressed to the glass.

Willard raised his revolver and grinned. Randy's mouth grinned too. For a man without eyes, Willard was unerringly accurate. His shot hit the Bandito leader between the eyes, and the biker's brains left home through the back of his skull with a slushy rush, came to rest on the sleeve of the one called Cooter.

"Man," said Cooter. "Radical."

All the bikers with guns opened fire. Slugs hit Willard and Randy repeatedly, but their flesh spat out the buckshot and revolver loads. Even that damn popcorn tub on Randy's head had become flesh, molded into Randy's skull, and it too regurgitated lead.

Willard raised his revolver and emptied it. Hitting a biker each shot, killing two of them, wounding one. He was empty now.

Or would have been, except for the tattooed bandolier across his chest. He reached up, pinched six dark loads from it, shoved the fleshy projectiles into the revolver, which puckered open to receive them.

This was the bikers' clue to zoom out of there. Motors roared, bikes whirled, and they were off. The one called Cooter made a quick turn in front of Bob's truck and Willard fired in the general direction. The bullet came out of the barrel, hung there a moment, then it was a streak and gone. It went around the edge of the truck in hot pursuit and I heard Cooter yell.

I went across the camper, shared a window with Bob, who was also checking it out, and there was Cooter's bike still going down the row, veering slightly to the left. But the biker lay on the ground, face down, the top of his head gone. The bike hit a speaker post, went up it a foot, turned sideways in the air, came down, slid across the path and slammed up against the back of a Ranchero, bounced back into the row and lay on its side like a small foundered horse.

I rushed to the other side to take a look at Willard. He was still firing his flesh bullets. They sought out their targets like heat seeking missiles.

When he was through firing, Willard lowered the gun and looked down. His stomach bulged. The tiger tattoo stretched its neck. Shoulders appeared, then a foreleg poked out. It was as if the tiger were climbing out of a deep, inky well. Another foreleg showed. The cat leaned forward, touched both feet to the ground, pulled the rest of his body out of Willard's stomach, growing in size as it did. It stood momentarily in front of Randy and Willard and swished its tail. Then, with a roar, it went after the biker who had been injured early on, grabbed him around the head with its jaws and bit down with a sound like a duck egg being swatted with a mallet. That was all for the biker.

The tiger pulled the biker inside the concession by what was left of his head (pieces were dropping here and there like china fragments) while Willard held the door open. The tiger deposited the stiff inside, came back out licking its lips. A paper bat exited with it, fluttered up beyond the blue glow, then flapped down again and went back inside the concession. Two skulls rolled into the doorway, looked out with empty eye sockets, chattered their teeth like sidewinder rattles, then rolled out of sight, not even venturing out of doors.

The tiger, as it moved outside the influence of the blue light, softened in color until it was almost light gray; it looked weaker. Then, as it returned, dragging another body by the noggin, it would gradually darken and hold its head higher, and finally, within the confines of the blue glow, it would turn its true color and look strong again.

As each corpse passed through the doorway, I became aware of a black dot, like a bee that had been in hiding, leaping from the bodies and going into Willard's bandolier—little bullets returning to their nests.

Finished with its work, the tiger jumped at Willard and it was as if someone had tossed a can of black paint. The beast splattered against Willard's stomach, made a blot that dripped like hot tar. Its whiskers twitched and it showed its teeth, then it went still and was nothing more than a vivid tattoo.

The other tattoos on Willard's body (they had been thrashing and lashing about) followed suit. The last of them to lie down were EAT PUSSY and KICK ASS. They had been walking across Willard's upper arms like tall, stiff ants.

Randy continued to look peaceful up there on Willard's shoulders, like a real estate agent who had just closed a big deal. I looked for a sign of my old friend in that wrecked one-eyed face, but saw not a clue.

Willard and Randy lifted a hand and waved to the left, then to the right. From my position I could see a few people waving back—reflex reaction, or maybe after seeing what these guys could do, they just felt friendly.

The mouth that belonged to Randy opened and a powerful voice came out. "I am the Popcorn King, and my rein has begun. I will take care of you."

"That's damn nice of him," Bob said.

Then the King ceased to wave and went inside the electrified concession. And so began the rein of the Popcorn King.

PART
TWO

THE POPCORN KING
(With Scabcorn and Other Bad Stuffs)

1

The Popcorn King was happy.

He was a smiley kind of guy—with both mouths—and he could talk that trash. I mean, say you're in this little universe of the drive-in, and maybe we should say the smaller universe of your car or truck, and all you've got is movies. You got no real food, and you got soft drinks for liquid, you're hypoglycemic to the max and your hope don't work no more. All you got is this voice, sleek as a starlet's thighs, soft as duck fluff, as intoxicating as rum and honey. A voice that oozes out of the speaker and flows in your ears, jells around your brain like candied fruit.

The voice of the Popcorn King, telling you how it is, offering you *truth*, telling you he loves you and will feed you and take care of you, and all you've got to do is love him back, and all you've got to do is understand that what you see on the screens are the visions of gods, the way it is, ole buddy, and the manner in which you should live, for so speaks the messiah, the Popcorn King.

Yeah, the Popcorn King was happy.

And he was crazy.

And he helped make everyone else more crazy than they had become.

Back up.

Speculate.

This is how I think it came about; the birth of the Popcorn King.

So Willard and Randy go up on the roof during the storm, wandering up there because they are nuts on junk food and high on a kind of love for one another that isn't quite homosexual, nor exactly the passion of friendship. They're parasites feeding off one another, trying to make something whole out of two halves.

They wander up there on the roof after they have cleared out the concession with the knife, after they have killed. And maybe somewhere deep down, they realize this is something they don't like, this killing. Or maybe, like me, they're so high on sugar it all seems hokeydokey. Or maybe they just didn't give a fuck all along.

Well, you add all that together, toss in their insecurities, and what you have here are a couple of buddies a couple bricks shy a full load. Or to put it in Yankee terms, "They are on the verge of a nervous breakdown."

There's this storm, and it crackles and hisses and fizzles and pops, brightens the sky. Sheet-metal thunder rolls. And these guys up there on the roof are working off little more than the impulses of the primitive brain; that part that takes care of raw survival.

And so they yell at the storm (they don't like the noise, see), call it names. And perhaps by design, because the B-string gods up there are looking for a twist in the plot, or maybe they just don't like being talked to like that . . . and maybe there are no B-string gods and my dreams were just dreams and Bob and I only thought we saw tentacles poking out of the blackness and it's nothing more than an accident that this bolt pops out and zaps the living shit out of our boys, makes them one creature full of power.

Down through the trap they go, smoking like bacon too long in a pan. And they are no longer angry and confused, but they're not just well done either. They have been given power, and this power has straightened their confused asses right out. It has moved through them like a quick, happy cancer, spreading little roots of energy from head to head, from toes to toes.

They are one sho'-ugly critter now, but they are not aware of that. They feel pretty. In their mind's eye they are darling. So sweet with that one eye in the center of the top forehead, and the other head without eyes, just two gaps dripping ooze, puffing smoke.

Their brains no longer work independently of one another; this happy cancer has spread its tendrils through them so that their gray matter operates as one. Randy's eyes are Willard's eyes. Willard's muscles respond to Randy's needs. So, instead of *they* and *them*, these two are now one, and say at his feet are a few stray popcorn kernels that are blossoming in the electrical current, popping high up to greet him ("take me, take me"), and he thinks, uh-huh, happy little subjects, these popcorns, and he names himself the Popcorn King.

The Popcorn King is very happy because he feels as if he has been told the ultimate joke by the ultimate jokester, and he has understood the punch line perfectly.

He knows now he is the Chosen One. Feels that what led him up that ladder, onto the roof, was more than just confusion. It was ordained. Destiny.

Yeah, that's it. He thinks it again. Destiny.

He can feel a network of raw power spiraling through him, replacing the blood and bones inside him with something new; something that makes him master of his flesh (tattoos wiggle like maggots in dung).

The air around him hums (no particular tune) with that blue electrical current. (And while I'm hypothesizing here, sports fans, let's have some of those paper bats —now real—flap around his head, let's have some paper skulls—now real—roll at his feet and nip at his heels like happy pups.) He walks among the carnage of the concession, sees:

the manager with his face through the counter glass, his blood having splashed the wrapped and boxed candies and congealed like cold gravy;

the little girl that was kicked to death, looking like strawberry pulp;

other dead folks, including the Candy Girl (later I would see her corpse in the window, hanging there like a prize cold cut in a butcher's display);

and he moves through the blue air, into the film room, (the bats at his head, the skulls at his feet), sees that there are three projectors, pointing like ray guns in three directions at three six-story screens.

He goes over to one of the little slots by one of the projectors and looks out, sees *The Texas Chainsaw Massacre.* He goes to another and looks out, sees the tail end of *I Dismember Mama.* He examines the last projector slot, sees *The Toolbox Murders.*

He sighs contentedly. This is his domain. His throne room. His damn concession stand. And all those people out there watching those movies are his subjects. He is their King, their Popcorn King. And he is a fun kind of guy.

But what's this? A bunch of fat men on motorcycles are riding around and around in circles out front of his palace, calling him names (had one of them actually called him "dog puke"? Sure sounded like it), yelling for him to come out.

The little people are upset. A rebellion is brewing. The peasants are revolting.

Time to nip this crap in the bud.

So he steps out with the gun fused to his hand, the tattoos shucking and jiving like snakes on hot glass . . .

And from there, I have given you an eyewitness account.

* * *

When it was over and the tattoos had settled down, and the King had waved, he went inside the concession and closed the door. And Bob went out of the back of the camper, sneaky-like, cranked the truck, turned right, bumped over the dead biker and his bike, worked us to the far end, turned right at the fence, found a front row in what was called the East Screen of Lot A. We parked in a slot next to a big yellow bus with CHRIST IS THE ANSWER IF YOU ASK THE QUESTION, THAT'S WHAT I'M TRYING TO TELL YOU written messily on the side in what looked like rust-colored paint. And underneath in dirty-white letters, much smaller, was AIN'T BEING A BAPTIST GRAND?

On the other side of us was an old Ford. It looked empty. The occupants were probably dead, or had joined up with some others and gone to a new location.

Bob got a speaker off the post, more out of habit than anything else, put it in the window, turned the dial high as it would go, and we watched, or rather looked at, *The Evil Dead*. Ash, the character in the movie, was sticking his hand into a mirror, and the mirror had turned into some kind of liquid.

We sat there feeling numb until Bob said, "I don't think coming over here is going to help much, but I'm sort of in the mood for a change of scenery . . . Maybe out of sight, out of mind . . . And I don't think his tattoos can come this far . . . too much distance between the concession and us."

"Agreed," I said.

It wasn't much, but comparatively, this was the best part of the drive-in for us to hide out. For some reason, East Screen had had a lot less badness going on. There had certainly been some stuff happening over here; Crier, who knew everything had told us about it, but compared to the rest of Lot A, and certainly B, it was pretty tame business.

The movies changed as usual, and I could imagine the Popcorn King in the film room, going from projector to projector, switching them as needed. (Didn't he need sleep?) That part of Willard that had been a projectionist was coming into play; he knew how to keep things going.

Bob and I dozed a lot, and when we were so hungry we couldn't take it anymore, we'd go to the camper and lie down and eat, chewing slowly, sometimes talking if we had something to say, listening to the movies filtering into the camper from the speaker in the cab window. It got so I was having a hard time remembering what life was like before the drive-in. I could remember Mom and Dad, but couldn't quite see their faces, recall how they moved or talked. I couldn't remember friends, or even girlfriends whose faces had haunted my dreams at home. My past was fading like cold breath on a mirror.

And the movies rolled on.

At certain intervals, the old yellow bus next door to us would crack its back door, and out of it would come this rail-thin man in a black coat, white shirt and dark tie, and with him was this bony, broad-shouldered, homely woman in a flowered housedress and false leather slippers. She walked without picking her feet up much.

They'd walk toward the center of the row, and there would be others there, and they would form a crowd, and the man in the black coat, white shirt and dark tie would go before them and talk, move his arms a lot, strut back and forth like a bantam rooster. He'd point at the movies now and then, then at the group. He'd hop up and down and stretch his facial muscles, and toward the end of this little exercise he'd be into so much hand-waving you'd think he was swatting marauding bees.

When he tuckered out, everyone would gather around him in a team huddle, and stay that way for some time. When they broke up, they all looked satisfied. They'd stand around while the rail-thin man bowed his head and said some words, then each went on about his limited business.

Every time this little event occurred, the couple coming out of the bus, I mean, and Bob saw them, he'd say, "Well, gonna be a prayer meetin' tonight."

It got so it irritated me, him making fun of them, and I told him so.

"They've got something," I said. "Faith. It's been ages since any of these folks have eaten . . . not since the King took over the concession, and look how they act. Orderly. With strength and faith. And the rest of the drive-in . . ."

You could hear screams and chainsaws frequently, and not just from the screen. Now and then a shot would puncture the air and there would be the sounds of yelling and fighting. But not here at East Screen.

"They've got food somewhere, Jack. Faith ain't gonna take care of an empty belly. Trust me on the matter."

"You'd have to have faith to know anything about it," I said.

"And I guess you do?"

"No, but I'd like to."

"It's all a lie, Jack. There ain't no magic formula, no way to know how to go. Astrology, numerology, readings in tea leaves and rat droppings, it's all the same. It don't amount to nothing. Nothing at all."

Crier came by to see us.

We were out leaning on the front bumper of the truck, watching the people over at North Screen running around like savages, killing one another, wrecking cars. Bob had his faithful twelve-gauge companion by his side, just in case radical company from over there should come by and want to kill or eat us.

None did.

I figured the reason for this was threefold. Each screen had sort of become its own community, and strange as it was, each tended to stick together; they liked killing and eating their own. Least at this point. Two, Bob had the shotgun and he looked like a man who would use it, and there was the fact that the Christians, as I had come to think of them, had formed their own patrol. The patrol walked around the perimeters of East Screen regularly, armed mostly with tire irons, car aerials and the like, but also a gun or two. The third reason they left us alone was just a surmise on my part. I figured they were patient and were saving us for dessert.

Well, anyway, as I was saying, we were out leaning on the bumper of the truck, and along comes Crier. He looked bad. His lips were cracked and his eyes had a hollow look, as if they were shrinking in their sockets. He was using the hoe handle to keep from falling over. He seemed to concentrate heavily just to put one foot after another. I wanted to give him a piece of jerky bad, but Bob, anticipating my thinking, looked at me quickly and shook his head.

Crier came up and sat on the bumper next to Bob, let his head hang, got his breath. "I hope you boys aren't going to kill and eat me," he said almost pleasantly.

"Not today," Bob said.

"Then you wouldn't have anything I could eat, would you? I feel like fly-blown shit. You boys look pretty good. Maybe you got some food."

"Sorry," Bob said. "We did have, but we ate it. We saved a little of what we got at the concession each time, but now that's gone. No more stash."

"Well," said Crier, "I always ask. It don't hurt to do that. Getting so there ain't no use my doing this anymore, this walking around to report the news. Everyone is news now, and no one wants to listen anymore. They just want to kill or eat me. This hoe handle has saved my life a dozen times. Maybe more. I did get beat up pretty bad, though. My ribs are cracked, I think. Hurts when I breathe too deep or walk too fast."

"What can you tell us about the Popcorn King?" I asked.

"He went in there and he hasn't come out. Nobody can get in there neither. That blue light around it would fry an egg. I know, I seen an old boy get his hand burned off trying to go in there after the King and some food."

"Then why doesn't it kill the King?" I asked.

"Don't get me to lying. I ain't got the slightest," Crier said. "Maybe conditions were just different then."

"So, that's it on the King," Bob said.

"Well, almost," Crier said. "Those bodies his tiger dragged inside . . . He's eating those. Got them hung up in the window there, and every time you look, there's less meat on them."

That would be right, I thought. Willard and Randy showing their power, showing that they have food, that it's behind glass, hung up nice and neat, and that the rest of us are lowlifes scrounging for popcorn kernels, killing one another and tearing the flesh off the bones like hyenas. But not him, not the Popcorn King. He's got it all fine and clean and well lighted, and he probably slices his meat off with a knife. Has soft drinks to go with it. Maybe some chocolate almonds for dessert.

"The concession at B?" Bob asked.

"Taken over again," Crier said. "But there isn't any food left. Those Banditos had already cleaned it out. Did I tell you I found a third of a bag of popcorn under a car a few movies back? Over at North Screen too. Just lying there, and hadn't nobody seen it. Kind of in the shadow of a tire, part of the way under the car. I ate that sapsucker on the spot . . . Man, you boys got it made in this section."

"Right now," Bob said.

"Why don't you stay over here then?" I asked.

"Got to keep moving. It's my way. Besides, I don't know that your neighbors would want me moving in. I've been coming and going as I please so long, they let me do that, but I don't know about moving in."

"A word from us wouldn't do you no good," Bob said. "We're sort of low man on the totem pole here."

"Don't need a word. No matter what happens, got to keep moving. I used to drive a beer truck, you know. Always on the road . . . Got divorced twice because I couldn't stay still. Had to stay on the go. Get home and I wanted to drive around. One reason I liked drive-ins. You came and sat in a car, and when you watched the movie it was like you were driving through a new world or something. All you had to do was put your hands on the steering wheel and imagine . . . Sure you boys haven't got a thing to eat?"

"Nothing," Bob said.

"Then I'll hobble on. Take care. Hope the next time I see you ain't neither one of us so bad we want to eat one another."

"Same here," Bob said.

Crier climbed the hoe handle and started off again, moving down the row of speakers, heading for the pathway between East Screen and North.

"We should have fed him," I said. "He looks bad."

"Everyone here looks bad, Jack. It ain't practical to go feeding folks. Even Crier. He gets good and hungry, he might conk our noggins and take what we got. He's all right, but he ain't nothing more than a human being."

"Which as a group you don't have a lot of respect for, do you?"

"It's damn near got so I don't have a drop," Bob said.

I thought about the Christians, their meetings, their faith. It gave me moral strength. Their attitude assured me that there was more to humanity than a

good meal, a cold beer and a roll in the hay. There was
something strong and noble there too, something that,
like a seed, needed fertilizing, and I told all that to Bob,
and he said he thought beer, a good meal and a roll in
the hay were just fine, and as for the seed that needed
fertilizing, he had a strong suggestion for the type of
fertilizer that would best be suited for such a seed.

You just couldn't talk to Bob. He was too narrow-
minded.

And so we got worn down and went to sleep, the
speaker rattling movie dialogue and sound tracks
through the camper as we drifted into nocturnal lands
of cold shadow and dark dreams. And it was then that
the Popcorn King came to us over the speaker, oozed
into our brains and outlined his plans for us, told us how
we fit into the scheme of things. And I will admit, they
sounded inviting, these plans. He would be there to
watch over us, feed us, give us a point on which to fix
our wretched lives. And finally there was that voice,
that lovely voice that was kind of Randy's and kind of
not; that other voice that was kind of Willard's and kind
of not, the one that hummed softly, shucked and jived,
put a word in edgewise in just the right place. Those
voices, those honey-poison, hot and cold voices of the
Popcorn King.

2

So spake the Popcorn King—first one mouth and then the other:

My little dearies, my little popcorn eaters and movie lovers, my little heathens and mortals, you who take dukies beside your cars, how are you, babies, how are you? And listen up tight now, 'cause you done gone and went and got yourself the Popcorn King here, and I want to whisper to you, tell you some secrets, make your life complete, and talk on a subject that is dear to both mine and your hearts.

Popcorn.

Food, my subjects. Chow. Grub. Chewables. Hit it, mouth number two.

(chuckachew, chuckachew, chuckachewchewchew)

Yes, brethren—

(pseudo organ music from other mouth)

—I am here to talk to you about how things are going to be. How things are, in fact, though you may not know it yet. But before I do, let me tell you about the corn, about the sweet, popping corn, hot and fine and ready to melt in your mouth; good ole popcorn the color of fresh bird shit, but the texture and taste of life.

Corn, babies, corn.

Hit it again, mouth number two.

(chuckachew, chuckachew, chuckachewchewchew)

So I come off the roof, and I'm feelin' wild, walk in the house, jive down the aisle. There's some blue air here, some blue air there, lots of dead bodies sho' every-where—

(chuckachew, chuckachew, chuckachewchewchew)

—blood on the candy, blood on the floor, dried and gone nasty, and there'll be more.

(pappapap, pappapap, pappapap, pappachew-chewchew)

Yes sir now, babies, friends and pals, gonna tell you a story 'bout the Popcorn King, how he rolled and walked and talked so clean, yessiree billy, I'm the Popcorn King.

(chuckachew, chuckachew, chuckachewchewchew)

Put your ears to the speakers, put your brain on hold, listen up, honeys, and don't get bold, popcorn's the magic and that's no load.

(jujujujujujujujuju-pap, pap, pap, pap, yeah, chuck-achew, chuckachew, chuckachewchewchew)

Yeah, Popcorn's the magic, it's the tiny bomb, when it sees your insides goes off like a four-alarm.

(chuckachew, chuckachew, chuckachewchewchew)

Now if you been eatin' your kids, dead dogs too, licking cold shit off the bottoms of your shoes, this oughta thrill you, oughta make you feel grand. I'm here to tell you Popcorn King is a friendly man—

(boop, boop, boop—tadtadtad tadachew, chucka-chewchewchew)

—gonna offer somethin' special, offer somethin' fine, gonna tell you a story of the popcorn kind.

(chuckachew, chuckachew, chuckachewchewchew)

Listen up tight, don't stray from me, keep them ears wide open and I won't tell you no lie.

(jujujujujujujujupap, pap, pap, yeah, chuckachew, chuckachew, chuckachewchewchew)

You ain't gonna make it, you don't be my friend, so better do what I'm askin' then.

(boop, boop, boop—tadatada, tadachew, chucka-chewchewchew)

Now we gonna close up shop with the rappin' man, gonna take us a trip to the Promised Land.

(bringing in the sheaves, bringing in the sheaves, we'll all come rejoicing, bringing in the sheaves)

Yes sir, brethren, I have come to you today with a line of pure truth. I come to fill your hearts with love or panic or hate or blood, whatever it takes. Listen up, sinners, let me tell you about the Lords of Popcorn. Let me tell you that those movies are lights from the very eyes of the Lords.

(amen, brother, amen)

Was a time, though I can only distantly remember it and can't make sense of it, when I was a man like you. Two men, to be exact. And sinners in the eyes of the Lords of Popcorn.

(amen)

Yes sir, a sinner, I surely was, a great sinner . . . a damn big sinner. Where's the amen corner?

(amen, brother, amen)

I didn't know the laws of popcorn and soda, of hot dogs and chocolate-covered almonds, didn't know blood and death were the paths to destruction, didn't know that the very flesh of man was salvation and that all we could do was to please our needs and instincts and all else was out the window. Yeah, didn't know love and beauty when it was looking me in my own eye.

(no you didn't, brother, no you didn't)

That's right, I didn't, so the Lords of Popcorn in their ultimate wisdom—blessed are those Lords—seen this, and chillun, they saw I was trying to live like everyone else, and they brought me here.

(yes they did, brother, yes they did)

And I was picked by those Lords as your messiah, your grand executioner, your grand lover, your Popcorn King. They gave me the lightning and the lightning gave me the powers, and these powers made me better than you, and that's all there is to that tune.

(tell it like it is, Brother Corn)

But I come down off that roof a new man made of two, and I come in here and I saw these movies and I knew the truth, seen it was all a sign.

(come to you in a flash of light, this sign)

That's right, it did. Say amen.

(AMEN)

Man but I feel good, sanitized and homogenized. Say it again, good brother.

(AMEN)

Oh, but I like the sound of that. One more time.

(AMEN)

All right, glory hallelujah, popcorn and corpses be praised.

(amen on that popcorn and dead folks)

You see, I saw these movies were the juice of the Lord's brains, the very juice done squirted out of their heads and onto them big white things we call screens. There is the way to live, brethren. It's a dog-eat-dog, folk-eat-folk world, and ain't nothing matters but one thing. That you ain't the one that gets et, if you know what I mean.

(that's the truth, Brother Corn, ain't no denying)

And I said aloud right off the top set of my lips—

(yes, you did)

—I have been sent down here from that roof a changed couple of individuals to make sure those little people out there who are not nearly as neat as I am have an example, someone to follow . . . someone with the corn. 'Cause this place is full of corn, my friends. You too can eat again, and not your neighbor. I'll eat your neighbors, just bring them to me when they go belly up . . . get tired of living, bring your own self, I'll be glad to kill your ass dead.

(be thrilled to do it, yes, he will)

And now you say, but what is the point of all this? It is confusing, Brother Corn.

(was gonna ask that)

Sure you were. And the point is I do as I like when I

like and you do what I like when I like. And there is just really very little that I want.

(ain't asking much)

No I'm not. Just that meat I told you about, alive or dead. And another little thing. The most important thing. I want you to know the movies to be real.

(just as real as can be)

They are the reality and you are the nonreality. You cannot prove your reality by touching yourself. That means nothing.

(go on, touch yourself, don't mean a thing)

It's what you can't touch that's real.

(can't touch reality, no matter how hard you try)

If you want to become as real as the lights on the screens, you have to give yourself to them, do as they do, live as they live. They are the scripture and I am their voice.

(talking for them just as plain as can be)

So come on over to the other side, Reality City. Embrace the truth of the flickering dream, hold on to reality and let the nonreality flow out of you like piss from a bladder. Take the first step toward gratification, toward becoming real. All you got to do to have this thing and the popcorn—

(bless that popcorn)

—is listen to me, dear hearts, the voice of the scripture. All you got to do is listen, and give me what I want.

(amen, Brother Corn, amen)

3

What the nutcase in the concession wanted was simple.

Power.

For the King, power was the end and the beginning —the snake biting its tail. There was nothing else. For in his brains were the distant and confused memories of Randy and Willard. Two people who had seen themselves as outsiders, felt like hitchhikers on the road of life, forever watching fast cars pass them by.

But now, *they* were the drivers, hands firm on the wheel. It was *they* who drove with the pedal to the metal, smiling, looking out at the pedestrians, passing them by, shooting them the finger, giving them a rude honk and a flicking wave.

And if you could have heard the King's voice, that incredible voice massaging your brain like a cat kneading a pillow, you could understand a little how he suckered those folks in, gave them the religion of violence and greed to believe in.

And if Bob and I hadn't had the jerky, the juice of it giving fuel to our thoughts, keeping our brains clearer than the masses (but not as clear as the Christians fueled on the higher octane of faith), we would have joined right up with old King, praised him on high, begged for the corn, worshiped the action on the screens and tried not to think about the time we would die.

And it must be said that the Popcorn King not only had the voice, he had presence. He'd stand out in front of the concession with smiles on both his faces, plastic bags of popcorn in all of his hands (both of Randy's and one of Willard's—the other being permanently full of .357), and he'd close his eyes and flex his body, and the tattoos would quiver, and he'd open his eyes, and the popcorn would begin to pop in the bags, bursting them, and the King would toss the bags forward, beyond the blue glow, and it would snow corn onto the asphalt and fights would begin (the King would chuckle) as people tried to secure the puffs. But there was always plenty—least at this time I'm telling you about—and the fights were more ritualistic than desperate, like punk rockers slam-dancing.

Then would come the buckets of soft drinks carried by the King. Big buckets with paper cups floating in the liquid. People would form unruly lines, come forward one at a time, take a cup, dip from the buckets and drink the syrupy drinks, increasing, more than satisfying, their thirst. But that was the thing that bothered me most as Bob and I stood at the back of East Screen looking over the hood of an abandoned car, those people lifting those cups and seeing little drips of liquid running down their chins. All we had for liquid was the juice from the jerky, but it wasn't water, and we were feeling the slow effect of dehydration. But still, we held out.

Then the weak and the dead would be brought to the King, laid before the blue glow like sacrifices, and the tiger tattoo would leap from the King's stomach, finish off the living, then drag all the bodies inside, where later they would appear in the window, gradually losing flesh in strips.

These eaters and drinkers were not only from Lot A, but B as well. They would all come to eat the King's corn and drink his soft drinks, and afterward go back to their cars and sit on the hoods or roofs and quote the lines in the movies. Quote them with the reverence of holy scripture.

And ole Popcorn King, from inside the concession, using the intercom, would talk to his congregation via the speakers, that hot-cool voice fogging their brains. He would quote the movie lines with them. He would turn the sound down, preach at them, rap at them.

This version of loaves and fishes continued for a time to the happy contentment of the followers, and then the popcorn stopped.

Zip.

Nada.

No corn.

The King did not appear in front of the concession, and his voice did not grace the speakers. There were just the movies rolling on and on, giving evidence to the fact that someone was changing them, keeping them in order, but the King did not make an appearance.

The faithful continued to gather outside the concession, and they would call to the King, but he would not respond. The calls turned to chants, and finally to angry cries, but still no King. The meat in the window gradually disappeared. Someone was eating it. (The bats and the skulls? Nope, cut too cleanly from the bone.)

Bob and I got brave, and we'd go over there for a look, standing behind that same abandoned car, but there was never anything to see besides that confused crowd and those pathetic bodies in the window. People looked at us, but they looked at the shotgun too. Bob made sure they saw it, displayed it like a proud rooster tossing his comb.

I always carried the baseball bat. I liked its weight. It was my friend, Louisville Slugger.

One time we're up there standing behind that old car (a Fairlane Ford with the windows knocked out, I might add), watching, not really expecting anything, but maybe hoping for something. Standing there with our mouths and throats dry as Kitty Litter, our bellies howling and rolling like a storm, thinking maybe how it would be to have something warm to eat and sweet to drink, thinking hard on that meat in the window there, when out of the concession steps the Popcorn King.

The King had turned quite a bit darker, both Randy's naturally dark flesh and Willard's. They had blended together to make a charcoal hue, except in spots where Willard's original flesh tone swirled amid the darker skin like twists of vanilla in a chocolate Bundt cake.

The popcorn tub hat was now amalgamated with Randy's head, and veins like garden hoses stood out from it and extended down his forehead and came to rest above the single eye. The eye itself reminded me of that old Pinkerton ad with the bloodshot eye and the slogan that read: WE NEVER SLEEP.

Randy's knees had blended almost entirely into Willard's chest and shoulders, and the back of Willard's skull had nestled deeply into Randy's crotch like a large egg in a nest. Willard's blinded eyes had sealed over, and there were holes where his nostrils and mouth had been. Even Willard's sex had dried up and fallen off, like the shriveled stem of an overripe apple.

The tattoos, as usual, were quite busy. The animal designs made the appropriate, though diminutive, noises, fussed and snapped at one another like ill-tempered neighbors. The rude arm remarks (KICK ASS and EAT PUSSY), the bandoliers and the like moved about as if looking for better terrain. The tiger on Willard's stomach was silent, however, and, except for the lazy blinkings of its eyes, remained stationary.

An involuntary cry went up from the crowd, and it was a ragged bunch. They reminded me of those photos I had seen of starved, mistreated Jews in books about the war. Some of the women had little round stomachs, and it struck me that they might be pregnant. My God, had we been in the drive-in that long?

The King held up both hands like a victorious prizefighter. His mouths smiled. And out of the top mouth came: "I have returned. I offer you manna from the bowels of the messiah."

With that he opened his mouths phenomenally wide, the teeth folding back against the roofs of his mouths like tire-buster spears, and with a rumble and a methane-ish stink we could smell from where we stood, out came *popcorn*.

Sort of.

The velocity of the vomit was tremendous, the well from which it gorged endless. The content of the vomit looked to be cola and popcorn. It hit the crowd like a fire-hose blast, dispersed them, knocked them down. It spewed all the way back to Lot B.

Then it ceased. The shaken crowd found their feet.

Again the King opened his mouth, and once more the vomit spewed. More powerful than before. And when it ended this time, the King said, "Take of me and eat."

The crowd, somewhat recovered, examined the corn, looked at it long and hard. And then one man picked up a big puffy kernel and closed his eyes and put it in his mouth and bit down. You could hear his sigh of contentment throughout The Orbit.

Everyone, as of old, began to shove and fight for the corn, and a stray kernel, perhaps launched by an excited foot, came rolling our way, went under the Fairlane and lay between mine and Bob's legs.

We looked at it.

We looked at one another.

We looked at it again.

It looked back.

It was the general shape of popcorn, slightly off-white in color with a sort of scabby look between the creases, along with thread-thin veins that pulsed . . . and in its center was an eye. A little eye that had no lid, but was instead a constant thing that matched the eye in the center of the King's top forehead.

Bob put his foot on it and pressed down. It was like

stepping on one of those big dog ticks that are flat and gray until they've fed and dropped off their hosts to lie big as plump raisins.

"It moved under my boot," Bob claimed. "I felt it."

"Jesus," I said, and it sounded like a plea.

We looked back at the people. They were popping the corn into their mouths, oblivious of its appearance, or not caring. Blood oozed from between their lips. I could see their bodies rippling as if a sonic wave were passing beneath their flesh. Their grunts and cries of satisfaction and anxiety came to me like hyena barks, their squeals and lip-smacking like the sound of hogs at trough.

And a part of me, the hungry part, envied them.

The King looked at us over the top of the Fairlane. It was a decent distance away, if not outstanding, and I couldn't determine with his features the way they were, if he recognized us. I doubted it. Least not in a way that really mattered.

"Come," came that sweet-sour voice, "join us, brothers. Eat."

"Not just now," Bob said. "Maybe later."

And we turned and walked quickly away, back to the camper. When we got there, Bob took some wire cutters out of his toolbox, went out and cut the speaker wire off at the post, flung the speaker far away from us.

4

That's when I made my decision to join the "church."

If I was destined to go down before evil, or simply to starve to death, I wanted to make sure I would be embraced by the arms of our Saviour, the Lord Jesus Christ.

It was odd that I hadn't seen this obvious truth before. Odd that it had always been right before me, and I had denied it. But now it was all very clear, as if a visionary light had opened from the blackness above, a light unlike the fuzzy blue lightning, but instead a warm yellow light that struck me in the top of the head, penetrated my skull and filled me with sudden understanding.

Shortly thereafter, for it took little to tire us, we climbed into the back of the camper to sleep, and when I heard Bob's breathing go regular, I got up and snuck out and went over to that bus.

As I was nearing it, the back door opened, and the contents of an improvised bedpan went flying. I was glad I wasn't along a little farther when this happened, or my first meeting with them might have been less than auspicious.

Watching where I stepped (for this bedpan procedure had been followed for quite some time), I went over and called just as the door was closing.

With the door half open, the woman of the bus stuck her head out and looked at me in the same way all the Christians looked at me. With that cold stare that told me I was an outsider. She had her hair up, and some of it had escaped over her face like spider legs. She was wearing an ugly duster and pink house slippers I hadn't seen before. They had MEXICO written across the top of the insteps.

"I want to be one with the Lord," I said.

She just kept staring.

"I am not a Christian, and I see that you folks are, and I like what I see. I want to be one of you. I want to join in salvation, and—"

"Hold it a minute," she said, turned back into the bus and yelled, "Sam!"

After a moment the door cracked wider and the scrawny man stood there. Behind him it was dark, but there was enough light from the storm overhead that I could see the bus's walls were lined with shelves and the shelves were full, though I couldn't tell with what.

I noticed the man's tie wasn't a real tie at all. It was painted on. He eyeballed me for a long moment. "Whatchawant, sinner?"

"I want to be a Christian."

"Say you do. Want to be baptized and the like?"

"If that's what it takes."

"Does."

"Then baptize me."

"That's the spirit. Come around front of the bus, I'll let you in."

"Sam?" the woman said.

"Now, don't you worry," he said. "This here's a nice boy. Besides, he wants to become a Christian. Right, son?"

"That's right," I said.

"See, there you are," he said to the woman. Then to me: "Come around front."

They closed the door and I went around to the door at the front side of the bus, and Sam opened it. I stepped inside and saw that a blanket curtain had been put behind the driver's seat, blocking off the rest of the bus from view. The woman was still back there.

There was a special seat bolted to the floor next to the one behind the steering wheel, and hanging from the mirror was a plastic Jesus that glowed in the dark, one of those things you buy across the border in Juárez. I had never wanted one. Lastly, in upraised rainbow stencil on the dash was this message: GOD IS LOVE.

"Sit down, boy." He patted the seat beside him, and I took it. "Now," he said, pursing his lips, "you want to become a Christian, do you?"

"I've been watching you folks . . . your meetings going on . . . Well, I like what I see."

"Don't blame you . . . I was a plumber, you know."

"Beg your pardon?"

"And a painter. Did plumbing and painting. Paint a little, plumb a little. Mostly plumbing, 'cause I'm kind of wiry, you see. Get up under them houses like a snake, fix them pipes. Some of the other plumbers called me that —Snake, I mean. They'd say, 'Snake, you sure can get under them houses,' and I'd say, 'Yeah, I can.' 'Cause I could."

"I see," I said.

"Painting now . . . that was different. I did it, but I didn't care for it. All them fumes make you sick, real sick. I'd sign on to paint a house, and I'd be sick through the whole thing. Not a minute's peace, just queasy and kind of headachy all the time. Even at night when I was away from it, after I'd cleaned up, I could smell that paint under my fingernails. It kind of hung on me like a cloud, it did. Much preferred plumbing. Sewer smell ain't nothing to a paint smell. Sewer smell is good honest smell. Human smell. But paint . . . paint is just paint, you see what I mean?"

I had begun to sense a parable. "Well . . . I suppose so."

The blanket moved then and the woman came out

from behind it. She had put on another duster, not any more attractive than the first. She had on the same house shoes. I noted that she kept the backs broken down so her heels could hang out.

"It was just awful when he was painting," the woman said, picking right into the conversation. "He wasn't no fun at all. Grouchy all the time, like a poisoned dog. Hi. My name is Mable."

"Glad to meet you," I said. "I guess this is your seat."

"Oh no," Mable said. "You just keep it. I'll stand right here. I'm fine. I used to say to Sam about the way he acted when he was painting, 'Now you gonna act like that, you go out and sleep in the yard.' Didn't I say that to you, honeybunch?"

"Yes, you did, dumpling. She'd just say it right out, and mean it too. 'You gonna act like that, Sam,' she'd say, 'then you go out there in the yard and sleep. Take your piller with you, but get on out of this house.' That would straighten me right up, it would. Couldn't stand to be without my dumpling."

I was beginning to suspect this wasn't a parable.

The woman moved close to him, and he reached up and put an arm around her waist. She patted him on the head. I thought maybe she would give him a dog treat next.

"Painting is why I got preaching on my mind," Sam said. "They used to say, 'Be a Baptist preacher and you don't have to do no work,' and that sounded good to me. So, I started trying to teach myself about it, just so I could quit painting, you see, and you know what, son?"

I said I didn't.

"The call come over me. I'd been reading the Bible, trying to get a handle on it, trying to get all them names separate in my head, you know, and one night I'd just finished all that—I'd been painting earlier in the day—and I was dozing, listening to the radio, one of them country and western stations, and God, the Big

Man himself come to me over that radio and told me some things he hadn't told none of them other preachers. Gave me some insights into His ways."

"Hallelujah, honey," the woman said.

"His name be praised. So God come to me over that radio, and I remember it was right in the middle of a pretty good ole song too, and he said, 'Sam, I'm giving you the call, and I want you to spread my word.' That was it. He didn't lay out no details or nothing, just matter-of-fact about it, and I packed up our things, built us a traveling home out of this bus—"

"They come and took our house 'cause we couldn't pay for it," Mable added.

"Yes, they did, didn't they, dumpling. And I got this bus fixed up, and we started traveling around the country, doing a little fixing here and there, plumbing mostly, little painting when I couldn't get out of it and we needed the money, and I did a lot of preaching."

"It paid better than the plumbing or painting," the woman said. "It was just a sight to see how full that offering plate would be after a night of Sam's preaching. People just loved him."

"But the money wasn't the important thing. The thing was, I was reaching people with the Lord, taking the offering to keep this bus running, to feed our faces and keep us at the Lord's work."

"Sam made so many conversions," Mable said.

"Yes, I did. And one night while we was traveling, we come by this place, seen all those cars in line, and I thought, now wouldn't this be a golden oppurtunity?"

"Them's the exact words you used, sugar," Mable said. "You turned to me and said, 'Wouldn't this be a golden oppurtunity?' "

"I thought during intermission I might turn on my loudspeaker and start preaching. Try to bring some souls to God. But then this thing happened, this thing of the Devil. He'll do that every time, son. You got some good designs, well, ole Devil will come right in there on

115

you, trying to mess things up. Even Oral Roberts, and you know how close he is to God, has problems with the Devil. Ole booger come right in Oral's bedroom once and tried to choke him, tried to choke the life out of him."

"But his wife run the Devil off and saved him," Mable said. "She come right in there and ran him right off." She patted Sam on the head. "I'd do that for you, wouldn't I, sugarbunch?"

"Yes, you would, dumpling, you surely would. But now, what we got here is a boy that wants to join our flock. Am I right, boy?"

"That's right," I said.

"Good, good . . . You ain't got no food on you, do you?"

"No," I said. I thought about the jerky back in the camper, but it was really Bob's and I couldn't offer it without his permission. Besides, I was afraid he'd shoot me.

"Well, let's get the baptizing part over with." With that Sam spit on his fingers and rubbed them across the top of my head. "I baptize you in the name of the Father and the Son and the Holy Ghost. Amen. Okay."

"That's it?" I asked.

"You were expecting a tub?"

"No . . . I mean . . . I guess it's okay."

"Sure it is. You feel any different?"

I thought about it. "No, not a thing."

"Just a little tingle or something?"

"Nope."

Sam looked distressed. "Well, sometimes it takes some time, so you give it some. Thing I'm gonna want you to do is go to the services a little later on. You come to that, son, and I'll hand you the Lord on a silver platter. Mable, bring the sand, will you, darling?"

Mable went behind the blanket curtain and came back with a big hourglass. The sand in the top half had almost run out.

"This here has come in handy. It was just one of them things we picked up once and hadn't never used, but since we been here in this outdoor picture show, we've used it quite a bit. It's an eight-hour hourglass. When it runs through twice, we have services. Unless we forget to turn it or we sleep through, but that ain't often."

We sat there a minute and he told me a couple of plumbing adventures, then he said he had to go get ready and he went behind the blanket curtain and left me with Mable, who took his seat in front of the steering wheel. She looked at the rainbow GOD IS LOVE on the dash for a while, then put her eye on the Jesus hanging from the mirror, and finally looked out at the wing mirror as if she might find a revelation there. Things being as they were, I was kind of short on small talk, and as the weather was constant, that was out. I was beginning to feel like an enormous jackass.

"You know," Mable said out of the clear blue, "wish I had me some ham bone and some dried beans—pintos. I think I miss that the most, ham bone and beans. I can make the best pot of beans. I just take me some pintos, the dried kind, and soak them in a pan of water overnight, then the next morning I start cooking them, making sure I don't let all the water boil down. I chop me up a bunch of onions, put some salt and pepper in there, and that ham bone, and just cook and cook and cook till that water gets real soupy. You fix you some cornbread with that, even hot-water cornbread, and I tell you, you've got major eating, mister. I just dream about food all the time. How about you?"

"I think about it a lot," I said. "Mostly hamburgers. Sometimes pizza."

"You do like pinto beans and cornbread, though?"

"I've got no complaints against it. Right now most anything sounds good."

She seemed to consider that for a moment, then she said, "You know, this is all the work of the Devil.

And we can beat the Devil if we try. My next-door neighbor back when Sam was plumbing all the time was named Lillie, and she had these Hell's Angel types move in across from her. Drove them motorsickles, you know. And she said they were worshiping the Devil, 'cause she could hear that loud rock music, you know. The stuff where you play the records backwards and it's got some sort of ooga-booga about the Devil on it. And she started praying, and darn if they didn't move. Just up and moved six months later, and she said it was on account of her praying all the time. The Lord heard her prayers, and those Hell's Angels just up and moved."

Right. Up and moved six months later. I wondered if Bob would do me the favor of kicking my butt around the camper a few times.

In the middle of an apple-pie recipe, Sam returned. He had on his coat; it sagged badly. He had on a different shirt, and though it was in pretty tough shape, it did look better than the other one. Even the tie was painted on better. It must have been the shirt he used for Christmas because the tie was bright red.

Mable went behind the curtain then to do "a little touchin' up," and Sam sat down behind the steering wheel and looked at me like a loving, but stern father.

"Son, I want you to know that now, no matter what happens, you are in the hands of the Lord. If something really ugly should happen to you . . . if a ton of bricks fell out of the sky and crushed you flatter than a pie pan, you'd be one with the Lord. He's waiting on you, son. Waiting for you to join His kingdom. What do you think of that?"

"It's a comfort," I said. I wondered if Bob would loan me his shotgun so I could shoot myself. I had been a bean head to see anything wonderful about these people and their way of life. The truth was I was going to die, and there wasn't any heaven to go to. Unless it was some sort of B-string heaven for extras in bad movies. That's what this all had to be. A bad movie.

When Mable came back she had on a long overcoat, and I could tell the pockets were filled with something, but I had no idea what.

"Well, how do I look?" she asked Sam cheerfully.

"Like a million dollars, sugarbunch, like a million dollars." He smiled at her, then looked at the hourglass. "Almost time. I got to go next door and tap on Deacon Cecil's car window, get him to get everybody ready for tonight's services. You're gonna like this, son. It's gonna put you straight with God."

I was beginning to doubt that. If these were God's chosen people, He had poor taste, and if I wanted in with them, then I had even poorer taste. But as it stood, in for a penny, in for a pound. It wasn't like I had a pressing engagement elsewhere, but I was beginning to plan one. Maybe Bob would like the idea. We could maybe find a hose somewhere and run the exhaust fumes into the back of the camper. Just go to sleep and not wake up. It sure seemed like a good proposition to me.

Sam got up and I let him pass by me and out the door to get Deacon Cecil. When he was gone, Mable shrugged and said, "Well, here we are."

She told me a story about how she'd won a baking contest in Gladewater, Texas, once, and by then Sam was back.

"Are things ready?" Mable asked.

"Ready," he said, and looked at me and smiled.

I smiled back.

We went out of the bus, and as we walked, Sam put his arm around my shoulders and told me about the Kingdom of Heaven. None of it was particularly inspiring. The smell from his armpit kept my mind off what he was saying and made me woozy.

As we neared the selected spot, I could see a number of the Christians strutting rapidly toward it. They really seemed worked up and excited this time, like they'd just arrived at the company picnic.

On the other hand, I was considerably less than worked up. My entire religious experiment so far had been a vast disappointment. Sort of like when I found out my pet gerbil wouldn't live forever, and later, after I'd cleaned the little turds out of his cage for what seemed like an enormous period of time, thought the little fucker would never die.

When we were all gathered there, Sam introduced me as a "boy who wants to join God," and the others told me how nice that was, and a girl who might have been pretty, had she not been so thin and her hair so greasy, said, "A fresh one, huh?"

"You know," Mable said, looking up at the lightning flashing across the blackness, "this reminds me of when we used to camp out, and sometimes it looked like it was going to rain. And we'd build us a big fire anyway, and we'd take some coat hangers and straighten them out and roast wienies over the fire. It was so much fun. We'd just let them cook until they were black, and they tasted so good. That just don't make sense really, 'cause if you burn them at home they aren't any good at all, but out there on an open fire you can cook them black as a nigger, and they're just as fine as they can be."

"We'll start the services with a little round of prayer," Sam said, "then we'll have communion."

At mention of the word "communion," a collective sigh went up from the crowd. These were some communion-loving folks. I remembered the sighs from the Popcorn King's followers when they were eating the results of his vomit. There hadn't been a lot of difference in sounds.

"God," Sam said, "you sure have allowed some odd things here. In fact, I would say you have outdone yourself. But if that's your will, that's it. Still, sure would like to know the why of it . . . We also have this young fella amongst us, just baptized and craving the Lord, and we thought we'd bring him to you . . . It would certainly be nice if you'd do something to that old Popcorn King, by the way. Like maybe kill him. And it wouldn't hurt my feelings, or the feelings of anyone here, if you'd make this black mess go away and give us back our highway and things. Amen."

"Amen," said the crowd.

"Bad as things is," Mable whispered to me, "you got to be thankful. Things will work out, I know they will. I had a cousin, her name was Frances, and she didn't have good thoughts on nothing or nobody, and she got this rash on her foot and it got infected, and she wouldn't do nothing but wear this old sock on it, day in, day out. It just stunk something awful. I'd say to her, 'Frances, you need to go and pour you some chemicals on that thing. It's done gone and got infected.' But you know, she wouldn't listen, and her foot got so infected they had to cut it off. Had a foot one day, next she didn't. Just had this little stub and they got this leather thing they put over it, and she had to put on this artificial foot, and she'd pull a stocking over that and she could slip a shoe on, you know, and it looked almost real. But when she walked, she walked something like this." She showed me how her cousin Frances walked. The congregation and Sam had stopped to look at her, but she didn't seem to notice. She did a sort of stiff step with one foot and dragged the other after it. "That's how she looked. And there's some little ole mean kids that live down the block from her, and they'd get up behind her when she was walking to the store, and they'd all walk like her." She showed me the walk in more exaggerated form. "It was just like a bunch of crippled ducks following their ole crippled mama. They'd been my kids I'd have worn their little hind ends out so bad they couldn't have sat down for a week. But the reason she got her foot rotted off like that and got mocked by them children is because she didn't have no faith and doesn't look on the bright side of things. God keeps score on them kind, you can bet he does."

"Mable," Sam said patiently, "if you're through

with the story about your cousin's rotting foot, we'd like to continue."

"Oh, I am sorry," said Mable. "Don't you pay me no never mind. Ya'll just go right on with your rat killing and I'll hush and listen."

"That would be nice," Sam said.

Then came the sermon. It had a lot of storm clouds, sinners, fire and brimstone and the work of the Devil in it. Sam hopped around and waved his arms a lot. But somehow it wasn't very exciting. There were quite a few references to plumbing and painting and a parable about a little girl that got hit by a truck, which I couldn't seem to work into the rest of the sermon or find the point of.

A man beside me leaned over to another and said, "I'm really sick of this crap."

"It's a thing to get through," the other man said.

Finally Sam's sermon sort of petered out, like maybe he couldn't keep it on his mind anymore. He said "amen" and called his flock to him. This was the huddle I'd seen, and Mable put her arm around me and pushed me toward it. In the huddle it was hot and full of sweaty pits, unwashed clothes and bad breath; all this ganged up on me and I felt dizzy and weak, and before I knew it, I was in the center of the huddle and hands were touching me, then suddenly Sam stepped forward and kicked my feet out from under me. I went down hard and hit my head, tried to rise, but Sam shoved me down with his foot, and the next thing I know there's two guys holding my arms, and the girl with the greasy hair has one of my legs and Mable has the other.

"What in hell are you doing?" I yelled.

"Communion," Sam said. He took a tin of sardines out of his rumpled coat, and that made me aware suddenly of what was filling that shabby coat of Mable's. More sardine tins. "We been sharing these with the congregation," Sam said. "Folks have been real nice about it too, especially since they know I got the bus rigged up with a bomb, and they mess where they ain't supposed to be messin' when we're away from there, and BLAM!"

"That's got nothing to do with me . . . Tell these people to let me go."

"It's got everything to do with you. We also drink a little of each other's blood."

"Like this," Mable said, and she put her knee over my ankle to hold me down and produced a penknife from the pocket of her coat. She opened it smoothly and drew it across her palm. A line of blood appeared there and she held her hand up without looking and a man who was standing above her grabbed it and put his mouth to the wound and sucked. He trembled he was so excited. Mable's tongue worked from one corner of her mouth to the other and her eyes closed.

A man in the crowd began speaking softly. "Yeah, brother, get it, get it, go, go."

"Oh yes," Mable said, "Oh yes, yes, yes. Suck, suck, oh God in Heaven, suck, yes, oh yes."

Then other knives and razors flashed and flesh was opened and mouths were pleased. It sounded like a convention of leeches, or an orgy—or, to be more precise, both.

Sam squatted down close to my face. There was blood on his lips. "You see," he said, patting my chest. "We made a pact. We wouldn't let nobody else in. We would convert them if they wanted, but they couldn't join us, and we'd eliminate competition. It's a tough thing to do, but the Lord moves in mysterious ways his miracles to perform . . . and food lasts longer this way."

A man took Mable's place holding my leg and she inched down to me and held the penknife where I could see it. "And we have to take advantage of any food that comes our way," she said. "It would be sinful to waste . . . and we've had our eyes on you and your friend for a while."

"We just didn't want to get shot," Sam said. "Your pal never seems to leave his shotgun."

"But you're Christians," I said.

"That we are," Sam said, "and that should make you feel proud and special. You'll be with God in Heaven in a short time now. He'll embrace you and—"

"Then why don't you go join him," I said. "You're holier than me, you should go first."

Sam smiled. "It isn't my time."

"It's a little thing," Mable said. "Nothing to it, really. We got to do this thing, and you've got to accept it . . . And this here knife may be small, but it's sharp. It won't hurt much. They say the blood goes out of you fast when it's done right, that you just get terrible sleepy, then it's all over. I've cut many a hog's throat in my day, and though couldn't none of them tell me if it was sleepy or not, they seemed to go pretty peaceful, wouldn't you say, Sam?"

"I would," Sam said.

"But I'm no hog," I said.

"Cut the gab," a man said, and he dropped a rusty-looking hubcap beside my head; it clanged, rattled, stopped.

"Turn him," Sam said.

The two holding my legs let go, and the men who had my arms flipped me onto my knees, pulled my arms back so hard behind my back my shoulder blades met. They pushed me forward so that my face was over the hubcap.

"Won't none of you waste," Mable said. "I thought you'd like to know that. We'll take the blood to drink, then we'll have us a little ole cookout with the rest of you."

"Mable can cook like the dickens; don't matter what it is, she can cook it."

The greasy-haired girl who had held one of my legs earlier came around and bent down to look me in the face. "I'm gonna love you, sugar. I'm gonna just love you to death. Gonna wrap my lips around you, and chew and chew and chew."

"Get on with it, for Pete's sake," the man who had dropped the hubcap said.

Mable grabbed my hair. "Just think about something pleasant, like good ole turnip greens and black-eyed peas. It'll be over quick-like."

I closed my eyes, but I didn't think of turnip greens and black-eyed peas. I tried to remember how things were before the drive-in, but nothing would come. There was only the dark behind my eyelids, the sound of all those hungry Christians breathing, the smell of their bodies. Mable lifted my head more to expose my neck. I hoped it would be quick and that I would not have to hear my blood draining into the hubcap for very long.

And just when I expected to feel the blade, there was an explosion, a thud in the hubcap and I was warmly wet from chin to forehead.

PART THREE

THE ORBIT MUST DIE
(Death and Destruction and School Bus-Fu)

1

I thought my throat had been cut and the blood from the wound had sprayed my face, and that simultaneously there had been a loud clap of thunder, though it didn't sound right, not even for the artificial thunder of the drive-in.

Against my will I opened my eyes, saw lying in the hubcab beneath me a hand, and lying next to it in a little pond of blood was the penknife.

The men had let go of my arms and I was able to rock up on my knees and see Mable. She was still on her knees, but now she was holding her arm in front of her, minus her hand, and watching blood leap from the wound like freshly tapped oil.

Mable looked at me and said, "Oh my."

A number of the congregation dropped down to try and suck at the stump of her arm, and the girl with the greasy hair began lapping at the blood that had sprayed my face. Her tongue was rough and dry, like a cat's.

"Who's next?" a voice called, and I turned to see Bob standing there with the shotgun, a wreath of gunsmoke about his head. With his hair and beard grown long, his sweaty hat drooping, he looked like an old-time desperado. At his feet two men lay holding their heads. He had apparently cleared himself a path into the huddle with the stock of his gun.

"Mess with me," he said, "and I'll shoot you just to check the pump action on this baby."

Mable said, "Sam, Sam, my hand's done come off . . . Do you think we can get me an artificial one?"

"They cost too much," Sam said, and Mable fainted forward on her face. The stump-suckers stayed with her, working on her arm, pushing and shoving each other out of the way, tongues darting and colliding as they pursued the taste of the hot blood.

"Quit that sucking on her," Bob said. "Get away from there." He stepped in and gave one of the lappers a quick kick to the seat of the pants. "Spread the hell out."

They did.

"And you," he said, giving the greasy-haired girl a kick in the ribs, "you quit licking his face."

She scrambled away. I sort of hated that. I was beginning to like her.

A guy tried to pull a pistol on Bob, and Bob saw him out of the corner of his eye and gave him the stock of the shotgun to eat. The man went down and the gun slid across the asphalt. Bob looked at the greasy-haired girl and said, "Do me a favor, sugar, hand me that gun. Easy-like."

She gave it to him without protest and he put it in his belt.

"All right, all other weapons hit the deck," Bob said, "or I'm gonna start opening up heads."

Another pistol dropped to the ground. Can openers, knives, clubs, coins in socks. A condom full of marbles.

Bob nodded at the pistol. "I'd like that one too, sugar. Okay?"

The greasy-haired girl gave it to him. He put it in his belt next to the other one. Now he did look like a desperado.

The crowd had spread out, and I got up. I felt a little on the limp side.

"Take off your belt, Jack," Bob said, "and give it to

that preacher fella to put on the woman. He doesn't make her a tourniquet pretty quick, she's gonna die."

"She's gonna die anyway," a man in the crowd said. "Why don't you just let us go on and eat her, and you two can join in. Hell, you can go first."

"That's a good idea," the greasy-haired girl said.

"No thanks," Bob said.

I took off my belt and gave it to Sam. He got down on his hands and knees and applied it to Mable's arm, about six inches above the wound. It cut off most of the bleeding.

"I think you're supposed to let that off now and then," Bob said. "You don't, she'll lose her whole arm . . . if it don't kill her."

"I got some idea how to do it," Sam said. When he leaned over to make an extra adjustment on the belt, a can of sardines tipped out of his pocket. All eyes went to that can.

"They've got a lot of those," I said to Bob. "That's how they've been holding things together. And nobody's tried to take it away from them because they've got the bus rigged with a bomb."

"You don't say?" Bob said. "And here I was thinking this was all just the power of the Lord, and it's cans of sardines."

"You mess with that bus," Sam said, "it'll blow you out of this drive-in."

"That's an idea," Bob said. "Okay, Mr. Preacher, get your wife there. Jack, give him a hand. Ya'll come with me. Rest of you Christians just sort of lick up here while we're gone."

Sam and I got our arms around Mable and got her up. She came to briefly, but she couldn't walk. We dragged her away, the toes of her house shoes scraping the asphalt. I looked back over my shoulder as we went away from there, and the greasy-haired girl grabbed the sardines and tried to make a run for it. She was swarmed. At the bottom of the mound of thrashing arms and legs you could hear her yelling, "Mine, mine."

The guy who had dropped the hubcab snatched Mable's hand from it, sprinted off tearing at it with his teeth. He rounded an elderly Chevy, practically leaped from one row to the other, weaved into some other cars and disappeared into shadows, perhaps to lie under some automobile and chew on his prize like a contented terrier.

A middle-aged woman in jean shorts and a red blouse dove down on the hubcab and began to lap at the blood there. A man dropped to his knees to join her. They growled at each other like Dobermans.

"Praise the Lord," Bob said.

"Oh, shut up," I said.

When we came to the bus, Bob made Sam put Mable down and give him the key. Sam said he would give him the key if he was going to be so foolish, but he would rather be shot point-blank with the shotgun before he would open it himself. The results would be too terrible, and the death of all of us would be on his hands.

Bob put the key in the lock and opened the back door.

He looked at us and smiled. "Boom," he said.

"Well," Sam said, "it worked up until now."

Bob climbed inside and we went after. The bus had shelves and the shelves had wire over them, and behind the wire were oodles of canned goods, mostly sardines and Vienna sausages. Two of my all-time nonfavorites under normal conditions. Right now they looked rather attractive. My stomach growled like an attack dog.

"Comfy in here," Bob said.

Sam and I helped Mable over to a bed that folded away from the bus wall, and Sam got a bucket and put that by the bed and took the pressure off the tourniquet. Blood shot out of the wound and into the bucket. "We were afeared of a nigger takeover," Sam explained as he tightened the tourniquet again. "Figured it came down to us or the niggers, we'd have this food put back, and that would hold us for a time."

I looked around more now that my eyes were adjusted. There was all manner of stuff in there. Plumbing tools, carpentry tools, painting equipment, even a welding torch and the tanks to go with it arranged on a dolly.

"Guns?" Bob asked.

"We hadn't gotten around to that," Sam said. "That was next."

"Wouldn't lie to me, would you?"

"I'm telling the truth . . . Damn you, why'd you have to shoot Mable's hand off?"

"Seemed sort of necessary," Bob said. "She was about to cut my buddy's throat. Though I figure the dumb sucker deserved it. Christians, my ass."

"Watch your language," Sam said. "If it had been her foot, that wouldn't have been so bad. But her hand. She likes to cook and give me back rubs, and she needs two good hands to do them things right."

"She wasn't holding the knife with her foot," Bob said. "Just be glad I'm shooting slugs, or you'd have all got peppered."

I looked at Mable. Her face was as pale as a baby's ass, and her eyes were foggy. I figured she wasn't going to make it.

About then she opened her eyes and said, "You know, the thing that would do me some good right now is a chicken fried steak. Maybe some mashed taters and cream gravy and rolls with it. Big ole glass of ice tea."

"Rest now," Sam said.

"It's the batter does it on them steaks," Mable said. "Don't got that right, it ain't worth eatin'. You dip the steak in the milk-and-egg batter, then into the flour, then back into the milk and egg, then back into flour. Makes it extra crispy."

"Ssshhhh, now, sugar bee, you rest."

"Don't do it that way, you don't get that good flaky crust, and I do like a good flaky crust."

She passed out again.

Bob came over and gave me one of the pistols from his belt. "Here, you might want to shoot someone later."

I took it and walked to the open door at the back of the bus and looked out. The Christians were fist-fighting, probably over drops of blood on the asphalt, or what was left of the sardines Sam had dropped. I could see the greasy-haired girl lying on her side with her eyes wide open. There was a young man with a knife cutting strips of meat off her legs. I took a deep breath and closed the door.

2

Bob and I ate sardines while Sam lay asleep on the floor near Mable, who now and then came awake and gave us in great detail one of her favorite recipes. We had been through cherry pie, buttermilk biscuits, chili and hominy cakes.

"I feel kind of bad eating another person's food," I said.

"They were going to eat you," Bob said. "Look at it that way."

"A point," I said, and ate a little faster.

"You're going to need your strength when the Christians come for us. They're not going to be worried about the bomb anymore. They'll have it figured now, since we didn't get blown up."

"How'd you know the bus wasn't rigged with a bomb?"

"Just figured . . . didn't know for sure . . . Hell, Jack, I don't care anymore. If this is life, it ain't worth living. I think what you and I ought to do is something real foolish. Otherwise, we'll end up licking blood out of hubcaps."

"What you got in mind?" I asked.

"Destroy The Orbit symbol."

I mulled that over awhile. "It has a ring to it. Any reason?"

Bob looked back to make sure Sam and Mable were still sleeping. "Come with me." He pulled the lever and opened the door and we went outside. "You've been a mite busy to notice, but when I woke up and seen you were gone, I figured you'd joined the Christians."

"Okay, I was a jackass. Happy?"

"It's just your way, Jack. I'm used to it. Anyway, I woke up and come out of the camper and the first thing I seen was that."

He pointed at The Orbit symbol. "And it's worse now than when I'm talking about."

"God Almighty," I said.

The Orbit symbol had turned a hot blue, so blue it hurt my eyes. It was getting the juice from the tentacles —there were twelve of them now and I couldn't think of them as anything other than tentacles—and they were twisting and lashing across the blackness, spitting lightning from their tips like venom, and this lightning no longer ran the length of the pole, but just gathered in the symbol alone, and the symbol was spinning very fast, hurling more lightning than ever from it, striking the concession. The concession glowed so violently that at any moment I expected it to move, like amputated frog legs hopping in response to a live wire. The marquee was no longer there. I figured it had exploded and crumbled down, like a charcoaled stick.

"I figure something new is about to happen," Bob said, "and I'm not sure it's worth waiting around for. Last time we had something like this we got the Popcorn King."

I agreed with Bob. I felt it was gearing up for something bigger and more catastrophic. I tried to figure exactly what it was with the symbol and why the power from the lightning concentrated itself there before going to the concession. A number of B movie possibilities presented themselves: The symbol had accidentally been made from smeltered iron ore that had been mixed with some strange and horrid sentient metal that had come to earth in a meteor, and once it had been converted to The Orbit symbol it had awakened from a long sleep and was now tormenting us earthlings for lack of anything better to do. I figured being a chunk of rock, or even a sign, could get pretty boring. It was the sort of thing that could give you a bad attitude. And I thought again of the B movie gods, and that idea appealed to me most of all. Their motives seemed to fit in with those of most low-budget moviemakers. Bring it in on time. If it doesn't make sense in spots, well, make it pretty or exciting. Don't let them think about it too long.

"You getting hypoglycemic again," Bob said, bringing me up from the pit of my thoughts.

"No," I said. "I was just thinking."

"About what?"

"About rewriting the script."

"The script?"

"Let's just say this is a movie and those tentacles—"

"Just drips of goo, Jack."

"—belong to the B movie gods, and they're manufacturing all this, using us as actors, only we're not acting, and they're making up the script as they go. They've isolated us, they've given us our monster, the Popcorn King, and now they're looking for the big finish, and I don't think they've planned a heroic ending. I think this is one of those downbeat films."

"Always got to have something to believe in, don't you, Jack? Astrology, Christianity, now B movie gods."

"Give me something to blame all this on. A random universe with no god, evil or otherwise, is just too much for me. Just let me say it's the B movie gods and they have this bad scenario planned, and you and me, we're not going to stand for it. We're going to destroy the symbol . . . Hell, let's do something even if it's wrong."

"Believe the ghost of Elvis is doing it if you like," Bob said. "It don't make a hang to me. But I've got a plan for taking that symbol down."

* * *

Bob woke Sam up when we got back to the bus. He pulled him up front and said, "You know how to use that torch and stuff?"

"I don't just carry it around, boy. Sure, I know. But I ain't got a hankering at the moment."

"I'm going to give you a hankering," Bob said. "We're going to cut The Orbit symbol down."

"Have at it," Sam said.

"We want you to do it. You know how to use the equipment."

"After what you done to Mable, you think I'm gonna help you? You shouldn't oughta shot her hand off, little buddy."

I thought he might add "nahnuhnahnah," but he passed on that.

"We want to cut that sucker down and drop it on the concession," Bob said. "See if we can smash the Popcorn King . . . Christ, we want to do something besides wait to get eaten, or end up eating one another. What say, Sam?"

"Don't use the Saviour's name in vain . . . I don't know. You have to cut it just right, get it to fall that way."

"That's why we need you," Bob said. "You're the expert."

"Well," Sam said, rubbing his fingers along his chin, "it might not change a thing, but it sure could give a man peace of mind for trying, now couldn't it?"

"Our point exactly," Bob said. "You'll do it then?"

"All right, but this don't mean we're friends."

"Wouldn't think of it . . . One more thing. We're gonna need this bus, and when we finish with it, it won't be in any shape at all."

"No sir," Sam said, "you ain't gonna . . ." Then he

looked hard at Bob and the shotgun. "It don't matter what I say, does it? You'll take the bus anyway."

"We'd like to have your permission," Bob said, "just to be sociable."

Sam nodded wearily. "Well, tell me what you're gonna do to it."

The bus was part diversion, part weapon.

We tore the wire off the shelves, took the food and put it in a couple of blankets and tied it up, pulled it to the rear of the bus. We took the wire outside and Sam welded it into a kind of pen on the hood of the bus while Bob watched with his shotgun, just in case we had visitors. When Sam finished, I brought all the cans of paint thinner he had and put them in the wire enclosure, made sure they fit snug by pushing a couple of moldy pillowcases in between them.

"When the front end hits that electrical field," Bob said, "it'll blow. And if we can get enough momentum behind this baby, really put the hammer down, it'll run on into the concession and the gas tank will go. We're lucky, that'll get the Popcorn King. Or the symbol will when it comes down. The idea here is to try and hit him with both things at once. I've got a flare gun in the camper, and I'll give that to one of you. When the symbol is about to drop, shoot off the flare and I'll put my foot through it, put this sucker in his lap."

"And how will you get out?" I asked.

"I'll jump. I'm a jumping sonofabitch, didn't I tell you?"

"No. I knew you could hide under mufflers good, but I didn't know about the jumping."

Bob smiled. "If Wendle was here right now, big guy or no big guy, I'd kick his butt . . . after I had me something to eat, that is, like about ten cans of those sardines in there."

"I don't doubt it," I said. "But right now, let's kick the King's butt."

"I'll get the flare gun," Bob said.

Bob got the flare gun, then we took the blankets of food over to the camper, trying to make sure no one was watching, but not worrying too much about it. It was most likely a formality anyway. I didn't really expect to be coming back. If our plan failed, the Popcorn King would have plans for us—lunch, probably.

Fact was, I figured our time was running out anyway. So far the King had been patient, waiting for us to get hungry enough to join his flock, or maybe not thinking about us at all. He didn't seem to have any master plan. Feed the flock, and gradually feed on the flock. An insane demigod without true design; a voyeur of human destruction; the Jim Jones of Popcorn.

When we got back to the bus Sam was sitting on the bed beside Mable. "Died," he said. "Just gave her buttermilk-biscuit recipe and died. Didn't quite make it to the part about how long to keep them little buddies in the oven."

Bob nodded and went to the front of the bus.

"You did this, cowboy," Sam yelled at Bob's back.

Bob pulled the door lever and went outside. I went after him. He was leaning against the bus, the shotgun cradled in his arms. He was watching the movie. It was *The Toolbox Murders.*

I went up and leaned beside him. "You saved my life. I'm sorry you had to shoot the woman, but thanks for saving my life."

"I never said I was sorry for shooting her," Bob said, but he didn't look at me.

We leaned that way for a time. "Movie any good?" I asked.

"It's all right," Bob said, "but I've seen it."

I laughed and clapped him on the shoulder. "Come on," I said. "We've got things to do."

We went back inside the bus.

Sam looked at me and snarled. "Damn you, if you'd just gone on and cooperated, we'd have eaten you and things would have gone on like they were . . . least for a while."

"I have days when I'm obstreperous," I said.

"To hell with this talk," Bob said. "We're going on with it, Sam, with or without you even if I have to teach myself how to use that torch by trial and error and let Jack drive the bus. So how's it going to be? You in or out?"

Sam turned to look at Mable. He closed her eyes with his fingertips, then looked at us. "I'm in," he said.

Bob nodded. "Now . . . what would you like to do with her body?"

There was no way to bury her, and options were few. We could toss her into the acidic blackness or we could leave her on the bus to burn when it exploded. (If it exploded. Just because we had a plan didn't mean I had a lot of faith in it.)

Sam preferred to leave her on the bus. He got some cans of sardines out of her overcoat pockets (he wasn't so sentimental as to leave those), and put some old clothes on top of her to help her catch fire. He took some plastic plumbing pipe, couplings and pipe glue, used a hacksaw to make her an artificial hand. Or that's what it was supposed to be. It looked like a dull garden rake to me. He tied it to the stump of her arm with some rounds of twine and a twisted coat hanger.

Finished, he put a blanket over her and tied it and Mable to the bed with some strips of old sheet, changed out of his festive-tie shirt and put back on the one with a black tie. He said some words over her, then changed back to the shirt with the red tie painted on. I presumed that was also his welding shirt.

"Sam," I said, "I'm not one to meddle, but I've been meaning to ask you. Why do you paint those ties on your shirts?"

"Can't tie the knots," he said.

Made sense.

We ate some sardines, talked the plan over one more time, then Sam and I lowered the dolly with the welding equipment on it out the back of the bus.

"Go for it," Bob said. We shook hands and he gave me the flare pistol. I slipped it into my belt next to the revolver.

"Let's get on with it," Sam said. "I ain't gonna shake hands with nobody."

I took hold of the dolly, cocked it back and started pushing it across the lot at a dog trot. Sam ran alongside me, wheezing like a tire going flat.

3

We weren't too worried about the Popcorn King noticing us. We were a good distance away, and hey, it wasn't like there wasn't something strange going on all the time anyway.

But the closer we got to the little fence that led out to the stretch of concrete where The Orbit symbol was, the more nervous I became. My courage began to falter, and I wanted to go back to the truck and get into the sardines and eat those, and just hope for the best.

Still, I kept running, and Sam was staying up with me. We saw the Christians here and there, standing around, watching, wondering, I suppose. None of them waved. Stuck up.

I looked toward the concession. It glowed beautifully against the blackness, like some exotic gem on black velvet. One of those little winds that kicked up out of nowhere from time to time started going and it carried the stink of the no-longer-used toilets to me, and the smell was as hard and mean as a head-on collision.

In the window of the concession I could see the bodies hanging, like big fish in a market. Some of them were little more than skeletons.

We came to the wooden fence and Sam got up there and straddled it, and I pushed the dolly up where he could get hold of it and twist it over, lower it to the other side.

Sam followed after it and I took his place, straddling the fence. I looked out at the great tin fence surrounding the drive-in (except this area that led out to The Orbit symbol), and saw the cruel blackness beyond. I saw some of the screens and their movies and wondered how they had gone on so long without being destroyed. But then I knew. They were light. They were holy shrines to a mad god. I wondered how it would be if we managed to destroy the concession here in Lot A and the three movies went out. Once in darkness, would it all end, like bad dreams tumbling down the throat of sleep?

Nope. Lot B would be the center then, for how ever long that lasted. Lot B with its empty concession and its manned film room, carrying on with or without the King until there was mass murder and/or starvation and finally over there the lights went out as well.

I could see people moving around the drive-in, a number of them moving toward the concession. Probably time for the next meal of popcorn vomit. I figured some of the patrons could see me up there, but it most likely wouldn't excite them much. Many had gone over the fences and out into the blackness, and in their eyes I'd just be one more quitter.

"You gonna lay an egg up there, or what?" Sam said.

I went on over and took hold of the dolly and started pushing it out on the spur toward the symbol. It was brighter out there because of the lightning, and the ozone was so thick it smelled like a wound being cauterized.

The spur narrowed as we went and the ebony pudding was close on either side of us, and I thought about how easy it would be to end it all. I mean it was right there taunting me, inviting me to freedom. But I kept pushing.

When finally we made the tall, tapering pole that held the symbol, I looked up at the tentacles (liked to think I could see suckers on one side of them, like on an octopus) and the lightning coming out of them, watched the bolts strike the symbol, spin off and engulf the concession. Looking up at that great light, those tentacles, made me feel small and weak and hated.

Sam tried to arc a spark on the torch, but wasn't having much luck. He talked to it. "Come on, now, be good. Come on. Hot A'mighty, that's the way."

A spark jumped to the torch and he turned it up and the flame licked out and he put it to the pole, began to cut through. "Might as well get comfy," he said. "This is going to take a while."

I remembered it was not wise to look at a torch without goggles because a spark could jump to your eyes, and I didn't want to watch Sam work without goggles. The way he was squinting at the flame made me ache. I turned and looked at the blackness, but that was too dreary and it had a siren's call, so I turned and looked at the fence and the back and top of the concession. I could see the upper half of one of the screens beyond that and I tried to watch the movie, *Night of the Living Dead*, but it seemed too much like reality and I knew all the lines by heart. I closed my eyes and tried to think of nothing, but there was just too much in my head for that. I wondered what Bob was doing and how he felt sitting there in the bus, waiting for our signal. I wondered if he really would jump. I figured he might have already turned the bus toward the concession, and he would be watching the symbol, waiting for our flare. God, I hoped the bus would start.

Then I didn't think about that anymore. I thought of Randy and Willard and I felt pity, something I was afraid I might have lost, then there were tears in my eyes and they might have been for Randy and Willard.

"Getting there," Sam said.

I thought, no, the tears are not for Randy and Willard, they are for all the good dreams I've dreamed, for all the good gods, who do not exist, for all the good in man that is only social conditioning to keep the bigger man from breaking his head. Yes, that was what I was weeping for, mankind. The fact that *man* is not *kind* at all. But then I knew that was malarkey and that I was weeping for myself, all my loneliness, disappointment, the awareness of my mortality, the realization that the universe was a dark, empty place and life was nothing more than a carnival ride and that when the bell sounded to end the ride and you got off, you stepped out into nothing. It was all over then, all there was was ended, flesh and soul might as well have never been.

Even the B movie gods could not be proved except in my dreams. Maybe they were not gods at all but some sort of life-form that was far enough advanced that they served the purpose of gods—counterfeit deities. Alien filmmakers. Youthful aliens who have had an interesting accident with their chemistry set. Or nothing more than my need for there to be reason and design where there was none; I so desperately wanted there to be gods and magic, even if they were bad.

"Timber," yelled Sam.

I turned and looked up and the pole was starting to go, dragging its lightning after it.

"The flare," Sam said.

I pulled the flare gun, lifted it and fired at an angle, not knowing the height of our sky. The flare went bright red and pretty against the dark and the strands of blue lightning. I dropped the gun and started running for the fence, Sam behind me, wheezing. Before we made it there, the symbol came down, and it lost its lightning; it was like the lightning was bubble gum and it had been stretched too far and had popped free. The symbol came down on the concession with a crunch, and there was a momentary crackling and sizzling that hurt my ears and made my flesh feel warm, then debris flew and the lights of the projectors went out.

I got hold of the fence and pulled myself up, strad-dled it. There was still plenty of light from the lightning overhead, and I could see that Bob had gotten a late start, but was coming. The old bus whined like an unpleasant child, the lights shone like miniature suns. The bus hit the concession with a screech and a blast, and a rush of flame went through it, blew the windows out and wrapped around the roof, kicked the back door open. All manner of crap propelled out the open door and went sailing, including the bed Mable was strapped to. It skidded across the asphalt, twisted sideways and struck a Volkswagen, ricocheted back toward the burning bus, stopped spinning halfway there, sat smoldering like a cheap cigar. The blanket had been torn partially free, and Mable's arm with the plumbing-pipe hand came out from under it and struck the ground, lay there like a stiff white spider unable to run. The recipe cards had also escaped from beneath the blanket and they were fluttering down. Some had been flame-kissed and were nothing now but blackened wisps.

I saw Bob. He had jumped. He was on his feet and limping toward me. He had the shotgun and he was still wearing his hat. I felt like cheering, but before I could celebrate, the debris shifted, boards lifted and dropped as the Popcorn King stood up out of the rubble. He was charred from head to foot. That part of his head that was the popcorn cup had a lick of flame fluttering out of it like a feather in a fez. A board had gone through his top chest. Glass poked out of his flesh. He looked very unhappy, and he was looking directly at me.

He reached up with his top right hand and pulled the board out of his chest and tossed it aside. He started walking out of the debris, toward me.

"Get away from there," Bob yelled. "Run."

But I was frozen, watching the King. He was moving slowly, staggering. He no longer had the blue glow. He looked more like a bad acrobat act, a little guy on a big guy's shoulders.

The King opened his mouth and coughed out smoke. He fell to his knees and the tattoos dripped off him like melting licorice and formed a dark pool on the ground. The King lay face down and quit moving.

I got down off the fence and went over there. I could hear Sam calling to me to help him over, asking what was happening. I could hear Bob telling me to run, but I didn't pay either of them any mind.

I bent down to the King and whispered, "Randy?"

The head lifted slightly. The single eye looked at me. I couldn't tell if there was recognition there or not. Maybe it was just confusion. A tooth fell out of his mouth and clinked on the asphalt, was followed by a little lake of vomit in which one of the cyclopean popcorns floated; the eye was dead and filmed over.

"Eat and be fed, brother," the King's upper mouth said.

"I don't think so," I said.

"Turning down a sick man," the King said, and it was the lower mouth this time. "That's a hell of a note."

He laid his head down gently, his face in the vomit. His head was turned so I could still see the single eye. He opened his top left hand and there was a crumpled paper skull in it. "Second-rate materials. Second-rate effects," Randy's voice said. "I could have done better with household supplies."

The one eye closed. The Popcorn King was dead. But Mable wasn't. About that time she screamed.

4

When I turned, I saw that at Mable's scream Sam had made it over the fence and sprinted over to her. Bob was ahead of him, tearing off the smoldering blanket. Sam and Bob got arms around her and lifted her up and Sam said, "Oh, honey bugs, I thought you were croaked. Done gone to be with Jesus."

Mable was clutching one of the recipe cards in her good hand. She looked at it there in the light of the burning concession and the lightning overhead. "Polk salad," she said. "Now that's a good one, if you get it when the shoots are young. Don't, you might as well cook you up a mess of Johnson grass."

I started over to join them, stopped. The patrons of both lots were coming out of the shadows, into the light of the great fire, coming toward us. A more unpleasant crowd I'd never seen. The patrons from Lot A no longer had their movies, and neither lot had their King and their popcorn.

Sam and Bob saw me looking, and they swiveled Mable around so that they were all facing the crowd. I pulled the pistol from my belt and held it against my leg and walked over there.

Bob and Sam gently lowered Mable to the ground. She sat there reading the polk salad recipe, nodding over it.

"It ain't over," Sam said. "It ain't never over."

"The King," went the cry from the crowd. "The King."

Then they swarmed us. I heard Bob's shotgun roar and I got off one shot—and missed. In a crowd, no less. Jack the deadly gunman. Sweaty, hot bodies piled on me and I struck the ground hard and someone said an obscenity in my face and some other smart aleck twisted the gun out of my hand and hit me with it, which is kind of humiliating, getting clubbed with your own gun, I mean. Next the crowd started dribbling me around the lot with fists and feet and I got beyond pain and entered into nice, dark, cozy unconsciousness.

But that didn't last long.

Lot A built a bigger and better fire out of the smoldering lumber of the concession stand so they would have plenty of light to work by, but they managed to save enough of the lumber for cooking and building.

What they built was crosses.

They got some nails out of the wreckage and someone had a hammer, and they stripped us naked and held us down and crucified us. That hurt bad enough, but when they dropped our crosses into the holes the concession pilings had been in, that was real pain. It shook my entire body until I felt as if the tips of my teeth would bulb up and squirt blood.

They packed the holes tight with junk from the concession, then piled lumber around the bottoms of the crosses and looked up at us like chefs contemplating the larder.

The nails hurt something awful, but worse was the racking pain throughout the body and the pressure it put on the lungs. Now and then I had to make my legs work so I could force myself up on the nail through my feet and get some good breaths. I'd stay that way long as I could until the muscles in my feet cramped and I had to let go. Then I'd have trouble breathing again, and I'd get my strength back just enough before my lungs collapsed, and I'd push up once more. I had just thought Coach Murphy's calisthenics in PE were tough.

They got the Popcorn King's body, put it on a pole and stuck it upright in that part of the wreckage that wasn't on fire. The King had gone seriously ugly. The tattoos had fallen off him and lay like ink pools on the ground where he had lain. That part of the body that had been Willard was pink again; he had even lost the tattoos he had come to the drive-in with.

Members of the crowd took a blanket and put it over the King's head so his face would show, and they took a nail and nailed through it into the top of his hat so it wouldn't fall off. Then they stretched the blanket behind him so that he looked like he was standing there wearing a hooded robe. One young woman with spiky hair claimed she had been possessed by the King's spirit, or some such thing (I wasn't in the mood to take it all in, actually), and she floundered around and did a kind of Jezebel dance by the body, and after a while she let her voice go deep, though it cracked some, and she gave the impression the King was talking through her. The crowd liked that, and she got behind the body, under the stretched-out blanket, and patrons would come by and ask the King questions and she'd answer for him and everyone was pleased with this oracle. They did this until it got boring and they turned back to us and started piling more lumber. One of the pilers was especially annoying. He kept singing "Mama's Little Baby Loves Short'nin' Bread," and he couldn't carry a tune in a safety-deposit box. It just wasn't the way for a man to die. On a cross, about to be cooked, with some idiot singing "Short'nin' Bread."

I could turn my head and see the others to my left. Sam, Bob and Mable. Mable, who had lost her plumbing-pipe hand, had gotten nailed through the wrist a couple of times and I think she was bleeding worse than the rest of us. She cashed in early, her last words being something about how to wrap tamale meat in corn shucks. I kept expecting her to come alive again and start on some other recipe, but this time she was dead

151

for real. Her shapeless white body hung out from the cross like a swollen grub.

When Sam knew she was gone he went to preaching. Said something about Jesus and the thieves on either side of him.

"Ain't stole nothing in my life," Bob said. " 'Cept maybe your bus and sardines, and I don't think that counts."

Sam went on with his story, said those suckers on either side of Jesus had repented and Jesus had saved their lives and they went on to Paradise. Being as I was in the thieves' position, I could sympathize with their line of thinking, but just having had a rather uninspiring religious experience, I declined to join Sam in Paradise.

But Sam kept at it. I couldn't figure where he was getting the wind. I could hardly breathe at all. I reckon he felt like a big wheel because he was in the middle. He preached for quite some time before his mouth went dry and he couldn't say anything else, which I was grateful for.

I blacked out off and on, and once I had what might have been a dream. In the dream the lightning overhead ceased and out of the blackness came a face, an indescribable face, but a face that had the look of someone, or something, with a mission. He opened his toothy mouth and roared, "Over budget, you fools. Over budget. Cut. Wrap." Then the face withdrew into the black and there was light. The dream ended.

I opened my eyes and saw below that the patrons were piling more wood around me, and that one of them had a piece of board wrapped in a shirt and it was on fire. He was about to put it to my pile of lumber. I hoped fire was quick. I had read somewhere that it was a tough way to go, and that smoke inhalation killed you first. I decided I would breathe a lot of smoke quickly, get it over with.

And then there was a change. I looked up. The lightning was still there and so was the blackness, but there was something bright moving behind it, a red glow that was expanding.

I looked down at my captors, at the faces of those close to the fire and at the shadowy shapes of those beyond; the more clearly outlined, if distant, shapes over in Lot B, where the movies still rolled. They all seemed to be looking up.

I lifted my head again. It wasn't just delirium. It was lighter up there and growing lighter still. Then it looked as if a great apple broke through the chocolate pudding, but it was the comet tearing through the poison sky. Down it came, dragging daylight behind it, white clouds, the sun.

The drive-in went red and the comet smiled.

Up it whipped again, this time pulling the blackness with it. Up, up, up and away, until it was not even a speck against the bright blue sky, and there was nothing left but a fine warm day with the smell of trees in the air and the touch of hot sun on our faces.

It was nice, but I didn't feel like a picnic or nothing.

The patrons just sort of stood there for a while, marveling at the world beyond the tin fence. There were lots of trees visible. Big trees. The guy with the burning board dropped it—not on the wood pile, fortunately. People began wandering off, some began to run. Cars were cranked. Engines seemed to be working fine. Like a line of insects the cars and trucks rolled out of the drive-in. Some people whose cars had been totaled walked. Some hot-wired and took other cars. Everyone was in a hurry to get out of there. They didn't mention getting us down. No one waved or shot us the finger as they went by.

A tall, skinny man with long hair and a hoe handle for a cane came up. He looked up at Bob. "How's it going?"

"Hanging around," Bob said, not missing a beat.

"Maybe you'd like down?" Crier said.

"That would be right nice," Bob said.

Crier got down on his hands and knees and started pulling the junk out of the piling holes and pretty soon the crosses were wobbling and then Crier pushed us down. When I hit the ground I thought my arms and legs would come off.

Crier went away for a while and when he came back he had a hammer. He used the claw end to free us. It hurt like hell. He got Mable free last, since she wasn't in any hurry.

"I broke into your camper to get this hammer," Crier said to Bob. "I figured you'd have one. Hope you don't mind."

"Nah," Bob said, "it's insured."

My hands and feet hurt so bad I couldn't move them and I couldn't walk, least not without help. My legs seemed to have died. Sam looked walleyed and had gone to singing "The Old Rugged Cross" in a whispery kind of voice, and that wasn't helping my nerves.

"What you driving?" Bob said.

"Well," Crier said, "this is kind of odd, but I can't remember what car I came in. Can't remember who I came with."

"Don't matter," Bob said. "We'll take the camper. You can drive, can't you?"

"Is it an automatic?"

"Yep."

"I can drive. I remember that much. But you don't look like you got a key on you."

"There's one underneath the dash in a magnetic box. Doors aren't locked."

"Okay," Crier said. "I'll drive it over here and pick you up."

"You wouldn't just drive off and leave us, would you?" Bob said.

"Gone this far for you, might as well go the whole hog."

When Crier came back with the truck, Bob said, "There's some blankets in the back. There's a knife back there too. We can cut a hole in the blankets and slip them over our heads."

"Why the trouble?" Crier asked. "You boys got dates?"

"Just a thing I prefer, if you'll do it," Bob said.

Crier found the blankets and the sardines and the knife. He brought the sardines out and we ate all we could stand, Crier feeding them to us, as our hands didn't work so good.

He cut the blankets and pulled them over our heads. Sam didn't even notice. He was trying to sing "When the Roll Is Called Up Yonder."

"What about her?" I asked, nodding at Mable.

"Dead, ain't she?" Crier said.

"Maybe you could pile some boards on her or something, set her on fire if you had a mind to. She ought to have some kind of burial."

"Ain't you something," Crier said.

"And the Popcorn King," I said. "He ought not just be left."

"You're kind of tight with everybody, ain't you?" Crier said.

"Before he was that, he was two friends of ours," Bob said. "I know it's a bother, but could you?"

"Hell," Crier said. "Good thing you boys are paying by the hour." He piled some boards on Mable and set fire to her and she caught poorly at first, but after a time was blazing away. It didn't take so much to get the Popcorn King burning. He caught quick and flared like a torch, the blanket whipping to flame immediately. Black smoke churned up from the corpses and floated up into the clear sky and faded.

"Now," Crier said. "Any little ole chores you boys want performed? Just anything would be all right. Maybe you'd like to see if I can make a few laps around the lots."

"Would you?" Bob said.

"You know what you can do," Crier said.

Crier helped Bob and Sam into the back of the truck and led me around to the cab. It seemed to take forever and my feet felt like raw stumps. I had Crier on one side holding me up, and the truck on the other. I touched the truck with my elbow because my hand wouldn't take it. I still couldn't open or close either one of them. They looked like talons.

Inside the cab, Crier started the truck again, leaned on the wheel and looked around. "Strange, I feel funny leaving."

"Maybe you can get over it," I said.

"Maybe."

"One thing, Crier," I said. "You saw what that crowd was about to do to us. I know you couldn't have stopped them, but would you have helped eat us? Could you have done that?"

"Been the first in line if I could have. No sense missing a free meal, even if it is made up of a couple of guys I kind of like."

"Well," I said, "that's one way of looking at things."

Epilogue

I leaned against the door and kept my sore hands in my lap. As we started rolling, I looked around at all the vacant cars, many of them wrecked. There were also lots of bones. You could see that clearly now. We drove by one car with its roof decorated with human skulls wearing popcorn sacks, and there was another car with a baby seat sitting on top of it with a little skeleton in the seat holding a rattle.

I glanced through the gun rack and the back glass, saw Bob and Sam stretched on the floor of the camper. Bob was up on one elbow, gingerly managing sardines from a can Crier had opened and left for him. Sam wasn't moving. Later Bob told me he died before we got out of the lot.

We went through the exit, and though the highway was there, the yellow line had faded and the concrete had buckled and grass grew up through it in spots. Nothing else was remotely familiar. I wasn't in the least bit surprised. I remembered what Sam had said: "It ain't over yet. It ain't never over." No, it wasn't over. It was time for the second feature. A lost world movie. As we drove, a massive shape stepped out of the jungle foliage at the right of the highway and Crier eased on the brake and we watched. It was a *Tyrannosaurus rex* covered in batlike parasites, their wings opening and closing slowly, like contented butterflies sipping nectar from a flower.

The dinosaur looked at us in a disinterested way, crossed the highway and was swallowed by the jungle.

"I don't think this leads home anymore," Crier said, and eased forward again, started picking up speed. I looked in the truck's wing mirror and I could see the drive-in in it, one of the screens in Lot B. The projector might still be running back there, but if it was, I couldn't make out a picture. The screen looked like nothing more than an enormous slice of Wonder Bread.

CUT/FADE-OUT

THE
DRIVE-IN 2

*This dog-and-pony show is dedicated
with love and respect to that smart writer-gal
from Texarkana, Texas, current of Gulfport, Mississippi,
Mignon Glass.*

Acknowledgments are in order for Jeff Banks, Keith Hamrick, Jerry Heilman, Gary Raisor, David Webb, Ed Gorman, Dean Koontz, Neal Barrett, Lew Shiner, Karen Lansdale, Pat LoBrutto, and "The Hungry Guys" (you know who you are) for their encouragement and/or helpful criticisms. And, of course, a whole lot of credit must be given to me, my own self, because I had to write the sonofabitch.

I'd also like to note, that though part of this novel takes place in my hometown of Nacogdoches, Texas—and I stand by my comments both pro and negative about the place—the scene with the firemen and the burning frat house is purely imaginative. I went for the broad and the comic, and I have nothing but the highest regard and respect for our fire department and its underpaid personnel. I like old houses too. Frats I'll have to think about.

Everything human is pathetic. The secret source of Humor itself is not joy but sorrow. There is no humor in heaven.

MARK TWAIN
Pudd'nhead Wilson

Fade-in/Prologue

Pay attention. When I'm through there will be a test.

One day suddenly you're out of high school, happy as a grub in shit, waking up with a hard-on and spending your days sitting around in your pee-stained underwear with your feet propped up next to the air conditioner vent with cool air blowing on your nuts, and the next goddamn thing you know, you're crucified.

And I don't mean symbolically. I'm talking nails in the paws and wood splinters in the ass, sore hands and feet and screams and a wavering attitude about the human race. It's the sort of thing that when it happens to you, you have a hard time believing ol' Jesus could have been all that forgiving about it.

It hurts.

Had I been J.C., I'd have come back from the dead madder than a badger with turpentined balls, and there wouldn't have been any of this peace-and-love shit, and I would have forgotten how to do trivial crap like turn water to wine and multiply bread and fishes. I'd have made myself big as the universe and made me two bricks just the right size, and I'd have gotten the world between the bricks, and *whammo*, shit jelly.

It wouldn't do to make me a messiah. I've got a bad attitude.

I do now, anyway.

It isn't that I expected life to be so sweet and fine that I'd grow up sweating pearls and farting peach blossoms, nor was I expecting to live to be three million and have endless fan mail from long-legged, sex-starved Hollywood starlets telling me how they'd like to ravish my body and bronze my pecker. But on the other hand, I was expecting a little better than this.

Me and my friends went to the drive-in to see movies, not to become part of them.

The evening we drove into the Orbit things started going to hell in a fiery hand-basket. We had just gotten settled in, and this big, red comet came hurtling from the sky like a tomato thrown by God, and then the comet split apart and smiled rows of saw-bladed teeth at us.

And when I thought the comet would hit us and splatter us into little sparklers of light, it veered upwards and moved out of sight. What it left in its wake was some bad business.

The drive-in still had light, but the light came from the projectors and the projectors didn't seem to have any source of electricity. We were surrounded by a blackness so complete it was like being in a bag with a handful of penlights. The blackness beyond the drive-in was acidic. I'll never forget what it did to that carload of fat people that drove off into it (or what I assumed it did), or the cowboy who put his arm into it and got his entire self dissolved.

Anyway, we were trapped.

Things got nasty.

There was nothing to eat in the drive-in besides the concession food, which was bad enough, but when that got low, people started eating one another, cooked and un-cooked.

Then two of my friends, whacked out from lack of food, got hit by this strange blue lightning (Randy was riding on Willard's back at the time) and it fused them together and made them uglier than a shopping mall parking lot and gave them strange powers and they became known as the Popcorn King. They weren't friends of mine and Bob's anymore. They weren't anyone's friends. They were now one creature. A bad creature.

Hello, permanent blue Monday.

The Popcorn King used his weird powers and unlim-ited popcorn to control the hungry crowd, and Bob and I might have joined them if it hadn't been for the jerky stash Bob had in his camper truck. The meat kept us from having to eat the King's popcorn, which had grown kind of funky, and from having to eat other folks, which was a thing the King encouraged.

But me and Bob were realistic enough to figure eating other folks and each other was just on the horizon, so to speak, so we decided, live or die, we were going to destroy the Popcorn King, and we did, with the help of this evangelist named Sam and his wife, Mable, who we thought was dead at the time. But that's another story and I've already told it. Let me just say that Sam and Mable together probably had a lower IQ than the foreskin on my dick.

To shorten this all up, we killed the Popcorn King, smashed him with a bus and blew his ass up, and for our efforts, Samaritan as they were, the King's followers stripped us naked, called us some real bad names, crucified us and started building bonfires at the bottom of our crosses so they could have us for lunch.

Then the comet decided to come back.

The big red bastard couldn't come back before we were crucified. No sir. It had to wait until we were up on those crosses with nails in our hands and feet and our bare asses hanging out before it chose to make an appearance.

But, I suppose I shouldn't complain. The bonfire didn't get built, and consequently, we didn't get eaten.

The comet did what it had done before, only this time when it went away the blackness around the drive-in went with it and folks got in their cars and trucks and drove off.

A fella named Crier, who was kind of a friend of ours, but who was planning on eating us if we got cooked, took us down from the crosses. Mable, who got crucified with us and was really dead this time, wound up burned and buried under some lumber left over from where the concession exploded while we were in the process of killing the Popcorn King. Sam died shortly after all this, about the time he got loaded in the back of the camper, but I didn't know this at the time.

Crier had to help me and Bob to the truck, and Bob got put in the back with Sam, and I rode up front with Crier, who did the driving. My feet weren't in any condition to push pedals. Getting crucified is not like stepping on a sticker or having a splinter in your palm, I'll guarantee you. It takes the rhythm out of your step and saps your will to clap to inner music.

So Crier drove us out of there, and at first things looked fine as the missionary position, but when we saw that the highway was buckling and cracking and grass was growing up between the cracks and on either side of the concrete was thick jungle, none of us had to be a nuclear physicist to know things still hadn't gone back to normal. And while we were contemplating this, letting those old inner wheels turn and squeak, a Tyrannosaurus Rex came goose-stepping out of the jungle on one side of the highway, looked at us with contempt, and disappeared into the foliage on the other side.

It was an exhilarating experience. Scary too.

And that's where this part of my story takes up.

SHOWTIME

FIRST REEL

(A Burial, a Tree House, a Burned Man,
and Titties Close Up)

1

There was some nice scenery out there. Big trees that climbed to a sky bluer than a Swede's eye, and next to the highway was some grass growing so tall and sharp it looked like green spikes.

After being cooped up in that drive-in for who knows how long with the tar-colored sky overhead and people so close together you couldn't scratch your ass without elbowing your neighbor, I suppose I should have been grateful. No one was trying to crucify and eat me, and that was worth something, but even with everything so pretty, it had a sort of landscaped look about it that I couldn't explain. You know, like a movie set that could afford to use real trees and grass and what looked like a real sky but struck me as a little too blue and perfect. It put me in mind of an old woodcut I saw in an art magazine once. The woodcut was from the sixteenth century, I think, maybe earlier, and there was this monk on his hands and knees and he was poking his head through the fabric of a night sky and looking at all manner of gears and machinery on the other side, stuff that made the world work, that swung the sun and moon across the sky and popped out the stars and turned things light or dark.

As we rode along, I thought about the dinosaur, and the way he walked, and thoughts spun through my head like pinwheels in a blue norther. The Tyrannosaurus Rex had moved smooth, all right, but slightly mechanical, and had I heard a sort of hum as he crossed the road, like the soft buzz of a battery-powered watch?

Probably not. But I had dreamed off and on that there were these many-tentacled, bladdery, eyes-on-stalks aliens that were doing this to us, making us the stars of low-budget movies they were filming. And if my dreams were, as I suspected, more than dreams, were in fact my tapping into their thought processes, then they could be doing to us again what they had done with us in the drive-in. Didn't low-budget movies nearly always show as part of a double feature?

Odder than the dreams was me wanting to see someone. Meaning not someone from the drive-in. They were on my shit list. But I wanted to see someone out there, someone who could make me feel this was more than a movie set. I think I might have felt better if I'd at least seen some beer cans or Frito wrappers lying out beside the road or thrown up in the trees. It would assure me that humanity was out there, ready to start fucking up anything it could get its hands on. There's nothing like pristine wilderness to incite in human beings the need to start chopping down trees, tromping grass, killing animals and throwing down beer cans, so I was pretty certain there wasn't a human being within a hundred miles of us.

Not counting the folks who left the drive-in ahead of us, of course. They hadn't had time to respond to natural tendencies, and after our ordeal, it was doubtful anyone had a beer can or a wrapper to toss. Everything that could be eaten or drunk had been consumed at the drive-in and the containers and wrappers tossed down there.

So the people ahead of us were forced to fight their instincts to litter, though I figured in time the urge would become too strong, and they'd start throwing their clothes out, or pulling over to the side of the road to burn their spare tires and leave the blackened, rubber-dotted rims to mark their passing.

We drove on for quite a time, and when it was getting near dark, Crier said, "Think we ought to find a place to hole up for the night?"

"I doubt we're going to come across many motels," I said.

The sun was going down in what struck me as the north, and I mention this because when we went into the drive-in the highway ran north and south, and when we came out we were heading in what was formerly a northerly direction. But being a creature of habit, and not wishing to give any alien movie-makers the satisfaction of letting on I noticed, I reoriented myself and called the direction in which the sun was falling west.

Besides, you never knew when someone might ask you directions.

Crier found a place off the highway where the jungle cleared out and there was some tall grass that went on for a ways, and he pulled over and parked, came around and helped me out of the truck.

My feet were sore and stiff from the crucifixion and I couldn't walk, but I could lean a little when propped against the camper.

As our duds had been stripped off us by the mad drive-in crowd, Crier had cut holes in blankets for me, Bob and Sam, and slipped them over our heads to serve as clothes, and I took this moment to lift my stylish wardrobe's hem and take a whiz.

Crier went around and opened the back of the camper and helped Bob out, and that's when Crier and I found out about Sam.

"We hadn't no more than gotten started back there," Bob said, "when he snorted once, shit on himself and went on to glory. Or wherever assholes like him go. I won't miss him."

Bob was sentimental like that.

When Crier got Bob propped up next to me, Bob lifted his blanket and took a leak too. If I had waited a minute or two, we could have gone together.

Crier had gone back to the rear of the camper, and Bob called to him, "I know it's a bother, and I hate to ask, you having been so nice to us and all, but—"

"Would I clean Sam's shit out of the back?" Crier said.

"And they say there's no evidence for ESP," Bob said.

Crier took Sam by the heels and dragged him bumpity-bumpity out of the camper and onto the ground. Sam hit hard enough to make me wince. Crier pulled him over to the grass and dropped his hold on the old boy's heels. He peeled Sam's blanket off and went back to the truck and used it to clean the mess up as best he could. It still wasn't going to smell like the perfume counter at J.C. Penney's back there, but it had to beat leaving things the way they were.

Bob began to ease down so he could sit, and I did the same. We managed our legs out in front of us without wincing and moaning too awful much.

Bob looked over at Sam's body in the grass and made a clucking sound with his tongue. "Hell of a thing, ain't it Jack? Life's hard, then you die, then you shit yourself. There's just no dignity in dying, no matter how you look at it."

"Might not be any dignity," I said. "But at least you don't have to get phone calls from aluminum siding salesmen anymore."

"Got news for you," Bob said. "We won't be getting those anyway, and we're alive."

"It's because we don't have a phone," I said. "If we come across a phone, you can bet we'll be hearing from them."

Bob called to Crier. "You're gonna bury the old fart, ain't you?"

Crier came around from the back of the camper. He was a sight. He was scrawny as a month-old corpse, but didn't have as nice a complexion. He still had his clothes and shoes, but they seemed to be held together by little more than body odor and hope. His hair was long and shaggy and thinning. His beard looked like a nest. He had the shit-stained blanket in his hand, and he gracelessly tossed it into the grass, an act that gave me some hope. Humanity was once again on the roll.

"You're kind of pushy, Bob," Crier said.

"I ain't saying you have to bury him—"

"That's big of you."

"—I'm suggesting it. If I had two good hands and two good feet, I might do it."

"Uh-huh."

"Let your conscience be your guide."

Crier said something under his breath, then went to the back of the truck and came out with a tire tool.

"Hey, forget it," Bob said.

Crier used the tool to pop the hubcap off the rear right tire. He took the cap out to the grass and tossed it down next to Sam. He began pulling the grass and cussing while he did it. It was pretty interesting to watch. Once in a while he'd toss a wad of grass, dirty roots still intact, toward Bob, and it would land near his sore feet or slam into the truck beside him. Bob started moving his head like a nervous anaconda.

Actually, I think Crier could have hit him if he'd wanted to. It wasn't that far a shot. Instead, he was trying to make Bob nervous, which I could kind of understand. Bob didn't always bring out the best in a person.

As for me, I tried to sit casual with my punctured biscuit hooks in my lap, looking at the crusty wounds on the backs of my hands where the nails had come out and gone into the wood of my cross.

When Crier had a good patch of grass pulled, he took the hubcap and used it to dig with and his mouth to cuss with. He worked the dirt between his legs like a dog burying a bone.

It was almost solid dark when he finished the grave. It wasn't much, more of a shallow trench, really. The moon came up in the north, right where the sun had gone down, the place I had decided to call west before, and I had a vision of my real or imagined multiple-eyed, many-tentacled, bladder-shaped aliens pulling levers and pushing buttons and causing gears to creak and crank and start the final descent of the sun and the rise of the moon, which spilled its light into Sam's final resting place like thin cream.

Crier hooked his hands under Sam's chin and pulled him over to the trench. Sam's body rustled through the grass like a snake. Crier rolled him into the hole face first. Sam's legs stuck out at one end, and his left arm flopped from the grave and lay in a manner that suggested he was about to push up and get out of that hole as soon as he gathered his strength.

"You're gonna have to dig some more," Bob said.

Crier turned slowly and looked at Bob. The moonlight on his face made him look like the man most likely not to give an ax. I hoped he knew that Bob's sentiments were his own and that I was an independent.

"Maybe not," Bob said. "Hell, just throw some of that grass over the spots that don't fit, and fuck it."

Crier turned back to his work, took hold of Sam's free arm and brutally twisted it behind Sam's back like a kid working his end of a wishbone. When the arm cracked loud enough to run a cold tremor up my spine, Crier pushed it down against Sam's back and put a foot on it and pressed, rocking back and forth on it until it stayed in place. He bent Sam's overlong legs at the knee, folded them to where the soles of his feet touched the back of his naked thighs, sat on them and bounced hard.

Every time Crier got up to examine his handiwork, the legs would creep up slowly. Finally Crier had had enough. He hopped on them one last time, got up and grabbed the hubcap and started scraping the dirt into the trench and topped it off by tossing loose grass on it.

I guess it was an okay grave, in that it beat lying naked in the grass with a blanket full of your shit nearby, but it was disconcerting to see the top of Sam's feet and part of his ankles sticking up in the moonlight. If any of Sam's relatives had been around, I don't think they'd have liked it.

I suppose it got to Crier too, because he took the hubcap and set it on the soles of Sam's feet as a kind of marker. And though it wasn't perfect, it did sort of tidy things up.

Without saying a word, Crier went around on the other side of the truck and got in. I could tell from the way the truck moved he had lain down in the seat.

Bob leaned over to me and said, "Think it would be okay if I asked him to help us into the camper?"

"Maybe not just now," I said.

From inside the cab we heard Crier say something about "goddamn ingrates," and Bob and I went very, very quiet.

2

We crawled under the truck and tried to sleep. The grass made it pretty soft, but there were bugs crawling on me and it began to get cold and I was feeling stiff in the hands and feet. One thing I had gotten used to in the drive-in was the constant moderate temperature, and that made the chill seem even chillier.

I got one of the larger bugs off of me and crushed it with my thumb and forefinger, a movement that made my sore hand throb. The bug's body collapsed like a peanut husk. I tried to look at it closely, but under the truck with only a stray strand of moonlight, there wasn't much to see. It looked like a crushed bug. Maybe I was expecting little silver wires and a battery the size of a pinhead.

I suppose Crier started feeling guilty, because in the middle of the night he came and woke us up and pulled us out from under the truck and helped us into the camper, which he had, in fact, cleaned out quite well, though the odor of Sam's last bad meals clung to the interior like moss.

Still, it wasn't cold in there and the bugs, real or synthetic, weren't crawling or biting.

After we lay down, and Crier was about to shut the back of the camper, Bob said, "No kiss and story?"

Crier held out his hand, palm up, made a fist and let the cobra rise.

Bob looked at Crier's stiff middle finger and said, "That's not nice."

Crier shut the back of the camper and went around to the front seat and lay down.

Bob managed to get up on his knees and thumped his forehead against the glass that connected the camper to the cab.

Crier sat up and turned to look. I've seen more pleasant faces on water moccasins.

"Night-night," Bob said.

Crier did the trick with his finger again, only with less flourish this time, then lay down out of sight.

Bob wiggled onto his sleeping bag, got on his side and looked at me and said, "You know, I like that guy, I really do."

That night the dreams came back, the same sort I'd had in the drive-in. They seemed more like visions than dreams, like I had tapped into some consciousness that controlled things. Bob and Crier didn't have the dreams, so I could only guess that through some quirk of fate, or by alien design, I had been given this gift. Or, I was as crazy as a cat in a dryer.

Hot-wired to aliens or not, the dreams/visions were clear. I could see the aliens in them, their bulbous heads sporting wiggling tendons tipped with eyes, tentacles flashing about, touching gears and punching buttons. Lights and buzzers and beepers going off and on around them. And them leaning forward, conversing with one another in a language that sounded like grunts, squeaks, burps and whines, and yet, a language I could somehow understand.

And some of the things they were saying went like this:

"Slow, uh-huh, uh-huh . . . that's it."

"Nice, nice . . ."

"Very pretty, oh yes, very pretty . . . tight and easy now . . ."

"All right, that's it. CUT!"

Then the connection was cut as well, and the dream, or whatever it was, ended. The next thing I knew it was morning and Crier had joined us for breakfast, such as it was: a can of sardines that we had taken from Sam's bus before we blew it up.

Afterwards, Crier got us out of the back of the camper and made us take turns walking, him supporting us, so that we could exercise our sore feet. Mine had started to curl like burned tortillas, and Crier said if I didn't make them work, they'd quit on me, and that at best, I'd end up having a couple of lumps that had all the mobility of potted plants.

I believed him. I exercised. So did Bob, though he grumbled about it.

Worst part about the exercise, worse even than the pain, was the thirst. It had been a long time since I had had a drink of water, and of course, this was true of Bob and Crier too. In the drive-in, for a time, we existed on soft drinks, and later on, Bob and I had nothing but the juice from jerky, and now the liquid from sardines.

If that doesn't sound so bad, go out some summer evening and do some kind of hard work, like say hauling hay, then try quenching your thirst with a big glass of soy oil or meat broth.

The bottom line was we were dehydrating, starting to look like flesh-colored plastic stretched over a frame of coat hangers.

"I figure," Crier said, after we got through exercising and were sitting with our backs against the truck, "any place as full of trees and grass and critters as this, ought to have water."

I wasn't so sure. I wouldn't have been surprised to come to what looked like a stream only to discover it was colored glass or rippling cellophane.

We were looking at Sam's grave while we talked, examining his ankles sticking up, his feet wearing the hubcap, and all of a sudden, we grew silent, as if possessed of a hive mind.

"I could have at least spoken some words over him," Crier said.

"And who the hell would you have been talking to?" Bob said. "Sam? He don't give a damn about nothing no more. God? Personally, I'm not real fond of the sonofabitch. Or wouldn't be, if I thought he, she, or it, existed."

I didn't say so, but I was in Bob's camp. Like the drive-in patrons, God was on my shit list. I had tried religion during our stay in the drive-in, and it hadn't exactly been a rewarding experience.

I had decided that if there was a God, he was a cruel sonofabitch to allow the things he allowed. Especially since he claimed his name was synonymous with love. It seemed to me that he was little more than a celestial Jack the Ripper, offering us, his whores, rewards with one hand, smiling and telling us he loved us, while with the other hand he held a shiny, sharp knife, the better with which to disembowel us.

"I don't know what I believe anymore," Crier said, "but I feel I owe the ol' boy some words because he's a human being. It doesn't matter if I'm talking to the wind, or just myself. I didn't give him the best kind of burial, so it's the least I can do. And who knows, if there is some God out there, maybe he'll be listening."

Crier said this soft and solemnlike, and you could

almost hear the organ music in the background. I think Bob was as affected as I was by Crier's remarks, because he didn't say anything rude, and something of that sort was always on the tip of his tongue. A lump, like a crippled frog trying to make it downhill, moved in my throat.

Crier went over to the grave and looked at the hubcap, picked it up and looked at the soles of Sam's feet, put the hubcap back, sighed, looked at the jungle.

"I'm here to say some words about this man, but nothing much comes to me. I didn't really know the poor bastard, but from what I could tell, he was about the dumbest sonofabitch that ever shit over a pair of shoes.

"Still, he was a man, and he deserved better than this. I'm sorry I couldn't get him buried proper, couldn't get his feet to stay down, but I did get his arm in the grave, and that was a job. I hope he rests in peace.

"I'm sorry about his wife, Mable. She wasn't any better or smarter than he was, from what I could tell, maybe a damn sight dumber. But I guess she did the best she could, like all of us. She's back at the drive-in, burned up under some lumber pieces, just in case you care.

"And listen, God, if you're out there, how about some relief around here? Lighten up. Things are multiple-fucked-up, and if anyone can put things straight, it ought to be you. Right? I mean, you hear what I'm saying? Give us some sign of good things to come. It would be appreciated. Okay, that's it. Amen."

Crier walked back to the truck, and about the time he reached it, the jungle parted and out stepped a nasty red-and-blue dinosaur that was probably a baby Tyrannosaurus Rex, or something close enough to be a double cousin to one.

Whatever it was, it stood on big hind legs and held two

puny forelegs in front of itself as if pleading. Its face was mostly teeth.

Toothy sniffed the air delicately, scampered over to the grave, snapped at the hubcap with its mouthful of big, sharp teeth, and managed to gulp it and Sam's feet down with very little chewing.

After a moment, Toothy coughed and spat out the hubcap, which now resembled a wad of aluminum foil. He used one clawed foot to scratch Sam out of the grave the way a chicken might scratch a worm from the dirt, bent and bit into Sam's corpse. With a series of rapid head-flipping motions, he proceeded to gobble the old boy so viciously that pieces of Sam flew out of Toothy's mouth and sprinkled the grass.

Finished with his repast, Toothy eyed us, as if giving the dessert counter a once-over.

We stayed very still. Rocks couldn't have been that still.

He let out a little honk that shook the truck, then started to turn toward the jungle.

A weight watcher, to our relief.

But before he could make a complete turn, he froze, turned his head slightly to the side and acquired a look akin to that of a patient who has just experienced the greased finger of the doctor up his ass. Then with a grunt, Toothy leaned slightly forward and cut a monster fart that was reminiscent of an air horn, but with more tonality.

When the fart was finished and Toothy had adopted a more satisfied and comfortable look, he moved into the jungle and out of sight.

After a moment of silence, Bob said, "Well, Crier, hope that wasn't the sign from God you were waiting for."

3

We drove along for a while, and finally Crier, who had been looking pretty distressed for a time, pulled over and killed the motor.

"What's up?"

"Sam," he said. "I can't get him out of my mind."

"Hell, you buried him, didn't you? Wasn't your fault all you had was a hubcap. And that dinosaur even gave him a musical salute after he ate him. Tomorrow sometime, Sam will be fertilizing a patch of ground. What more could you ask for?"

"Fuck Sam. It's me I'm talking about. I don't want to end up buried alongside the road like that."

"You aren't dead, Crier."

"But I might get that way, and I don't want to end up in some trench next to the highway where something can dig me up and eat me."

"Something doesn't dig you up, the worms are going to take care of you, so what's the difference? Maybe we could just leave you where you lie and save the dinosaurs some digging."

"That's nice. I'm pouring out my heart here and you're making fun. I don't want to be left beside the road and I don't want to be buried beside it neither."

"Perhaps we could arrange for you to be whisked away to heaven."

"I want to be carried to the end of the highway."

"Keep driving, and if we don't run out of gas, that's a wish you'll get. You don't even have to be dead. Have you noticed the gas mileage we're getting? It's got to be super or the gas gauge is fucked."

"Forget the goddamn gas gauge and the mileage, I'm serious here. I get croaked, you guys make sure I get to the end of the highway. Something about that appeals to me. I like the idea of finishing things. Dinosaur eats me there, so be it."

"Crier, if you're dead, it doesn't matter if fifty naked girls with tits like zeppelins are at the end of the highway ready to suck your dick until your balls cave in. You'll still be dead."

"Promise me that should something happen to me you'll make sure I get to the end of the highway to be buried."

"Okay."

"Okay what?"

"If you get killed, I'll see you get to the end of the highway and get buried or cremated or something."

"Not cremated. I don't like that."

"Tried it?"

"Just bury me. I'll make you the same promise if you like."

"Something happens to me, leave me in the bushes. I'll be past caring."

Bob rose up in back and tapped on the glass with an elbow, held out his hands to question why we had stopped.

Crier waved him down, started up the engine and pulled back onto the highway.

"I'm going to talk to Bob about it too," Crier said. "Think he'll do it?"

"Who knows about Bob?" I said.

We finally came to a clearing on the right-hand side of the highway. There was grass, but it wasn't high, and I figured a lot of critters had been grazing on it. In the distance I could see the blue of a great lake. Or what looked like a lake. I still felt as if I were on a movie set. Reality was not to be trusted.

Crier turned off the highway and drove over the grass, and it seemed like it took forever to reach the lake. He parked about six feet from it, jumped out and went belly down on the bank and stuck his face into the water and began to drink.

It was real water.

I opened my door and tried to get out, but it was too far a step and too much pressure on my feet to manage it.

I sat and waited for Crier to finish drinking. If there had been any moisture in my mouth I would have salivated.

When Crier was done he came over and got me out of the truck. The grass was soft and I found I could hobble across it without too much support from Crier.

"I couldn't wait," Crier said. "Sorry."

"I'd have done the same," I said.

The water was cool and sweet, and pretty soon Crier had Bob beside me, then all three of us were lying there on our bellies drinking. I was the first to overdo it. I puked up the water and the sardines on the bank, and Bob and Crier followed shortly thereafter.

We finished puking and went to drinking again, slower this time, and when we were finished, we pulled off what we were wearing and went into the water, Bob and I entering it on elbows and knees, looking like pale alligators.

Waterlogged, we climbed on the bank and lay on our backs and looked at the sky. The sun went down—in the south, go figure—and the lake went dark and the moon rose up—in the south, go figure again—and the water turned the color of molten silver.

After we had talked a while about this and that, Crier said, "I'm one tired sonofabitch, boys. Let's call it a night."

Crier got us in the camper and stood at the tailgate. He said, "I'm in no hurry to leave. I like that water. What say we stick around a while? The highway's out there when we decide to try it again."

Sounded good to me, and I said so.

"Yeah," Bob said. "The idea of going off and leaving all that water doesn't excite me right now. Maybe just because I been thirsty for so long. But yeah, let's wait a while."

Crier nodded and went around to the cab to sleep. I lay down on my bedroll, and for the first time since before the big red comet, I felt a stirring of hope. Or maybe I had drunk too much water.

Whatever, it wasn't so exciting it kept me awake.

4

Next day Crier drove the truck to the other side of the lake, near the jungle, and that became our home. In spite of the water, we hadn't planned to stay as long as we did, but one day rolled into the next.

The jungle provided all kinds of fruit, and in defiance of the age of dinosaurs, all manner of recognizable animals from rabbits to squirrels to monkeys to snakes. All of these were good to eat, but in the beginning we left them alone. Not out of any respect for the lesser species, but simply because we couldn't catch the little bastards and had nothing suitable to kill or trap them with. Also, Bob and I were still crips, and you've got to have legs to run critters down.

Crier made a spear by breaking off a long, thin limb in such a way that it left a point. He put fruit rinds in the lake and stood in the water with them floating around him. He waited for fish to come and nibble at the rinds, then he tried to spear them.

Sometimes it took all day for him to get one, but he stayed with it. He was so determined that sometimes dinosaurs would come and stand off in the distance and watch. I think they were amused.

As time went by Crier got better, and later he changed to a more successful method. He got some strong vine and whittled a hook out of wood with a beer can opener he flattened and sharpened with a file from Bob's tool box. He used bugs and worms for bait. By the end of the day, he'd have a pretty nice mess of fish.

I was the fire builder. I'd pull grass and let it dry for a day or two, always keeping the supply ahead of the demand. When the grass looked brittle, I'd take two files from the tool box and knock them together until they made a spark, which I directed into the grass. By blowing on the spark, I could get a blaze going, and then I would feed it twigs, then larger kindling, and finally big hunks of wood. Before long, I'd have a good fire going.

Bob cleaned the fish and cooked them by spitting them on a green limb and hanging the limb between two upright forked sticks. The fish tasted pretty good. Every night, before bed, we ended up with a pile of fish bones and fruit rinds around us.

In time, Bob and I healed, and once we could get around, we turned industrious.

With what we had in the tool box, we managed to make some simple tools for cutting and splitting wood. And damn if we weren't making crude lumber, notching it and pegging it and building a two-story house at the edge of the jungle. It wasn't anything to impress *Better Homes and Gardens*, but it was all right. We managed to use the limbs of this big tree as part of it, and the tree's foliage was so thick the house blended into it. We christened the place Jungle Home. It made me feel like I was a relative of the Swiss Family Robinson. A poor relation, to be sure, but a relation.

The upper floor was the sleeping nest, and by stuffing it with leaves and dried grass and putting the sleeping bags and blankets on top of that, we had a pretty comfortable place.

We also built a deck of split wood and bamboo on either side of the top floor, and it gave us a place to sit and feel the wind.

It wasn't paradise, but it beat being jabbed in the eye with a number two pencil.

But, as a great philosopher once wrote over the urinal in Buddy's Fill-up, "Things will go and change on you."

Crier and Bob had gone off hunting, since Crier had finally made a bow and a few arrows, and from here on out the animal populace was no longer safe. It was going to be roast rabbit and roast squirrel to go with the fish from now on.

Or so said Crier.

I had my doubts, since I had seen Crier practicing with that thing. It didn't look to me that he could have hit the side of a barn with a cannon, let alone a squirrel with a dull arrow. Still, I was hoping for him. I was beginning to tire of fish and fruit, fine as it had once seemed.

Isn't that the way of humans? They're never happy. One day I'm living off sardines and jerky with no water, and the next thing you know, I'm complaining about having fresh water, fish and fruit. Before long, I'd probably want a sauna in Jungle Home and someone to cater my meals.

Anyway, Crier and Bob went off on safari, and I was home filling some water containers we had made out of thick cylinders of hollowed-out bamboo.

I finished the job, stripped off my blanket, and went out and sat on the deck and dangled my feet over the edge.

I had no more than gotten comfortable, when I heard a car out on the highway, the engine straining and knocking as if it were about to explode.

I found me a good spot between the limbs and leaves, zeroed in on the highway, and saw a battered green Galaxy. It was coughing gouts of black smoke from under its hood and pooting a matching concoction from its tailpipe.

The driver hit down on the horn for some reason, and the horn hung.

This wasn't the Galaxy's day.

It slowed, turned off the highway onto the grassland, started weaving and picking up speed again.

I could see a figure in the front seat, fighting the wheel as if it were some rare breed of poisonous hoop snake. Then the driver lost it or quit, because the Galaxy veered to the left toward the lake.

The closer it got to the lake, the more speed it lost. It got down to a crawl. But it still made the water and dipped its nose in. Hot black smoke hissed up in a cloud, and the Galaxy began to slide languidly into the water.

And I was moving.

I had minded my own business so long, I was somewhat surprised when my Good Samaritan urges came back to me like a return bout of malaria fever. I went down the ladder two steps at a time and started running across the grassland toward the lake.

Owing to the gradual slope of the shore, the Galaxy had still not eased all the way in. The back right window was open, and I climbed through that.

The backseat was little more than springs and foam rubber. On the floorboard was something that looked like burnt sticks and brush. Another look and I knew it was human. Its skin was burned the color of neglected bacon. There was no hair, features or genitals. One of its arms was lifted, fingers extended and frozen in a pose that made the hand look like a miniature weed rake.

Water began to trickle in the back window. Already the

front seat was filled. The thing on the floor didn't look alive, so I was about to go over the seat for the driver when the garden rake took hold of my ankle.

I jerked and flesh came off of the ruined hand and ran down my ankle like dirty Jell-O. I looked at the thing and it opened its mouth, made a croaking noise that sounded like "Kill me."

The water would take care of that. I couldn't. I went over the seat and into the water and found the driver, fearing he or she would be like the burned creature on the floorboard.

I got the driver's head out of the water, saw it was a woman. I started pulling her into the backseat by the chin. The rising water helped me.

The car was going under now, and I had time to get one deep breath before the whole kit and caboodle sank to the bottom of the lake.

The mud was stirred up down there and it was like being in creamed coffee. Somehow I got out the open window and tugged the woman after me, tried to kick to the surface.

The woman was deadweight and I couldn't get us up. We sank to the bottom. Since we were near the edge of the lake, it wasn't too deep, so I buried my toes in the sand and flexed my knees and shot us to the surface.

I managed her on shore, rolled her on her stomach, got hold of her arms and worked them some, pausing to push in the middle of her back. She puked.

I turned her over, cleared her mouth with my fingers and started mouth-to-mouth. It was a stinky job and tasted of vomit, but after a short time she coughed hard once and started breathing regularly.

She blinked at me. "Timothy?"

"He the burned guy?"

She nodded.

"He's still down there."

"Best," she said, and tried to get up on her elbows. She looked at that part of my body I least wanted her to look at.

"Small," she said.

"It's cold, for Christsakes."

But she wasn't listening. She had fallen back and was out of it.

5

Considering the way she had insulted my anatomy, I wasn't in any rush to pick her up and carry her to Jungle Home, but I finally gave it a try. She was a pretty hefty gal.

I put her down, went back to Jungle Home, found the keys to the camper and drove over there and got her, loaded her into the back, letting her head bump the tailgate only a couple of times.

When I got her stretched out, I moved her hair out of her face and took my first good look at her. She wasn't bad-looking. Somewhere between eighteen and twenty-one. Guessing ages is not one of my better attributes.

Under the wet clothes her breasts looked nice and so did the width of her hips and the shape of her thighs. I thought about getting her wet clothes off to make her more comfortable, but I feared an ulterior motive.

I left her there in a puddle and went back to Jungle Home, stopping on the way to look at myself in the truck's wing mirror. My hair was wet and twisted and my scraggly little beard looked like a smear of grease. If I was going to have whiskers, why couldn't I have a full set like Bob and Crier.

I did the best I could combing my hair with my fingers,

then went on up to Jungle Home and put on my blanket
and tied it around my waist with a belt I had made of vines.
Then I lay down on my sleeping bag and found that all that
exertion had worn me out. I went right to sleep.

Next thing I knew, Bob and Crier were back. They had
a vine basket of fruit, but no game.

"The great hunters return," I said.

"He saw a bunny," Bob said, "and couldn't shoot it. He
got all dewy-eyed."

"It had a little pink nose," Crier said. "After all that's
happened, I just couldn't kill something."

"Think those fish you catch live happily ever after in
our bowel movements?"

"They aren't cute like bunnies," Crier said.

"Boys," I said, "there's a girl down in the camper."

"Don't joke me," Bob said. "I see a fork in a tree and
I get hard."

"I'm not joking," I said, and told them the story.

We brought the basket of fruit with us, and when we
got around to the back of the camper and looked inside, it
was empty. There was a pool of water where she had been
and her clothes and tennis shoes were laid out on the
tailgate.

"Melted, I figure," Bob said.

"I'm right here."

We turned. She was about ten feet away, wearing only
faded blue bikini panties. Her blond hair was dry now and
somehow she had combed it out. It fell to her wide
shoulders and tumbled over them and, much to our
happiness, stopped just before covering her breasts, which
were firm and full with areolae the size of half-dollars and
the color of warm beef gravy. The nipples were thick and

firm, like the tips of pointing fingers. She had a narrow waist and her ribs showed from having lost too much weight. There were faint, pink bands here and there on her body, as if she had been lashed with something. She had her hands on her hips and was looking right at us. If she was embarrassed, I couldn't tell it.

"Christ," she said. "Haven't you boys seen titties before?"

"There's titties," Bob said, "then there's titties."

"This is my first time, ma'am," Crier said. "I've heard of them, of course."

"Fuck with me, any kind of way," she said, "and I'll break your legs off and shove them up your assholes."

"Me first," Crier said.

But the way she looked at us then made us step aside. She came over and got her clothes and started putting them on.

"You boys enjoying the show?"

"Very much, yes," Bob said.

She finished dressing, sat on the tailgate, and looked at us. I guarantee we weren't as pleasant to look at as she was.

She said, "Had a cousin told me about a boyfriend she'd had. Said he was so horny he'd go to the ocean and fuck the water in case there might be a shark out there that had swallowed a girl. Know what she meant now. You could at least close your mouths."

"We're not so bad," Crier said. "We brought you some fruit."

She eyed the fruit we had left on the tailgate and said, "It isn't full of dick holes, is it?"

"Oh, come on," I said, "we're not that bad. All things considered, we're doing okay. We're not trying to rape you, are we? Look here. I'm Jack, this is Bob, and this is Crier."

Her face changed a little then, and there was something behind that pretty skin and those green-gray eyes that wasn't so pretty. But whatever it was went away as quickly as it had arrived.

She took a plumlike fruit from the basket and bit out of it. The juice leaped from it in gold beads and flecked her lips and cheeks and she began to chew. After a moment, she spat out the seed, and went deeper into the fruit like a lion biting the innards out of an antelope's belly. When she finished that one, she ate another.

Somehow, watching her eat was as good as a peep-show. None of us said a word.

When she was finished, she said, "Now you've had a look at my tits and watched me eat. I hope you're happy. Had you showed five minutes earlier, you could have gone off in the bushes with me and watched me pee."

"You could have called us," Bob said.

"Nice dresses," she said, nodding at Bob and me.

"Let's not talk fashion," I said. "Tell us about yourself. Before the drive-in and up to now."

"Why would you want to know?"

"Entertainment," I said. "It's not like we have a pressing social calendar. We know more than we want to know about each other. Give us something new to think about."

"All right," she said. "Sit down and get comfy, because this is going to take a while."

SECOND REEL

(Grace Talks About Frat House Fires,
Raw Liver,
and a Nine Iron to the Noggin)

1

My name is Grace, and I come from a little burg called Nacogdoches. It's supposed to be the oldest town in Texas. We got a sign that says so, but it doesn't look that old—the town, I mean, not the sign.

The place is still kind of neat, but it's going to hell fast, and when I look at photographs Mom and Dad have of it twenty-five years ago, it really chaps my highly attractive ass.

It's one of those towns where the fine old houses and the massive trees have been torn or cut down so progress can slither in. You know progress. Burger King, McDonald's, and all manner of plastic eateries where the wrappers for the burgers and the lettuce inside them taste pretty much alike, and it's my opinion the wrappers have a more natural tint than the lettuce and are probably more nutritious.

These days the old houses are gone and you can stand in the parking lot of McDonald's on North Street and toss a dried Big Mac underhanded and bounce it off the front glass of Wendy's on the other side of the street. Or you can go over to University Drive and toss a pepperoni pizza, no anchovies, out of the driveway of Mazzio's Pizza and wing an innocent bystander on the table-laden deck of Arby's.

I went to high school and college in good ol' Nac. The college is called Stephen F. Austin University, and it's named after one of the guys that helped con Texas from Mexico.

I was majoring in anthropology/archaeology, but what I really wanted to be was a karate instructor, since my dad, who was a black belt in kenpo, had been teaching me ever since I was five. If it matters, I'm first degree brown belt now.

But like Dad, I couldn't see any real future in martial arts. Or to be more precise, I think I let Mom convince me there wasn't any future in it. She talked Dad into being a manager of an optical store and she wanted something like that for me, or as she always put it, "Kicking people is all right, but you can't make a decent living at it. You got to have something to fall back on."

Well, I had been hearing this speech since I was old enough to know which was the business end of a tampon, so when I saw this *National Geographic* special on archaeology on television, I thought it might be just what I was looking for.

There were these folks with tans about the color of fresh walnut stains applied to burnt mahogany, wearing khaki shorts and pith helmets, and they were swarming all over these ruins. Fire ants couldn't have been any busier.

They were doing a lot of pointing and writing in notebooks and looking intelligent. There were close-ups of pottery shards from pots that had been made before Jesus was old enough to suck Mary's tit, and there were skull fragments and pieces of bones from the guys and gals that had made the pots.

The show ended with a close-up of this woman with sweat running from under her pith helmet and onto her face and mixing with the sand there, and she was looking out over these little fragments of walls, looking soulful as a Baptist preacher, contemplating the past and all the great civilizations that had arisen there and folded back in on themselves like a card table.

It was inspiring.

Thinking back on it now, she may have been looking out over that sand waiting for somebody to pick her up in an air-conditioned truck and drive her over to a Mideast Hilton.

But the desire to dig holes in the ground and hold the bony remains of ancient pottery makers in my hands had come over me like the Holy Ghost. I couldn't think of anything else. I checked out archaeology books and read them cover to cover and started envisioning ancient civilizations marching ghostlike through Nacogdoches, throwing down pots and bowls and breaking them so I could find them a zillion years later.

What I didn't get from those books, or refused to get, was how goddamn hard archaeology is. And it's dirty work. Those people on *National Geographic* weren't just deeply tanned, they were downright filthy.

At the end of a day, having sifted through enough sand to fill Galveston Beach, the sun burning through my clothes like an X ray, it was hard for me to take a whole lot of pride in a few broken pieces of pottery that some prehistoric dude had marked on with a pine needle.

Looking back on it, it was pretty wonderful stuff, I guess, but I don't like working in the heat and getting so dirty you have to use a putty knife to get it off your elbows. And I didn't even have a pith helmet. Just a cap that said Nacogdoches Dragons on it, and they weren't winning many ball games.

If someone from *National Geographic* had showed up right then, I'd have stuffed a year's run of magazines down their throat and kicked them until they shit a single bound volume.

It's not that I'm a weak sister. I'm not. Karate gave me patience as well as determination. But it's mostly clean work. A little sweat and dirty feet is all. And I did my workouts in our air-conditioned garage or the college gym. If you have to use martial arts on the street, it doesn't take but a few moments to open up a can of whup ass, then you can find some air-conditioned building to cool off in when it's over.

Even indoor archaeology is hard.

On one dig I found some pottery pieces, and I was assigned to try and reconstruct them. That's like giving a blind, crippled monkey a hammer, a bag of nails, and a pile of lumber and telling him to build an A-frame. I'm the gal who still has an unfinished fifty-piece puzzle of a white cat in my closet at home, and I got that puzzle for my tenth birthday.

I'd go to the lab every night and try to do that pottery, and I'll tell you, after fifteen minutes of that I was dangerous. I wanted to kill something and drink a couple of bottles of Nervine.

Bottom line is, I quit. And that was the turning point. Had I stayed in archaeology, I'd probably have been home studying, or up at the lab, destroying my nerves with that pottery instead of meeting up with Timothy and Sue Ellen and tooling on over to the Orbit Drive-in that weird Friday night.

2

So, on the night after I'd given up archaeology and my chance to have something to fall back on, I was out riding around in my old Chevy Nova trying to figure out what I was going to do with the rest of my life, and I'll tell you, what I was coming up with was not pretty.

I thought about all those stories I'd heard about college dropouts and how they spent their lives working behind the counter at K mart or pulling the train for the football team during off season. I could envision myself standing on the corner of North and Main with a cigarette jutting out of my mouth, one side of my lip pulled up in a permanent snarl, and me thinking how I can get a few dollars so I can go over to the 7 Eleven and buy me a bottle of Thunderbird wine. Nothing would be too low for me to do: prostitution, theft, drug-running, murder, working as a used-car salesman. In time I would be shunned by winos and Baptists alike.

On the other hand, I was also thinking about whoever had inherited my prehistoric pottery shards, and I felt a wicked elation that while I was out tooling around, someone was hunched over those shards with their eyes twitching, their hands shaking, wishing I had quietly pushed those fragments down a gopher hole.

Anyway, I was riding around, taking back streets mostly, thinking, and I came up on this fire.

There were cars pulled over to the curb and people were standing on the sidewalk and out front of their houses, watching a frat house burn down.

I pulled across from the house, behind the string of parked cars, got out and leaned on the Nova and watched.

The fire department was there and the firemen were jerking hoses, yelling and hopping on the lawn like grasshoppers. Every now and then one of them would erupt from the doorway of the burning structure like the end result of the Heimlich maneuver, land in the yard on his hands and knees, and crawl about feebly, coughing smoke like a little dragon.

I had never seen a fire like that before, and it didn't take Smokey the Bear to tell me it was some kind of serious. A blazing paper hat would have been easier to save.

While I was watching the frat joint burn up—hating that it was an old house of the sort the city council loved to see go so an aluminum building the shape of a box could take its place, or some concrete could be laid down for a car lot—a tan van came down the street and stopped at the curb and three guys fell out of it yelling. Frats, I figured. Most likely they had gone for a six-pack, or to work their version of heavy machinery, a Trojan dispenser, and had come back to find they had forgot to turn the fire off from under the chili, and now their pad was on its way to becoming air pollution.

Two of them sat on the curb and started crying and the other one rolled around on the lawn and whimpered like a dog with glass in its belly. A fireman came over and yelled at him and kicked him in the butt. The guy crawled off and joined his comrades at the curb and they cried in trio.

I hoped like hell there wasn't anyone inside that house. If so, they wouldn't be graduating.

I was about to leave when I was touched lightly on the elbow and a voice said, "You start this one, baby?"

"Nope. I'm all out of matches."

"Then you got nothing to worry about."

I turned and looked at Timothy. I had known him all my life, had been over to his house to play when we were kids, and he had been over to mine. There had never been anything romantic between us, though when I was twelve I talked him into playing doctor and discovered what I'd heard about boys was true: They were fixed up different from girls.

"Good to see you," I said. "It's been a while."

One of the firemen came coughing out to the curb across from us and sat down next to one of the frat boys. The one who had been rolling on the ground sobbed and said, "They gonna save it?"

The fireman took off his smoke-stained hat, coughed, and looked at the frat the way some people look at retarded children. "Son, we'll be lucky if we save the mineral rights on that sonofabitch."

The three frats really started to cry.

The roof collapsed then and the sparks from it rose up to heaven and turned clear like the souls of fireflies gone off to meet their just rewards.

"Last time I heard," Timothy said, "you were digging holes in the ground or something. Had some night classes too."

"A lab," I said. "Archaeology in the daytime, labs at night. I had to let it go."

Then I told him the whole story.

"I quit too," he said.

"I never knew you started."

"It was the math fixed me. Never could understand how X could be some other number. It always looked like X to me. I couldn't make sense of it. If X was ten one time, how could it be fifteen the next? Who the hell could keep up with what X was if it could be anything?

"What I should have taken was all P.E. courses and majored in golf. I can't make X and Y add up, but by God, I can knock those little white balls to Dallas."

And he could. I had played golf with him before. My golfing style was akin to a frightened matron trying to beat a rat to death with a curtain rod, but I had played enough to know the good stuff when I saw it, and Timothy had the good stuff. A number of pro golfers had made the same observation, and Timothy had mentioned more than once that he was thinking about taking his clubs on the road and seeing what he could do.

"We're on our way to the Orbit," Timothy said. "Want to go?"

"We?"

"Sue Ellen. She loves that horror stuff."

Sue Ellen was Timothy's little sister. She was twelve. Last time I'd seen her was two years back, and she wanted me to explain why Barbie and Ken were smooth all over. I didn't remember having any answers.

"I doubt she even remembers me," I said. "She might feel uncomfortable."

"She remembers you quite well."

"She's sort of young for blood and guts, isn't she?"

"Tell me about it. Mom and Dad think I'm taking her over to see *Bambi*, *Cinderella*, *The Fox and the Hound* and assorted cartoons in a Disney dusk-to-dawn extravaganza."

"Wonder how they got that idea," I said.

I took my car home, told my parents where I was going, not mentioning that Sue Ellen was waiting in the car with Timothy, and we went over there in the Galaxy.

When we got there, the line was as long as the Macy's Thanksgiving parade, and, of course, we got a place near the end of it. The flashing blue-and-white Saturn symbol of the Orbit was far enough away to look like a Ping-Pong ball with an oversized washer around it.

It was warm and the air was full of mosquitoes. Rolling up the windows made you hotter, and rolling them down fed you to the mosquitoes. Timothy talked about giving it up and going home, and I was for it. But not Sue Ellen.

"You promised me, Timmy. You said you'd take me. You know I want to see *The Toolbox Murders*."

I turned and looked at Sue Ellen perched in the middle of the backseat. She was blond and fair and had moist blue eyes and a freckled pug nose and a red bow mouth. Course, it was dark enough you couldn't see all this, but you knew it was there, and telling her no was a lot like kicking a puppy for licking your hand.

"We'll be miserable," Timothy said. "Besides, *The Toolbox Murders*? How'd I let you talk me into that?"

"You promised, Bubba. And if any of it bothers me, you can explain it to me."

"That's choice. I might need you to explain it to me."

"See, I'm old enough."

"One word about mosquitoes, one complaint, and we're out of here."

"Deal."

Had the weather been hotter, the mosquitoes thicker, or if Sue Ellen had had all the charm of Dr. Frankenstein's hunchback assistant, we might have cut for home right then. Sue Ellen would have grown up to break hearts,

Timothy would have gone on to hit little white balls across great expanses of greenery for unreasonable amounts of money, and I might have ended up with my own karate studio.

3

All right, I'm going to stop with Grace's story now. For all you dipshits in the back row who haven't been listening—Leroy, quit playing in that pile of shit. Put that stick down. Yeah, well, screw you too, little buddy. I hope your balls get covered in ants.

Now, all you bozos keep interrupting my reading here and I'm tired of it. You keep saying, "What about the comet? What about the comet?" Well, I've got no new news on the comet, okay? You've heard it all before. I've told you that story half a dozen times. I started this story with the comet. Remember?

No, I don't change it as I go along, Leroy. Look, I don't make you come and listen, do I, huh?

Why did all this happen?

We've been over this part, Leroy, back when I read you the first half of this story, the one I call THE DRIVE-IN, A B-MOVIE WITH BLOOD AND POPCORN. Yes, the one written on the Big Chief tablets. But to answer your question why . . . I don't know. It's like why do turds come in different shapes and colors. I can't answer that. It's one of life's big mysteries, and the comet is an even bigger one.

Here, listen. Do you remember those sayings I taught

you? The ones the Christians are fond of. Remember, we talked about Christians. Good? Now, those sayings. Let's use them to get things on the roll and because they're all-purpose. Repeat after me: THERE ARE SOME THINGS MAN WAS NOT MEANT TO KNOW, *and* I FEEL IT IN MY HEART. *Later I'll teach you about* Faith, *that way if you don't know how to explain something, say, I've got faith. That covers a lot of bases and cuts down on argument.*

What do you mean that doesn't work for you? Is this going to be like yesterday's conversation, Leroy? The one about Why Is There Air and Why Do Boys Have a Pecker and Girls Don't? Good, because I'm not going to get into that. I've got a story written down here and it's the story I'm going to read. It's a good story and I've recorded it as best I can, and it's almost the truth. If you want to hear it, fine, if not, I'll read to myself. I do this for me, not you, so you want to hear the story you got to listen. What, Leroy?

Uh huh, that's right. Why don't you go ahead and find your stick again and stir the shit pile. At least you were quiet. I wish I hadn't disturbed you.

Yeah, that's okay, use your finger. Let me get back to Grace—

Okay, maybe I don't remember what Grace said word for word, but this is pretty close. Trust me.

Food started running out at the concession, so we used Timothy's pocket knife to cut strips from the leather seat covers. The leather must have been coated with something (a dirt-resistant spray?), because it made us sick at first, though after a while we got used to it. When we still had Coke from the concession, we'd soak it in that and chew on it, maybe finish off with a few chocolate almonds. But when everything was gone at the concession we had to eat the strips straight out.

All around us people were losing it, going nuts for food, killing one another and eating one another. Sue Ellen wasn't doing so hot either. She seemed addled most of the time and kept insisting we take her home, that Mommy and Daddy would be worried. She said she didn't like the movies anymore. She missed her dog. She said lots of things.

I had to use my martial arts a few times to keep from being hurt by nuts who wanted me for either sex or food. We never got the situation clear; I pounded their heads briskly and they went away. But in time I got too weak for the martial arts, and a lot of the folks around us were too weak to do much of anything either. I guess you could say it was a kind of trade-off. I didn't feel so good, but the folks that might have done me, Timothy and Sue Ellen harm, weren't exactly up for the Boston Marathon either.

Then along came the Popcorn King.

Now he was one weird sonofabitch, looking back on it, but I'll tell you, when those two guys were fused together by the lightning and they had all those powers, tattoos coming to life and running around and the like, I wasn't even surprised.

Weird was the status quo, right?

What did surprise me was when he used those powers of his to supply us with popcorn and Coke, and he started talking that stuff about how he was our savior and that the movies were reality and murder and mayhem were okey-dokey and our salvation, and by the way, got any dead bodies, bring them on over to me and I'll eat them. You know the rap.

When he stopped giving out the popcorn and disappeared inside the concession stand for a time, like Jesus gone off into the wilderness, I'll tell you true, I was some depressed. It was back to eating seat covers.

When he finally did reappear, he no longer had popcorn to give us. Least not the real stuff. Now it was that substitute crap he was vomiting up. And that had bloodshot eyeballs on it.

Weirdness suddenly reidentified and redefined itself. I wasn't going to eat that junk, no way, no how. And neither was Timothy.

Sue Ellen ate it. There wasn't any way we could stop her from it. We tried at first, but she got away and got to it anyhow. She said it was sweet as candy and ran around inside your head like a hot lizard; said looking out of her eyes was like looking through a projector, like becoming the light and sound that shot out of the projector and hit the screen; like being everything fast-moving and bright that ever existed. Stuff like that, not twelve-year-old talk. She said when she looked at us she saw little screens on our faces instead of eyes and on the screens she could see little picture shows of our past, and I guess maybe she could, because she told us some things we hadn't told her about the two of us, like about the time we played doctor.

Mysterious stuff. Popcorn magic.

And in time the eyeball corn didn't seem so odd. So what, big deal, the popcorn had eyeballs and it came from the King who vomited it up? So what?

The idea of crunching down on those eyeballs wasn't so weird anymore. I thought maybe in texture it might be like damp Cracker Jack. Was it the vomit that made it sweet? Did lights and shadows and sounds run around in your head like a hot lizard, as Sue Ellen said? Was it really like that? Would I know new and wonderful things?

I looked around at the others. They were eating the corn, but they didn't seem to be cruising through life any better than I was. They were weak and sick and malicious, always hungry. They were dying same as me except they were hiding behind the veneer of the King's chemistry, mixing it with his jive religion, but they were going to die same as me.

Still, you can only hold out so long. Hunger is the biggest monkey ever made. It can make heroin addiction seem like a Coca-Cola habit.

Timothy caved in. He got tired of chewing seat covers and listening to his belly rumble. He went the way of Sue Ellen and ate the vomit corn. First time he had it he came back talking about the color of lies. His breath was sewerish and his eyes were dull; I wondered what movies were showing on the backs of them.

I used my martial arts to keep me away from the corn. I was too weak to practice it, but I did the movements in my head, tried to fill the hungry thoughts with visions of me nude and strong and practicing every technique I knew, fast and slow and medium.

It worked well, but not well enough. In time my belly started to win over, and I would have gone for the corn had the man not come along.

This is hard to talk about, but it seems to me, bad as this was, it was better than the corn. The corn would make me sing the King's song; I wasn't ready for the color of lies and movies on the backs of my eyes.

Okay, here goes. Straight plunge.

Timothy and Sue Ellen were just back from the concession, sitting in the car, eyes closed, seeing whatever it was the corn made them see, and I was sitting there thinking of stripping off another piece of seat cover to chew on. There wasn't much left and it made me ill to think about chewing on that nasty stuff, but what else was there to do? So I'm thinking about this, trying to get the will to do it, when this man staggered by on my side, put his hand against the door frame, said, "Shit, this ain't heartburn," and fell over.

I got out of the car and looked at him. He was about thirty with long, stringy, grayish hair and he was lying on his stomach with his head turned to one side, his eyes open. But he wasn't seeing much. He had been correct. It wasn't heartburn. He was as dead as a dodo's agenda.

Sue Ellen and Timothy got out of the car and came around and looked at him, then looked at each other, and finally me.

We didn't say a word. We got hold of him and put him in the backseat and Sue Ellen got back there with him, and Timothy and I got in the front.

Of course, I knew what we were doing. We were saving him for food. I hadn't been willing to eat popcorn with eyeballs on it, but somehow this was different. It would have been a shame to let him go to waste when we were starving. And if we didn't eat him, someone else was going to come along and drag him off for just that purpose.

Hell, it wasn't like we'd killed him.

I remember sitting there thinking about this, turning from time to time to look at the body on the backseat, and finding that each time I looked, Sue Ellen had removed yet another article of his clothing. When he was completely stripped, she called for Timothy's knife, and he gave it to her.

My next memory is of holding the corpse's still-warm liver in my hands and rubbing it into my face, then eating it. Strength flowed back into me immediately, and for some reason my legs began to jerk spasmodically and my knees hit the bottom of the dash and caused the glove box to knock open.

Timothy kept a little mirror in there, and it was at an angle, and by the light of the pulsating Orbit symbol, I could see myself. My face was stained a rust color from forehead to chin, and my eyes were little pits.

I looked at Timothy and Sue Ellen.

Timothy was chewing on a bone with a few chunks of meat on it. He had his eyes closed, and when he chewed he made little orgasmic noises deep in his throat.

Sue Ellen was on her hands and knees straddling the body, and she had half her head buried in an opening she had cut in the man's stomach. She was rooting around in there like a pig.

I opened the door and fell on the ground and threw up.

I don't think Timothy or Sue Ellen noticed. They were too busy with lunch.

I crawled under the Galaxy and tried to wipe the blood off my face with my forearms, then lay on my side with my knees pulled into my chest, and shook.

A young man so thin his pants flapped around his legs like flags on poles, came by, dropped to the ground, and made a meal of what I'd thrown up. His face was turned toward me as he lapped. When he saw me, he lapped faster. Maybe he thought I wanted it.

He finally staggered off. Where my vomit had been was a damp spot.

I rolled on my back and looked at the underside of the car and tried to think about nothing, but all I could see was that man gutted from throat to crotch and Sue Ellen with her head dipped into him. And lastly, my own face in that mirror, smeared with blood from hair to chin.

Bones were dropped out of the Galaxy's windows on the left side, and I turned my head and looked at them and tried to determine if they were rib, forearm, or leg bones. I couldn't make a decision.

As I watched, people came along and snatched up the bones and ran off with them.

I lay there for the longest time, feeling very sick to my stomach and my soul.

When I heard Timothy and Sue Ellen getting out of the Galaxy, I refused to watch their legs go by. I knew they were going to the concession to get their vomit corn from the King. I had decided I would starve to death before I did that.

I don't know how long this went on, my lying under the car hoping to starve. It could have been thirty minutes or it could have been days. But Timothy and Sue Ellen came and went several times and I always felt dizzy, as if I were in the middle of some huge platter that was being spun.

But my starvation plans weren't working out. The hunger had a mind of its own, and finally I crawled out from under the car and tried to stand up. But couldn't. I was too weak. I got hold of a door handle and pulled myself up and looked in the window at the body on the backseat.

There was hardly anything left of the man. Even his eyes and genitals had been eaten. Only his pelvis, ankles and feet had flesh on them, and it was turning black.

I felt hungry enough to bite the toes off his feet, one at a time, and would have tried, but about the time I started to go after him, the concession stand blew up.

4

That was us that did it, of course, and no use going into that again. Anyway, we smashed the concession, killed the King, and for our fine work, the crowd got hold of us and crucified us. But, I told you all about that too.

Summing up this part of Grace's story, she didn't see what happened to the concession, but when she turned around it was in shambles and on fire. Of course the movies from the concession were snuffed too, though the projector over in B section of the lot was still pumping. But the thing is, we killed the King.

Grace's dizziness subsided, and she managed to walk toward the flames. She saw what was happening to us, but later when she met us, she didn't remember our faces. The crowd was about to put fires under the crosses and cook us, and the comet came back. The black goo went away, and the drive-in folks were out of there.

Grace wanted to help get us down. Her dizziness had passed, and she tried to talk Timothy and Sue Ellen into helping, but they had come back to the car and they were ready to leave.

Anyway, Grace said—

* * *

I got the keys from Timothy and pulled the body out of the backseat. Doing that made me dizzy again, but I put a hand on the side of the car and stood that way until it passed.

I went around back to the trunk and opened it. I wanted to find something I could use as a tool to get those people down off those crosses, but there wasn't much there. A tire tool, a spare, and a bag full of golf clubs. I leaned down deeper, seeing if maybe there was something way in the back, and when I did, my head felt as if it were flying apart.

And as they say in the old detective movies, I fell into a deep, dark pit and it closed around me.

"I didn't mean to hit you that hard," Timothy said.

"Someone meant to," I said. "What did you use?"

"A golf club."

It was bright daylight and I was stretched out on the ground beside the Galaxy, which was parked on the grass next to the highway. I felt a little too warm.

Timothy helped me to a sitting position and gave me a piece of fruit. After what we'd been eating, it tasted like heaven. I began feeling better immediately. Which is not to say the golf-ball-size lump (which was appropriate) had gone away.

"I panicked," Timothy said. "I was afraid it would go back to how it was. I'm thinking better now that I've had some food."

I looked for Sue Ellen and spotted her sitting in the shade of a big tree, eating fruit. She was rocking a little and humming to herself.

"She's not doing so good," Timothy said.

He got an arm under me and helped me to my feet. I

looked down the highway and saw nothing but more highway bordered by jungle and topped by blue sky.

"I've got to go back to the Orbit," I said.

"I can't do that," Timothy said. "Neither can Sue Ellen."

"Just take me back. You don't have to go in."

"We've come a long ways since I hit you."

"You owe me, Timothy."

He drove me back and waited while I went inside the drive-in. I thought maybe I could find something in a car there to use as a tool to get those folks down, if they were still alive. But when I got inside, the crosses were down and they were gone.

I didn't stick around to look at the empty cars or the bones. I went outside to where the Galaxy was waiting, and we started on down the highway.

Okay, gang, I'll interrupt here to say that we stopped Grace's story and told her that Bob and me were two of the folks on the cross, and Crier was the one that got us down. And when we finished that, she picked up with her adventures.

But before we get to those, why don't we take a brief intermission. My tongue is getting tired.

THIRD REEL

(Grace Tells of Tremendous Gas Mileage, Shit Town,
and Popalong Cassidy)

1

So we went on down the highway, traveling only a few miles a day, stopping to look around, relieve ourselves and search for fruit and berries.

I was amazed at the way the gas held out. It was like when we were in the drive-in and the electricity worked for no logical reason, and now here was the gas gauge showing us to be getting incredible mileage. It was going down all right, but slowly compared to the miles we were racking up.

Still, gas was going to be a problem eventually. But it was a problem that was solved when we came to a place with lots of cars pulled off the highway and parked along its edges and out in an area that had been partially cleaned by nature and partially by human beings.

A crude sign had been painted on a big, split limb and stuck up in the ground beside the road. It read:

S
H
I
T

T
O
W
N

People were living in their cars and crude huts. There
was a river nearby and they were getting fish out of it. And,
of course, there was abundant fruit.

You wouldn't call it a harmonious little town, but it
seemed to be doing well enough, considering a canopy of
doom hung over it; a canopy knitted stitch by stitch by dark
experience.

We stayed on a while, living out of our car, watching
the place try and become a real town.

One night this guy about my age got a rope from
somewhere and went out to the edge of town and picked
this big oak and threw the rope over a limb and fashioned
a noose and hung himself.

Next morning he was dangling there, purple-faced,
looking like some odd-shaped, overripe fruit about to drop
from the vine. The log he had stood on and kicked away at
the last moment was about six feet from where his feet
dangled. I wondered if in his last painful moments he had
looked down at the log with regret.

Timothy and I helped get him down and some others
got rid of the body, and the next night, a girl of about twelve
went out there and climbed up on the limb and put the
rope around her neck and hung herself.

In the morning she was discovered. Sue Ellen went
over to look at her. Neither Timothy nor I tried to stop her
from seeing the body. She had seen much worse than that,
and keeping her from it was akin to shutting the barn door
after the stock have run off. Still, the way she looked at the

dead girl's face made me shiver. You'd have thought she was gazing on the countenance of the Madonna.

No one cut the rope down. I think it was a way out everyone liked knowing was there, even if they never actually planned to use it.

New people joined the community regularly. They had all been down the road a piece and they had given up and turned back, coming rolling into Shit Town in cars propelled by little more than fumes. Or they walked in, weary and defeated.

I was still thinking about the end of the highway, so I talked to as many newcomers as I could. No one I spoke with had made it to the end. They said it got rougher and stranger as you went, and some of them felt certain the highway never ended.

The town grew and the rope became more popular. Sue Ellen spent a lot of time looking at it. I decided it was time to move on.

Timothy agreed. He spent his days gathering stones and taking them out to the middle of the highway and putting them on the fading yellow line and swatting them with a golf club. His strength, like mine, had come back, and he could knock them real far. He did that day in and day out until it was too dark to do it. He didn't talk much.

I talked to people in the town that had cars, asked if I could have their gas. A lot of them said they had gone all they intended to go, and they gave it to me. I managed to get a can and a hose. I siphoned gas from the cars into the can and transferred it to the Galaxy.

While I did this, Timothy golfed and Sue Ellen looked at the rope.

I put a can of gas in the trunk and some fruit too, then I got Timothy and Sue Ellen and drove us out of there. Timothy wasn't shit for driving anymore. He couldn't keep his mind on it, and the King's popcorn had done something to the both of them. They had flashbacks of a sort. Recited lines from the movies back at the Orbit. Sue Ellen could even do the nail gun noise from *The Toolbox Murders*.

Anyway, we drove on out of there, and I put the pedal to the metal and kept my eyes ever forward, searching for the end of the highway.

2

We went along quickly, stopping only to sleep and get fruit from the trunk of the car, but after a few days, things began to change.

It was getting along night when I first noticed it. As it grew darker the jungle grew thicker and great roots cracked the concrete and coiled onto the highway along with vines that twisted and knotted like threads in a complex tapestry.

When the Galaxy's tires went over the big roots, the shocks throbbed, and when they went over the larger vines, the vines exploded like garden hoses full of black water.

The sun, like a head full of fire, nodded out below the pinprick of the highway's horizon, and the moon rose up in the same spot like a mean little kid giving us a bent-over view of a pockmarked ass.

I turned on the lights and the trees on either side of the highway leaned forward and touched overhead making a tunnel of foliage down which the Galaxy was shooting like a bullet out of a gun barrel.

The wind picked up and leaves churned across the road and popcorn bags and soft drink cups and candy wrappers joined them and made a little twister that fell over the windshield of the Galaxy like an avalanche. I beat the refuse away with the wipers and went though another twister of the stuff, and yet another, each gaining strength and causing the car to shake violently.

I thought I could see drive-in screens, or fragments of old drive-ins, on either side of the road, but I couldn't be sure because of the shadows.

Something came blowing toward me and plastered to the windshield and there was no way I could make out for sure what it was before it blew away, but it looked like a movie poster, one of those garish ones you see in the horror movies.

I glanced at Timothy, but he had passed out some time back and was leaning against the door, snoring softly. Sue Ellen was stretched out on the backseat asleep.

Goose bumps went up my back, but I didn't slow down and I didn't pull over. I didn't know what I'd find out there if I pulled over, and the idea of slowing down bothered me, especially now that the shadows were growing thicker and looking funny, and I use the word funny in the loosest sense, because I wasn't laughing about anything. I wasn't even cracking a smile.

The shadows fluttered and rolled across the road like tumbleweeds and hit the car with a sound like wet blankets. They were very odd shadows indeed. Shadows of trees and leaves and men and women and giant apes and dinosaurs and flying things bigger than a double-decker bus.

I couldn't see the source of any of the shadows, but I had a feeling if they had a source, they lived lives contrary to the movements of their origins.

I thought I saw movements in my mirror, faces, reflections of things in windows, thought I heard whispers, laughs and sighs.

Then it started to get really bad out there. The wind

picked up and gathered in the shadows, the popcorn bags, candy wrappers, cups, and posters (I was sure now), all this stuff, and it began to hit the Galaxy and whirl about it and the wind sucked at the car and lifted it up and dropped it down, lifted it up and dropped it down, and once when it went down, the back right tire went with a noise like a six-gun shot.

The car swerved and I tried to turn in the direction of the skid like the handbook says, but the skid said "Fuck You," and the shadows sacked up the car and took away the light.

Round and round the Galaxy went, over and over. Timothy flew into me and we banged heads and the darkness outside became the darkness in me.

3

I woke up and found that the car had righted itself and that I was lying on the front seat alone. The door on the passenger side was open.

I sat up and clung to the back of the seat until I felt focused. I could see Sue Ellen's shape in the back, draped partially on the floorboard and partially on the seat. I reached back and touched her and she moaned and sat up slowly and held the side of her jaw.

"You okay?" I asked.

"The movie over yet?" she asked.

"Not yet," I said. I took her hand gently from her face and saw a thin cut running from the corner of her mouth to her chin, a scratch really. She didn't seem to be in any real pain.

"Wait here, okay?"

"You going to the concession stand?"

"I'll be right back."

"Where's Timmy?"

"I'm going to get him."

"Have him bring me a large popcorn, will you?"

I couldn't tell if the wreck had banged her around and thrown off her time frame, or if she was having another of those pop-backs. Maybe she was seeing a movie through the windshield of the car.

The wind was still high when I got out of the car, but not as bad as before. I held on to the door handle for a moment, edged my way to the rear of the car. The trunk was open and the keys were in the trunk lid. Timothy had gotten the keys and gotten back here. Maybe he wanted some of the fruit.

I got the keys and put them in my pants pocket and saw that his golf bag had been pulled from under all the fruit. It was sticking out of the back of the car by a foot. I knew then that he had gotten one of his golf clubs. If Sue Ellen was still at the drive-in watching movies, maybe Timothy thought he was participating in the Bob Hope Open, or whatever that golf thing is called.

There was mashed fruit all over the place and the gas can was banged up, but not open. I set it up and got a piece of fruit and ate a few bites out of it, and started looking for Timothy.

The wind passed on by, and the last of it let popcorn bags and debris flutter onto the car and ground. Plastered across the rear of the windshield was a poster. The moon was brighter, now that the shadows had fled, and I could read the printing on the poster. *Texas Chainsaw Massacre.* The words looked as if they had been written in blood.

Out in the trees I could see big hunks of whiteness. I decided they were fragments of drive-in screens—chunks of white painted wood.

Draped between the trees like Christmas decorations were lengths of film, the moonlight sticking through the sprocket holes like long, bright needles, and a sort of mist swirling about the film itself.

I didn't see any videotapes, and I didn't see Timothy. I went around the car a couple of times, examining it.

Except for a lot of bumps and a hairline crack in the windshield, it looked all right. It was no more than ten feet from the highway, and the ground between it and the highway looked firm enough to drive on.

I wanted to look for Timothy, but I didn't know if we might need the car in a hurry, and I wanted to be ready. I dug around under the fruit and the golf bag and got out the tire iron and the spare.

The jacking up and the tire changing went pretty quick, and I rolled the old tire off beside the road, tossed the tire tool in the back and closed the trunk.

I started looking for Timothy.

Out to the right there was a trail. Maybe dinosaurs had made it. Maybe cars had made it. There was no rhyme or reason to this place.

I went down the trail calling for Timothy. As I went the wind picked up again and it started to rain and lightning began to crackle in the heavens. Still, the moon held bright.

Something moved in the jungle, and I found a good-size stick and carried it with me. Martial arts or not, another equalizer never hurts. Course, if it was a Tyrannosaurus Rex, something like that, it would eat me and pick its teeth with my stick.

As I went along, the trail widened. I went over a little rise and down into a clearing. There was a lot of grass and there were posts for drive-in speakers, and a few of them still had speakers on them. There were rusted cars dotted about.

At the back, almost integrated into the jungle, was a drive-in screen. It was split open in spots and limbs poked through the splits and twisted upwards and spread out in leaf-covered branches that looked like bony fingers from which dangled tufts of dark flesh.

About ten yards in front of the screen, golf club in hand, on the tail end of a classic swing, was Timothy.

I stood and watched a while. He was golfing up dirt and leaves.

I called to him. He looked up, went back to golfing. I walked over and waited until he finished a swing, then I stepped in and took hold of his elbow.

"This is a tough course," he said.

"You can say that again."

"I don't think I'm doing too well."

"You're doing fine. That was the last hole."

"Yeah. How'd I do?"

"You beat the competition hands down. Come along, Sue Ellen is waiting for us."

I led him along and the wind picked up and the trash twisters coiled at our feet.

4

Serious rain.

Serious wind.

Serious lightning.

Serious lost.

"Where the hell are we?" Timothy asked.

"Well, Toto, I don't think we're in Kansas anymore."

"Kansas? We've been in Kansas? Who's Toto?"

"Just close your little mouth and walk."

Sometimes it doesn't pay to read or watch old movies. No one knows what you're talking about.

"Goddamn," Timothy said. "This is a weird course. What's that?"

It was shadows. They had collected in our path. On either side of us the trees whipped their heads up and down like drunk women with the dry heaves.

I threw my stick at the shadows and the stick went into them and was not seen again. The shadows flowed over us with a howl of the wind and they felt like wet felt where they touched us. But there was nothing more to them. They went through us, and I turned to watch them blow on down the trail like ink-stained ghosts.

The trail disappeared. It was as if the trees had pulled

242

up by the roots and repositioned themselves. Nothing was familiar. Strips of film dropped down from the branches and clung to us, and when I tore them off they ripped my flesh.

Timothy swatted at them with his golf club. The film wound itself around the club and jerked it away from him. Last sight of it was a silver wink in the moonlight as it disappeared into the rustling leaves of a dark, gnarled tree.

I grabbed hold of his wrist and tugged him. We went between trees and shrubs, wherever there was a space. Film ran along the ground and dropped out of the trees and tried to grab us.

Lightning flashed. I got a glimpse of the highway through the trees. Not much farther.

Timothy was pulled from me. I turned. The film had him by the feet and more of it had dropped down from the trees and coiled around his arms and pulled them up. A thin strip of it was twisting around his leg and working up his body. By the time I reached him, the end of it was tight around his neck.

I tried to pull it off of him, but more of it came up from the forest floor and snapped around me like the business end of a whip. Then my feet were held and my arms went up and more of it wrapped around my body. Where it touched my bare skin I could feel a sensation like dozens of tiny needles.

From where I stood, immobile, I could see a clear spot in the trees, and when the lightning flashed, I saw the highway, and out there on the highway was a black wrecker with its light on. A man was standing by the wrecker looking at the jungle and the wrecker door was open and I could see a naked butt rising and falling, and there was something between the butt and the seat, white-legged and thrashing, and I knew instantly that it was poor Sue Ellen.

And I knew too that the same lightning that had flashed and allowed me to see the man by the wrecker had allowed him to see me.

5

A flashlight bounced like a great firefly toward us. When the light reached the edge of the jungle I could see the outline of a big, broad-shouldered man and the outline of another behind him. Their shadows leaned together behind them like two happy thugs. When the men moved, the shadows moved of their own accord.

As they entered into the jungle the film crept out and grabbed at them and the biggest of the two men yelled, "Edit," and produced some large scissors and snipped at the film. The man behind him did the same with a smaller pair.

They clipped their way through, and one came up to me, the other to Timothy.

The one with the big scissors and the flashlight was the one in front of me. He put the light in my face and said, "How would you like to be cast in the part of prime pussy?"

Film crawled on his legs and he bent casually and clipped it. "Damn stuff," he said.

"This one looks like a dumb asshole," said the other.

Some of the old Timothy came back, and it couldn't have been a worse time. Timothy said, "Fuck you."

The man hit Timothy in the side of the head with the little scissors. Timothy nodded forward, made no further sounds.

The little scissors went to work on the film that held Timothy, and when it was snipped, Timothy fell down. The man picked him up and tossed him over his shoulder and headed toward the highway, kicking at the film as he went. Once he squatted with Timothy balanced on his shoulder, and used the scissors on a swathe of film.

"Snip, snip, snip, you little motherfuckers," he said. Then he and Timothy were out of the jungle, being pursued by both men's shadows; they moved out into the brighter moonlight which had replaced the dark and the lightning. Out on the highway the wind made little plumes of trash jig all around the wrecker.

The man in front of me cut a coil of film from around my neck and snipped an even smaller piece from that, held it three feet from me. It dripped blood.

"They're like leeches. They show best when they've eaten." He put the flashlight against the strip from behind and two hands holding a chainsaw came out on my side and ballooned to full size and the chainsaw buzzed and the hands shoved it at my face.

He turned out the light just in time. The buzz of the saw died, and where the hands and saw had been, were drops of falling blood. I felt them hit my shoe.

The man cocked the flashlight and said, "Good night, moon," and he hit me.

I was still bound when I awoke, but I was no longer in the jungle. I was tied to the wrecker, facing out. The wrecker was off the highway and a tarp had been stretched over it and the end visible to me was stretched down tight with stakes, and the center of it was poked up high with an antenna stalk that bloomed into a clutch of silver quills at the top.

It was warm under the tarp, and the warmth came

from fires built in the husks of a dozen television sets. Rain pounded the tarp and scratched at it like harpy claws. Some of it came through the holes in the tarp and hissed in the fire and hit my face and ran down it like tears. The televisions gave off greasy smoke and it fouled the air and made me woozy.

The side of my head hurt. It should. I had been knocked on it enough. But considering all that, I was lucky. My dad always said I had a hard head. On the other hand, I have dizzy spells from time to time even now. My vision gets screwy.

But as I was saying. My head hurt. Where the film touched me stung.

To the rear of the tarp, squatting in a semicircle, facing me, were four men. They were all dressed in ragged clothes and jeans. They were close-shaved and had bushy flattops that looked as if they had been cut with dull knives. They looked strong and well fed, or maybe just fed. Two of them were the men who had taken Timothy and me out of the jungle.

Behind them on the tarp were their shadows. The shadows were moving in defiance of the motionless posture of the men and the flickerings of the firelight.

I looked to the right of me and saw Timothy. He was tied to the wrecker by blue and red electrical wire. I assumed the same thing held me. Where the man had hit him with the scissors his skull had cracked open and a coil of his brain was leaking out like congealed oatmeal escaping from a crack in a bowl. Suddenly it was very hot. I thought I was going to faint. The wire was the only thing holding me up; there were no usable muscles left in me.

I took a deep breath and pulled some strength back into me from somewhere and looked to my left and saw Sue Ellen. She was tied to the wrecker by wire too. She had her clothes on now. Both her eyes had been blacked and her bottom lip was puffed. The front of her pants was dark with blood. She had her eyes open and she was looking straight ahead, but she wasn't seeing what was there. She was tuned in to something else. Maybe a flashback of one of the movies she liked. I hoped so. This little scenario was certainly a stinker.

Then the four in the back rose and their shadows went still and rigid. They were staring at me, or so I thought at first, but realized that they were in fact staring at something behind me. I could sense the presence of that something, and I heard movement on the wrecker and I could hear a sound like breathing through a bad drive-in speaker, puff and crackle, puff and crackle.

Goose bumps rose along my arms and ripped up my back and down my spine, felt as big as black berries. They were even on the backs of my calves. Then the sensation passed and the wrecker creaked and I knew that whatever had been behind me had moved.

I watched the heads of the men in back turn; watched the heads of their shadows turn. The fires flickered and popped when the cold rain came through the holes in the tarp and went into them and was turned to steam.

There was movement on the wrecker again, then whatever it was jumped to the ground between Sue Ellen and myself, and I got my first look at the thing I would come to know as Popalong Cassidy.

6

Leave It to Beaver was playing on his face and his face was a sixteen-inch screen with one of those old-fashioned glow lights trimmed around it, and this was all encased in a cheap brown wooden case. The character on the screen, Ward Cleaver, closed a door and said, "Honey, I'm home," and this was all faint, this dialogue, because there was lots of static right then. And behind all this, in the depths of that tube-face, I could see two red glows that might have been little tubes or eyes.

The television set was wearing a tall, black hat. There was a white scarf around a very human neck, and the rest of the figure was human too, and it was dressed all in black, drugstore-cowboy attire. The pants were stuffed into some tall, black boots and there was a black glove on either hand. He wore a black gun belt with some metal studs on it and there was a holster on each hip and in the holsters were pearl-handled, silver-tooled revolvers.

Television Face came and stood in front of me, and I saw below his screen, on the cheap wooden frame, two rows of knobs and dials. They divided suddenly so that they looked like top and bottom teeth, which in a way they were.

The thing was smiling. The wood was not wood.

A tongue made of tangled blue and red wires licked from left to right and disappeared. In its place came a voice full of static and high of tone. "Hi. My name is Popalong Cassidy, and I bet you think we are mean."

The hat lifted and I saw a set of rabbit ear antennas were responsible. They wiggled out cautiously, as if testing the air for radiation. The hat tipped way back but didn't fall off; it fit there like a flap of skin.

A blue arc jumped from the tip of one ear to the other and the arc rode down the middle space between the ears, then back up. *Leave It to Beaver* went away and on the screen there was a dumpy, ugly man down on one knee next to a Highway Patrol car. The car door was open and the man reached inside and took a microphone from off the dash and pulled it out until the wire was stretched. He said something into the microphone I didn't catch, ended it with "Ten-four." I realized then that he was down like that because on the other side of his car, way off the highway, hid out there in the brush-covered hills, there was supposed to be a bad guy with a gun.

I recognized the television series. It was an old black-and-white one I had watched on occasion. It was called *Highway Patrol* and starred Broderick Crawford.

I didn't get to find out if Crawford went after the culprit in the brush or not, because Popalong darkened his face except for a little yellow dot in the center, and that grew rapidly smaller until it too was gone. The rabbit ears slid back into the set and the hat fell back into place.

"It's okay if you think we're mean, you know. I don't mind." And with that Popalong backed away from me until he was up against the big antenna that punched up the middle of the tarp. There was a bar that ran through the bottom of the antenna, about four inches off the ground, and Popalong back-stepped onto that and reached his arms up and draped them through the antenna rods, hung his head to the side and let his body droop. Presto, a media Christ.

The rain plummeted the tarp and slipped through the holes and sizzled in the popping fires. Nobody said a thing or moved a muscle.

After a while, one of the men got up and raced to the wrecker and climbed on it. When he jumped off he had a big load of magazines under each arm. He went from TV to TV and put magazines into their blazes. I saw the covers of some of the magazines before the flames devoured them. *TV Guide, People, Tiger Beat, Screen Gems*, all of them decorated with the faces of movie stars and fading celebrities. I thought: Where in hell did that stuff come from?

When the fires were really popping and the air was tinged with smoke, the man darted back to his place with the others, and Popalong lifted his head and looked at me and turned his face on. A test pattern filled it. The dials below the screen split apart again and the tongue of tangled wire presented itself briefly and disappeared. "Don't think there's any hatred in my heart for you or anyone," Popalong said. "My heart has no room for that. It's full of electromagnetic waves and they jump about like frogs."

He got down off the antenna and came over and bent forward and looked at me, as if hoping to find something reflected in my eyes. The rabbit ears poked out from under the hat and touched my hair and I felt a faint electric sizzle ride the circumference of my skull. "You have no shadow, you know. It's because you haven't learned to belong. That's what I think. I think when you belong here you have a shadow. I think you earn it. You haven't earned anything. When you're like us you'll have a shadow, a familiar made up of the absence of light.

"Pay attention. Keep sharp. I jump around a lot. It's

the sign of a good mind. I'm trying to tell you there's a confusion about good and evil. We worry about which is which way too much. Let me just say that good is too easy. It requires nothing. No real commitment. You can't get the real good out of goodness until you know darkness. Death. Pain. These are instructive tools. Or as Dr. Frankenstein said in *Andy Warhol's Frankenstein*, 'To know death, you have to fuck life in the gall bladder.'

"I know this now, but all my life I have been looking for this truth and it's been under my nose all the time. The images taught me where it was at. There are good images and there are bad images, but the bad images make the best show, so I've opted for the bad images. I praise the Orbit for leading me to the truth. I praise the night I went. The Popcorn King was right. Movies are reality and everything else is fraud. But the King was not the Messiah, as I thought. He was John the Baptist. I'm the Messiah. I was given powers and position by the Producer and the Great Director, and they wanted a sci-fi horror picture. We're number two of a double feature.

"Why me, you ask? Because I have seen more hours of television than anyone. I can quote commercials by heart. I know the name of the Green Hornet's secret identity, the name of the sleek, black car he drives. I know the name of Sky King's niece and what Batman eats for breakfast. Everything that is important is in this square head.

"Let me tell you too, I was made for it. I'm a preacher's son. I grew up with fire and brimstone and channel nine, the only channel we could get at that time.

"My father spoke savagely to us from the pulpit and every Sunday afternoon after church he beat my mother with his thick belt, then came downstairs and beat me too. I never ran. I took it. He would beat me until his arm got tired, then he would switch arms and wear down. He left welts on my ass.

"When he was finished, he would become remorseful and read the Bible to me and pray. Then he would tell me to turn on my television set and watch it. That I was redeemed. That the sin was cast out of me by pain.

"My mother went away when I was eleven. I thought about her a few days after she was gone, but I never missed her. She had been nothing more than someone around the house, going this way and that in a plaid housecoat and slippers with the backs broken down. She ate a lot of sweets and drank lots of coffee and sipped Nervine that she poured from a bottle into a great big spoon. She seldom spoke to me and never fixed meals. I took care of myself. I grew up on Cokes and Twinkies. The characters on TV spoke to me in her place.

"When I graduated, passed more out of courtesy than for any other reason, my father took his belt to me and beat me until I couldn't get off my knees. He gave me a new Sylvania set and told me to be gone by morning and to never come back. He had taken care of my raising until I was a man, and now I was a man, and to go.

"I went. I couldn't get a good job. The people out there were cruel. Unlike TV, they expected things of you. They wanted college educations. I wanted a satellite dish and more channels. The chance to see time and again *Apocalypse Now, Taxi Driver, The Andy Griffith Show*. It really didn't matter. Just images. My images. Part of my holy communion. Kurtz and Opie, Leatherface and Lassie, side by side.

"I ended up working at a filling station. I could never get the work straight. I mostly put nozzles in gas tanks and dreamed of *Gilligan's Island* and a trip on *The Love Boat*, of chain-sawing pretty people and stripping their flesh so that I could wear it, jacking off in a gutted corpse. I missed my father's belt. Gasoline ran over my shoes."

As he talked, silent scenes from films and TV shows and commercials ran across his screen like track stars. I couldn't take my eyes off of them. Something about them tugged at me. I felt drunk. I wanted Popalong to turn his face off and shut up. I wanted a hot bath and a good meal and a hot fuck. I wanted to be home in Nacogdoches, tooling down Main Street with the car windows down and a hot wind in my face, looking to see what historical house or building they would tear down next.

But what I got was more of Popalong.

7

POPALONG'S STORY

But the boss kept me working even if I wasn't any good. It wasn't a place that got much business and nobody else wanted to work there because the pay was cheap. Lucky for the boss, I didn't need much and no one else would have me. He let me watch television there at the station between cars. I was between cars a lot.

The money I made kept me in Twinkies and Cokes, *TV Guide* and the cable. I saved up and bought a VCR. I bought a belt like my father used to beat me. I was cozy. I lived in a one-room, walk-up apartment that smelled like the winos in the doorways below. I often saw them when I was walking to work, shuffling ahead of me in search of a bottle. For some reason they made me think of Henry Fonda in *The Grapes of Wrath*.

At night I would take the belt like my father's and slap my naked back with it. I did this while I watched tapes of Hopalong Cassidy reruns. Hopalong had a face like my father's. Watching him made the beltings work all the better. I slapped myself until I bled. I tore pages from the *TV Guide* and stuck them to my back to stop the blood. Sometimes there were not enough pages.

When I finished, I would put the videotape of *The Bible* into the VCR and watch a few minutes of that while I knelt and held the box the tape had come out of. I prayed there would be no electrical blackouts while I was watching a movie. I prayed my television would not wear out until I could afford a big-screen TV. I prayed I would someday have a place of my own away from the noise of the winos, a place where I could have a satellite dish and fill my head with channels. I wondered who I was praying to.

So it went until a week before Halloween. I was on my way home from work, eager to get my belt and put in the Hopalong tape, and what do I see in the window of the costume shop between Sylvester the Cat and a pirate outfit, but a Hopalong Cassidy costume. I felt weak in the knees.

I went in there and blew all the money I had. I knew I would have to buy some cheap brand of soft drink and some sort of pastry that wouldn't match Twinkies, but I had my Hopalong suit, complete with hat and boots and holsters, though the guns in it were cap pistols.

When I got home I put the outfit on and looked in the mirror. I was disappointed. My shoulders were not as broad as Hoppy's and my face was nothing to look at. I didn't look like my father who looked like Hoppy. I looked like a weasel staring out of the woods.

I took off the suit and hung it in the closet and put the boots below and the hat on a shelf above. I discovered if I left the closet door cracked and turned on the end table light, or if the moonlight came through the window just right, it looked like Hoppy was standing in there, hiding, waiting to come out and beat me with a belt or shoot me with his pistols.

I liked that. The suit was not a total loss.

Then about Christmastime I saw this special on random killers. I noted that most of them had sad little faces

like mine. But here they were with their sad little faces
going out to millions while I lay in bed holding my dick.
They had done things like pump hot lead into warm bodies,
and all I could do was shoot a pathetic wet bullet onto my
sheets. What they had done brought camera crews out, and
they got their pictures taken. Got seen by millions. Got to
be stars. What I had was more laundry.

But when the special was over, I knew what I wanted
to do.

I had to save my money again, and this meant I didn't
eat very much, but I never really cared that much for eating
anyway. The more I thought about what I wanted to do, the
more excited I got, and the more I took the belt to myself.
When I showered it looked as if red paint were running
down the drain.

I took to wearing the Hopalong outfit. I didn't look any
better in it, but I didn't care anymore. I knew what I
wanted now, and knowing made me feel better about
myself.

First I bought a car from my boss for three hundred
dollars. A white Ford Fairlane. I was not a good driver, but
I knew how. I could get from one place to the next if I could
get my mind off television. I tried to pretend that I was part
of a television show like *Miami Vice*, and I was patrolling
the streets for crime. I drove every day so I could get better
at it, but I never learned to like it.

Then I saved up enough to get the rifle. A Winchester
with an old-fashioned lever. I had it replaced with a loop
cock like the one John Wayne had in *Stagecoach*. It was no
big problem to get the rifle. I merely had to sign some
papers. It didn't matter to me that later they would be able
to trace it. I wanted them to.

By the time the summer came around I was able to buy
two pearl-handled, silver-tooled pistols and enough ammu-

nition for them and the Winchester. Again, I merely had to sign some papers.

I went home and took the cap guns out of the holsters and put in the real .45's after I loaded them. I loaded the Winchester and put it in the closet. I watched a video of *The Wild Bunch*.

Next afternoon after work, I put the rifle in the trunk of my car and went back in and put the Hopalong outfit and gun belt on. The real guns weighed more than the cap pistols, but I liked their weight. It was like waking up and having muscles.

When I went out to the car the second time, a wino saw me. He said, "Man, who you supposed to be, Hopalong Cassidy?"

"That's right," I said, and pulled one of the .45s and shot at him. I missed him by a mile. The bullet went past him and smacked into the doorway of the apartment house. The wino ran around the corner, and I shot at him again. This shot wasn't any better. He got away. My marksmanship worried me some.

I drove out of town, and by the time I got to the overpass, it was starting to get dark. I pulled over next to the concrete wall and unlocked the trunk and got the rifle. It was dark now. I could see the lights of the cars, but to see who was in them I had to let them get pretty close to the overpass so the lights there would shine down on them and give me a look.

I watched a few go by before I shot at anybody. Guess I was getting the feel of things.

I picked one out and aimed between the headlights, then lifted the rifle barrel above that so I could center on the windshield, then I moved the barrel to the driver's position and pulled the trigger.

First time didn't work because I had the safety on. The car went beneath the underpass and on.

I took off the safety and waited for another car, remembered to cock the lever and jack a shell into the chamber. I felt like Lucas McCain, the Rifleman.

Next car that came I shot at, and I don't know if I hit anyone or not, but it veered off the road, then back on, and went under the overpass and kept going, very fast. Next car I hit someone because it went off the road and through a barbed wire fence right before it reached the underpass. I saw a man stumble out of it and fall down in the pasture and get up. I took a couple of shots at him, and I guess I finally hit him because he·fell down and didn't get up. I shot once more in his direction, then went back to watching cars.

A station wagon was next, and I put a shot into it and it ran into the side of the overpass and a woman opened the door part of the way and fell out. The lights from the overpass were bright on the windshield in the car, and I could see a child in a baby seat on the passenger's side. I could even hear it crying.

I leveled the rifle and fired until I finally hit it and it shut up. I figured I had done enough then. I was a celebrity, though no one knew it yet. I could just imagine being apprehended and handcuffed and the television cameras coming out and taking my picture in my Hopalong outfit, and then taking pictures of my pistols and my loop-cock Winchester. I hoped they'd let me see myself on television in the jail. But just knowing I was going to be there was a great thrill. I was, for the first time in my life, somebody.

At first I thought I should turn myself in, but this seemed too easy. I would let them come for me. I might take a few shots at them, then, if they fired back, I would toss out my weapons and say I quit; I had watched that sort

of thing on television more than once. They didn't kill you
if you quit. After I got on television, I didn't care what they
did with me.

I put the rifle in the trunk and drove away. I drove
until I came to a little serve-yourself gas station and
grocery. I was very hungry and I needed gas.

I went in there and got a Coke and a Twinkie and the
girl behind the counter stared at me. I liked that. I felt like
a movie star. "Who are you supposed to be?" she said.

"Hopalong Cassidy," I said, and pulled out my pistol
and reached across the counter and put it next to her nose
and fired just as she screamed. Blood went all over the cash
register. I went around and opened it and got some of the
money just to have something to do, got my Coke and
Twinkie and started to leave.

A man in a big black wrecker drove up then, and he
walked inside just as I was about to go out. He looked at me
and I saw his head jerk a little. He knew something wasn't
right. I pulled the revolver and shot him in the chest and he
went back against the glass door, hitting it so hard it
cracked. It swung open and he fell out on the ground. I
bent over him and shot him twice in the head.

Something about the wrecker appealed to me. I put
my Coke and Twinkie in the wrecker's seat and got my rifle
out of the Fairlane and put it in the floorboard of the
wrecker. I had some trouble driving the wrecker at first,
but I knew how. I had learned how to drive a lot of things
at the station so I could put them in stalls to have flats and
oil changed.

I drove along not thinking about much, and I saw the
Orbit drive-in. I couldn't pass that up. I had been away
from a screen too long and had begun to feel unreal. I drove
in there and watched the movies and waited to be arrested.
I thought I might not even wait. I thought I could get my

rifle and go behind one of the screens and poke a hole in it and start shooting at people in their cars like the guy did in *Targets*. Maybe Boris Karloff would show up to stop me. I would have liked that.

But before I could do anything the comet came and trapped us all in the drive-in. I wasn't going to be arrested. I wasn't going to be on TV. It was depressing at first, until I realized an incredible truth. I was living a movie. This wasn't like working at the filling station. This wasn't like walking home and seeing the winos. This was even better than watching television. It was like when I was shooting from the top of the underpass, only more so. This was constant, and everyone had to be involved, like it or not. The movie owned us all and you couldn't change channels or turn it off. Here was a movie with blood and guts and a wild monster, the Popcorn King. He was wonderful. He preached violence and religion. If he could have gotten wrestling into his talks he would have covered the three manias of television. I loved him. I wanted him to beat me with a belt. I quit wearing the Hopalong outfit. I stripped off and went around naked like a lot of the others. I was not ashamed of my body now. Everyone looked awful. The comet and the Popcorn King had made us all alike. My constant fear was a happy ending, which meant, of course, everyone would go back to what they were before. And for me, that wouldn't have been much.

But things did not last. The comet came back. I put my Hopalong outfit on and drove out of the drive-in behind the others. I figured the old world would be out there and the only thing I could think of that was positive about that was that I would eventually be arrested and my picture would be on TV, and I would be recorded on video for all time. I figured this would be even more likely if I wore the Hopalong outfit.

But the old world wasn't out there. There was this world. This double feature.

I became determined to drive to the end of the highway. Things got weirder as I drove along, and I wanted to see just how weird they would get. I wanted to be part of the weird.

Once, when I stopped to find fruit, I saw a crowbar lying on the bed of the wrecker, and I got it and used it to break the padlock off the big metal box welded below the back window. Inside was a tarp, flares, knives, electrical wire, miscellaneous items. I knew these would come in handy later.

The gas in the wrecker lasted a long time, and when I got to this place with the film draped in the trees, I knew I was on the right track.

I pushed on. I felt like Humphrey Bogart in *They Drive by Night*.

Though the shadows and the storms and the crawling film persisted, I began to see new things. Solid things. Munchkins from *The Wizard of Oz*, for example. I never saw a live one, just dead ones. They were lying beside the highway or in it, obviously having been hit by cars. They were smashed and/or bloated. Their little caps lay beside them like markers. I passed one that someone had propped up with a stick. They also had a stick down one of his sleeves and had rigged it so his arm stuck straight out; he looked as if he were thumbing a ride.

I passed cars beside the road. Empty. Came to one where a body was wrapped like a mummy in film; the film was pulsing like a tumor.

Cars passed me on their way back. None of the drivers waved.

Beside the road I saw what looked like a collapsed

water tower, but it was one of the Martian stalking machines from *War of the Worlds*. A squidlike creature was dangling out of an opening in the top of the machine, limp as spaghetti.

When the storms came now, they were more violent than ever. The blue lightning flashed through the films and the images on the films were cast onto the ground and into the trees and onto the wrecker. They lived and breathed during those brief moments of lightning.

The wrecker was rigged with an auxiliary tank, and I switched that on and kept at it. I finally had to stop and use the hose from the box on the wrecker bed to siphon gas from a couple of dead cars, which turned out to be the last ones I saw on the highway. What gas I got from them you could have put in a paper cup. But it was gas that got me to the end of the highway.

I got closer looks at the Munchkins. They were solid all right, but they weren't real after all. They were elaborate dummies. As I went, there were more of these, and not all of them were Munchkins. They were the sort of dummies they used to use a lot in old movies, when they wanted to have a body tumble over Niagara Falls for instance. I stopped in the daylight and looked at the Martian machines. Cheap wood painted silver. The Martians were rubber octopuses.

I liked that.

Finally I came to the end of the highway.

And there was the Orbit.

It was different in many ways, but it was the Orbit. The highway was a snake biting its tail.

Amid the wreckage that had been made by the fools who killed the Popcorn King were strips of film, more dummies, props of all kinds, lobby cards, TV sets and fragments of antennas. In several spots there were piles of

TV sets; piles that made pyramids that tipped through a continuous bank of dark clouds.

At night there were really violent storms. Worse yet. The wind blew popcorn bags and movie posters and soft drinks and movie magazines against the wrecker with a sound like wet towels popping.

When it rained, it rained chocolate almonds and popcorn and soft drinks—every kind imaginable: cherry, orange, Coke, Dr Pepper, Pepsi. I recognized the taste of these and more by drinking from puddles in the blacktop. Later I sat cups out at night and in the morning I drank from these, picked up chocolate almonds and popcorn and the occasional unwrapped Snickers for my breakfast. I confess, I longed for Twinkies.

I learned that the busted television sets grew up from the ground like sacrificial potatoes. Once birthed, the ground healed up behind them like a sore.

I checked out the concession over in Lot B, but though it was intact, it was a shambles inside; there wasn't anything of use in there. The projectors looked okay, but unlike when the Orbit was in that black stuff, they didn't work without electricity. It was a depressing discovery. All those films and no way to show them.

The lightning gave me glimpses of films, because of the way it made images jump, but it was really more of a tease than anything else. What I would have given even for a complete dog food commercial.

I picked magazines—*Screen Gems*, *TV Guide*, and the like—off the windshields of the cars and off the ground, and spent my days shaking the soft drinks out of their pages and reading them carefully. It was okay at first, but a lot of the magazines were the same. I began to get bored. This place was certainly like a movie set, but it wasn't as satisfying as before, not the way it had been when it was at the other end of the highway. Then it had been more than a set. It had been a movie that I was part of. There was action and drama and comedy, and now there was just me. I didn't care much for me.

I decided to climb one of the pyramids and go up into the constant cloud bank. I doubted it was high enough for me to need an oxygen mask up there, and then again, I didn't really care. I wanted to see where all the chocolate almonds and soft drinks came from, and it was something to do that was like being in a movie.

I started up by sticking my feet into the busted faces of the sets, clutching them like lovers. After a time I realized the pyramid was much higher than I thought. I began to get frightened. I was reminded of the movie *The Bible* and the scene concerning the Tower of Babel. Was I defying the gods? Or was it a test?

Once again, I decided it didn't matter. I was living a movie and that was what counted. I would rather die as part of a movie than live as part of the normal world.

When night set in with its storms of papers and its rains of soft drinks, chocolate almonds, and popcorn, I was not even halfway up. I found a twenty-three-inch television with the tube busted out and I crawled into the opening and pushed out the back and found myself in a den of sets and movie magazines. It looked like someone or something had been living in there at one time. I crawled back through some more sets and found a comfortable spot with plenty of room and stretched out on top of some magazines and tried to pull a few over me. I lay there pretending I was Stewart Granger and I was trapped in King Solomon's mines.

When I awoke the next morning, I felt awful. I let down my pants and took a shit, got out of there and started climbing. I went like that for three or four days, sleeping in what TV caves I could find, traveling as long as I could take it each day.

Finally I came to a wisp of cloud. I was right, the clouds were low. They were also made of cotton and they bunched tightly around the top of the pyramid. I pulled the cotton away to make the going easier, and kept climbing.

As I went up, I saw there were hundreds of thin, white strings holding the dark clouds up on either side of me.

I didn't go much farther before I came to a spot where the blue lightning jumped and crackled constantly and swarmed around my head like a halo. The electricity made my hair stand on end and push my hat up so that it seemed to be supported by porcupine quills. The hair on my body poked through my clothes like tacks.

Above me I could see an opening in the blue sky. I went up through that and felt my hair go soft and my hat settle down on my head. When I got through the hole I was at the top of the pyramid and I stepped off of it and found myself inside a tremendous room full of gigantic cameras, sound systems, and gadgets I couldn't identify. None of it looked designed for human hands.

Leaning against a distant wall was a backdrop. It was of the Orbit, and it was the Orbit when it was acidic and the Popcorn King had ruled. My favorite time.

I took the long walk over and touched it. It rippled under my hand and I was able to move into it. It was suddenly real. On the screen nearest me, *Night of the Living Dead* was playing. It wasn't one of the good parts. No one was getting ripped apart or eaten.

There were people moving about among the speakers and cars. They looked stunned, mechanical, thin and wasted. But they didn't look as bad as they were going to look.

When I turned, I expected to be trapped in the Orbit,

and I wouldn't have minded too terribly, but behind me was a backdrop of the room full of equipment. I reached out and touched it and walked forward, and I was out of the Orbit; it was a backdrop again. I was a free agent.

I looked around.

There was this hallway, and on either side of the hallway were painted backdrops. I went down the hallway and stopped to look at some of them. One that caught my eye was of a jungle.

I stepped into it. Immediately I was very hot and the air was full of the stink of mold and plants, and the trees were dripping water. I thought maybe this was a backdrop of the jungle below; maybe by stepping into this one, I was down below again.

I heard a cracking of trees and brush, and a red, blue and yellow Triceratops poked its head through some greenery and looked at me. I know they're supposed to be vegetarians, but I wasn't in the mood to find out. Besides, he looked as if he might charge. I wondered if he could charge right out of the backdrop. I turned quickly and stepped back into the hallway. When I looked at the backdrop, it was just a jungle. No Triceratops.

I walked down the hallway until a Western backdrop caught my eye. I stepped into a dusty street and began walking between rows of clapboard buildings. At the far end of the narrow street, a tall fellow with a gun on his hip began walking toward me.

I was dressed for the part, but I didn't like the looks of this. I turned around and walked back up the street and stepped back into the hallway.

When I examined the backdrop, there was just an empty street, of course.

The backdrops came to an end, and in their place were mirrors that distorted my appearance. No two had me looking the same. It seemed to me there was some great cosmic truth in this, but try as I might, I couldn't put my finger on it. I kept walking.

The hallway became filled with a large red ball. It towered high above me and touched the walls of the hallway. I put my hand against it and it felt as if it were made of cardboard. I pushed and it rolled back to reveal a split that widened and showed me several rows of jagged, poorly painted, cardboard teeth.

It was the comet that had smiled and turned the Orbit into a horror movie. I pushed the ball hard and it went rolling down the long hallway very fast and disappeared into the distance like the sun falling down the dark shaft of the universe.

I noticed now that the floor beneath me had changed and that I was standing on a dark rectangle and it was in turn linked to another and a series of these went on down the hall and disappeared into the same distance the comet had fallen. On either side and between the rectangles were gaps and out of the gaps poured a bright yellow light that hit against the ceiling.

The light became stronger and warmer. It worked through the rectangle and it worked through me. I fell face forward, went stiff and was enveloped by the flooring.

The light went out.

Lines I remember from my father and his Bible:
In the beginning God created the heaven and the earth. And the earth was without form, and void; and darkness was upon the face of the deep. And the Spirit of God moved upon the face of the waters.

And God said, Let there be light; and there was light.

I don't know about the waters, but there was certainly light, and plenty of it. It was stronger than before and warmer than before; it went through me like new blood. I felt as if I had never lived, except I had memories, and these seemed to belong to someone else and loaned to me. I felt as if I were a new creature in the eyes of the God (or Gods) of film; I was nothing more than a flat lifeless piece of celluloid with a great yellow light shining through me and the light was giving me life.

In other words, I was on a filmstrip.

I could hear gears grinding, sprockets turning, and the rectangle that was my home began to move. It rolled through what must have been a projector, because at some point the bright light became brighter and I hit a white wall and—

I was animated, cartoon style. I held my hand in front of me, and it was black-gloved like it was supposed to be but the hand was puffy and silly, as if it were really nothing more than a glove filled with air.

I was in a little room sitting on a stool, and all around me were white walls, and there were whisperings from somewhere, and occasional shadows, then in front of me was this little blue glow. The glow died down and in its place was a short, dumpy cartoon woman wearing a blue-and-white dress tied in back with a white cloth belt. Her hair was silver and done up in a bun. She was holding a wand tipped with a silver star and she was using it to scratch her ass.

In a voice that had been worked over with Brillo pads, she said, "I think it's the riding around on the film or the light that gives you the itch, but whatever, it's some kind of itch. Lot of us have it. But listen, kid, I'm not here to talk to you about ass itch. We know what you want and we want you to have it. You're made for the part, and I ain't blowing smoke up your ass. You're perfect. You see, the Producer and the Great Director want a show down there and we

think you're the one can give it to us. Kid, we're gonna
make you a goddamn star."

She took a pack of cigarettes out from under a roll in
the sleeve of her dress, shook one out and lipped it,
replaced the pack. "We give a man a job, we like to give
him the full run of things, see, and while we're talking here,
let me tell you something. You're ugly, kid. With a kisser
like that if you was a chicken you'd have to sneak up on a
pile of shit to peck a corn kernel out of it. But that's not your
fault. It's something we can fix."

She brought out a box of wooden matches and struck
one on her hip and lit her smoke. She puffed and tossed the
box on the floor. She pinched the cigarette between thumb
and forefinger and held the flame toward her palm.

"Tell me what face you want, kid. I want to show you
what we can do. Naw, don't tell me a thing. I know the face,
and it ain't pretty and it ain't ugly. It ain't really a face. You
want something everyone will look at. You want it so when
you step into a room all eyes go to you. Well, in the name
of the Producer and the Great Director, by the power
vested in me, and all that stuff, I give it to you."

She waved the wand. "The stuff dreams are made of,
kid."

I felt a rush of energy. I was a thermometer and I was
overheated and my mercury was about to explode out the
top of my head.

Next thing I knew, I was on the floor, then I was
coming out of darkness. I blinked and found myself next to
the hole that let in the tip of the TV pyramid.

I looked at my hands. They weren't animated now. A
big-handled mirror lay next to me. I picked it up and looked
at myself.

What I had for a face was a TV, and that suited me fine.

And my face operated like one. Inside my head was the mental switch, and with a twist of my mind I could tune into any movie, television show, commercial, or personal video I wanted.

And I could play it on my face and see it at the same time.

I was proud.

I tossed away the mirror and started down. I felt like Charlton Heston playing Moses in *The Ten Command-ments*. But I wasn't coming down from on high with the Ten Commandments. I had something better. Every movie, show and commercial ever made was tucked tight in my head, ready to explode onto my face at a whim.

It took me some time to get down, of course, but when I did, the drive-in was full of people. They had been wandering in for a time. They had built a stage of TVs in front of one of the drive-in screens, and they were taking turns going up there and acting out scenes from movies, quoting dialogue they remembered. They also did sound effects and screams. They weren't too good at it.

When they saw me they stood open-mouthed, and when I turned my face on and filled it with *Night of the Living Dead*, their expressions turned to rapture. I sat down on a TV set and crossed my legs and leaned forward and they gathered before me and squatted down and watched. And when *Night* was over, I gave them *The Texas Chainsaw Massacre* and then *The Sound of Music* intercut with *Zombie*. Now and then I gave them a commercial for GI Joe action figures and accessories, tossed in a California Raisins commercial, and one for some kind of shampoo. Things got cozy.

They loved me, and it was then that I gave myself a new name. I was in Hopalong gear and I had a TV face and my idol had been the Popcorn King, so naturally, I came up

with Popalong Cassidy. I told my audience that was what
they should call me, and they did. They would have called
me anything to keep those images coming; they had learned
that the images were the reality and all else was an illusion
they had to work to invent. My face did all the work for
them. It gave them all the reality they needed to know,
minus the effort.

I found that I no longer needed to eat food. All I
needed were the eyes and minds of those people on my
face. That kept me full.

In time, more people came to the drive-in, and they
too sat before my face and worshiped it, and I pulled energy
from them and felt fuller and stronger than ever before.

I was loved. Loved by those who sat before me and ate
the popcorn and candy that fell from the sky, drank the
drinks it rained. Loved, goddamnit, loved. Me, Popalong
Cassidy. Loved and admired and revered.

Course, there were some nonbelievers. They wanted
to stay away from my face. They saw it as bad. They blamed
the movies for what had happened to them.

This was nonsense.

I had my followers rip them open and eat their guts
and act out *Night of the Living Dead*. Then the heads of
those stupid dissenters went up on tall pieces of antenna
and we placed them all around the drive-in as a warning to
the nonviewers who might come, and as an inspiration to
the rest of us.

I had my followers strike sparks and set the TV
pyramid's on fire. They would have no other gods before
me. I was it, and I didn't want competition. No one else
would be climbing up there to see my Fairy Godmother; no
one else could have my prize.

This kept the drive-in a happy place. A new era had
dawned. I was its messiah. Offspring of the Producer and

the Great Director, whoever they were, and it was my job to make sure they were entertained. And I planned to give my heavenly parents a really big show.

Now let's pause for this brief commercial message.

8

GRACE TALKING

All the while Popalong had been talking, images were flashing on his face. Clips from movies and television shows. Now a series of commercials went lickety-split across the screen; everything from exercise machines to Boxcar Willie's Greatest Hits. Damn if I hadn't always wanted to try Boxcar Willie's stuff, though I hated to admit it. If I ever got home, I was going to order his album.

I suppose there were subliminals at work under all that film stuff, but maybe not. I like to think it had no effect on me because I'm just too much woman to be taken in by a subliminal message; I like to think Mom and Dad raised a pretty stubborn girl and that my martial arts training allowed me to maintain my focus on who I was and what I thought.

Course, maybe the only subliminal in the whole mess was for me to buy a Boxcar Willie album, and that seemed to be working. Maybe all those people who had fallen for Popalong's line of corn were just stupid. My dad always said, "Grace, most people are idiots."

It was kind of cold-blooded, but life seemed to sort of be bearing him out.

The commercials wrapped up, and in spite of myself I liked the last one. It had to do with these carrots, potatoes and bell peppers with stick legs and shoes and stick arms and gloves. They were hopping off the face of a box and dancing across a kitchen table on their way to leap into a pan full of water resting in the mouth of an open stove.

"My message is simple," said Popalong. "There is pleasure in darkness and pain. The light cannot be appreciated without the dark. Entertainment is where it's at. At the end of the highway I have formed a humble Church of Darkness and Pain. Services every day. It all plays on my face. And when someone, shall we say, becomes a star at the church, like those nonbelievers I told you about, we record their acting and play it again and again for our pleasure. No special effects. No wooden lines. No one pretending to eat guts. The real thing. It's addicting, I kid you not."

He leaned close to me. "Revolutionary, don't you think?"

"It bites the moose," I said.

"Now that's ugly," Popalong said. "After all I've shown you and told you, you're still an asshole. I'm afraid you'll have to be edited out of what you call life. But don't worry, I'll make you a star. I'll make sure your agony is recorded forever in the only way that really matters. On film."

He turned to Sue Ellen. "Her, I think she's got potential. I think she can see the light of my face and know it for what it is, don't you? I think she's rather pretty. She might make me a nice queen. I'd like that. I mean I may be a messiah, but to hell with this Jesus stuff where you don't get any pussy. I'm a new kind of messiah, and I say hey, what's the point in being a messiah with all kinds of control, if you don't throw some pork to the women. You see, I can give them any face they want while I make love to them.

Whatever star they want, man or woman, hell, Lassie or Rin Tin Tin, I can call them up on my screen, and presto, I'm who they want me to be."

The rain had stopped and daylight was creeping beneath the tarp and poking through the holes where the rain had come through. The fires in the television sets were dying down and the smoke from them was thinning and becoming lighter, going as soft and gray as the cottony strands of an old man's hair.

The shadows huddling against the back of the tarp were fading. Popalong's shadow was seeping into the ground at his feet like motor oil.

"They're fraidy-cats of the light," he said. "Roy, would you please get the gasoline."

The man who had cut me free climbed on the wrecker and came down with a five-gallon can.

"You should feel honored," Popalong said. "Rare as gasoline is. You know, this will be our last trip out from the church in the wrecker. When we get back we'll be near empty. It's a pisser not to be able to go out and spread the word, but what's a fella to do?"

"You're no fella," I said.

"You know, you're right. Soak her, Roy."

"Don't we get to fuck her first?" Roy asked.

"Now that you mention it," Popalong said, "I do seem to be ahead of myself. Everyone for fucking her?"

He held up his hand as an example. The four men put their hands up.

Popalong turned that sixteen-inch screen on me. "You're popular, what can I say. But you know, I'm going to pass. You have such a nasty disposition, I'm afraid I'd end up having to fake an orgasm. Roy, would you like to be first to crack open the box?"

Roy smiled and put the can down. He got a pair of wire

cutters out of his back pocket and went over and snipped what held me to the wrecker, but this didn't free my hands. They were fastened together by a separate bond.

"You going to record this?" Roy said.

"Whatever I see is recorded," Popalong said. "Bring her out from the wrecker, please, get her pants off, and get started. I'm sort of in a hurry to see her burn. Rest of you get that tarp down."

The three in the back went straight to the tarp and pulled it up and flipped it over the antenna in the middle and tossed it onto the wrecker.

Roy led me so that I was in front of Popalong's antenna. Popalong stepped up on his spokes and hung his arms in the rods. He looked at me and smiled his dials.

"Showtime," he said.

9

There was no wind and the dead air had turned warm and humid. Sweat poured off of me and my hair stuck to the back of my neck. I needed to go to the ladies' room.

Roy wasn't taking me real serious. After all, I was a girl. Maybe I was supposed to beg and scream like in the horror movies.

What I did when Roy reached out to take hold of my pants was swivel on the ball of my left foot and whip my head around and get my hips shifting, and I brought my leg up fast and loose and snapped it back so that the heel caught Roy directly behind his right ear and made a sound like big hands clapping.

Before Roy filled his teeth with dirt, I was moving. One of the men tried to stop me, but I jumped up and snapped out my right leg and caught him in the throat with the edge of my foot. I could feel something in his neck give, then I was down and running, hitting the jungle hard as I could go, keeping my balance as best I could, which wasn't easy with my hands tied the way they were. Then I was out of there, boys, prehistoric history.

10

At first I felt like Brer Rabbit in the brier patch, then I didn't feel so good. This was where the film crawled and sucked on you, where the bad storms blew shadows and trees moved.

But nothing of the sort was happening then. The film lay still at my feet and still in the trees. There were no shadows and no storms. I supposed those things were reserved for night.

I heard footsteps behind me and I only paused long enough to jump up and pull my knees to my chest and whip my bound hands underneath me.

I saw that my hands were tied with a piece of wire that had been wrapped around them three or four times with the ends twisted together. I pulled at the wire with my teeth as I ran and got it loose. I crunched it up and put it in my pocket so I wouldn't leave something on the ground for them to mark my passing.

Eventually I didn't hear them anymore, but I kept running. I don't know how long I went, and I had no idea which way I was going. I followed the path of least resistance.

When I felt certain they were no longer behind me, I

stopped and found a tree with low branches and swung up in that and climbed as high as I could.

I was shocked. I had looped back until I was almost to the highway. In fact, I probably wasn't far from where I had been captured. If I had kept running, I would have been out on the highway again in a matter of minutes.

I could see the wrecker at the edge of the highway and I could see Popalong's antenna, but he wasn't on it. I could see the Galaxy too. I couldn't see Popalong, his men or Timothy or Sue Ellen. I could see some dark smoke, but I couldn't tell what it was coming from. Its source was near the edge of the woods though.

I felt poorly, so I found a forked limb that had a lot of leafy cover and wedged my butt in the fork and put my back against a bigger limb and clutched a smaller one with the crook of my right arm. A wind began to stir, and that was all I needed to send me off to dreamland.

When I awoke my back hurt and my arm was stiff, but I felt rested. I had no idea how long I slept. It was still daylight.

I got out on the limb where I had been before and looked at the wrecker. Popalong's antenna cross was in the back of the wrecker, fastened to the wench post somehow, and Popalong was on it. He had this TV head turned in my direction, lifted slightly up, but I didn't think he could see me. One of his men was coiled at his feet like a house cat.

The wrecker started to move. I watched until it was out of sight.

11

At this point, some of this is bound to be obvious. Yes, it was Timothy that was burning. I found the guy I had kicked in the head dead in the bushes. The one I had kicked in the throat had been impaled on a piece of television antenna. Popalong didn't like failures much.

I guess I should have killed Timothy. That's what he asked for. But I got the keys out of my pocket and opened up the trunk of the Galaxy and took the gas can and poured it into the tank. I got my arms under Timothy and got him loaded in the backseat of the Galaxy. His flesh came off on my hands and I had to go out to the side of the road and wipe my palms in the grass; it was as if I had been holding greasy pork chops.

I got the car going and made a U-turn and drove us away from there. I talked about anything that came to mind, and Timothy when he did speak, said, "Kill me."

I didn't seem to know how to do anything but drive, and I did that through the day and through the night, finally stopping to rest. I kept going like that, kept talking and singing and reciting poetry to myself, and I don't remember eating or drinking at all.

There's not much to tell after that. My throat got

hoarse. The road pulled me on. When I was nearly out of gas I saw the lake—your lake—and I guess it made me realize how thirsty I was, and I went for it.

Next thing I knew Jack here was pulling me out and then I was in the back of your camper. I woke up and had to pee, and when I came back from that, you guys were here.

FOURTH REEL

(Titties Even Closer Up, Pants for Jack
and Bob,
and On Down the Road)

1

Bob said, "You're welcome to stay with us."

"Thanks. I appreciate it. But tomorrow, or day after tomorrow, when I'm rested, I'm going to start after Sue Ellen. I owe her that. I went sort of nuts when I found Timothy, panicked, took off in the opposite direction. But I've got to go back now and find her.

"You don't have a car," I said.

"If I can get to Shit Town, I think I can get a car and some gas. If not, I'll go on foot."

"I'm going too," I said.

"What?" Bob said.

"I can't sit here the rest of my life."

"See a set of titties and you go all to pieces, don't you?" Bob said.

"If what she says is true, we know what's at the end of the highway," Crier said. "So why go?"

"Let Grace be the White Knight," Bob said. "She's into that kind of shit. Kung fu lady and all that. We're into surviving."

"I may have to do some ugly things when I catch up to Popalong," Grace said. "It won't be an easy trek, especially if I end up on foot."

"Listen to her," Bob said.

"This isn't living," I said. "This is existing. It's giving up. I did that once before. I won't do it again. You're the one made me do something last time, Bob. You're the one pulled me out of just getting by."

"But this isn't so bad," Bob said.

"Maybe we can find a way home at the end of the highway," I said. "Maybe there's something more than what Popalong told her about. And there's that little girl, Sue Ellen."

"I'm not asking anything of any of you," Grace said.

"Not much you're not, lady," Bob said. "You know how to work things. I can see that."

"It's not her fault," I said. "It's what I want."

"Shit," Crier said. "We've been through some things together, the three of us. I feel like we're the three musketeers or something."

"Oh hell," Bob said. "Here it comes."

"We're all we got," Crier said. "I'd like to see us stick together. Hell, fellas, you're the first real friends I ever had."

"Well, fuck," Bob said. "Guess we could use a change of scenery. We can take the camper to Shit Town and try and get some gas there."

"Hey," Grace said. "I'm not asking—"

"Hush," Bob said. "I might come to my senses."

2

Up in Jungle Home I tried to sleep, but no dice. I got out of bed and slipped on my blanket and left Bob and Crier sleeping and went out on the deck where a warm breeze was blowing.

I went on down and walked over to the camper and touched it. It was cool to my touch and I got a mild sexual charge out of it, which made me feel pretty damn silly. I thought about what Grace had said about fucking the ocean in case there was a shark in there that had swallowed a girl, and suddenly it made a lot of sense.

I went around to the end of the camper. The tailgate was down. My mouth filled with saliva. I knew then that I was going to at least look inside.

I looked.

She wasn't there. There was just a basket of fruit. I guess my sexual charge had come from that or a horny spare tire.

Then I heard splashing. I think I had heard it before, but now it registered.

I walked around on the other side of the camper and looked out at the lake.

The moon was high and bright and it made the lake

287

slick as a mirror. Not too far out in it, halfway submerged, was Grace. She was slapping her arms on the surface of the water. Playing.

I went down there, and when I was fifty feet from the water, I stopped and looked at her sleek, marble-white back sticking out of the water like a flooded Grecian statue.

She looked over her shoulder and smiled.

"Out for a walk, Jack?"

"Sort of."

"Excited about tomorrow?"

"I guess."

"You saved my life today."

"That's all right."

"Of course it is. I got hot in the camper. Funny, Timothy's down at the other end of the lake and here I am playing in the water at this end. I never made love to him, you know."

"Did you want to?"

"I think I saw him as a brother."

"You telling me this for a reason?"

"I don't know."

She turned and started to shore. She came out of the water like Venus being born. The moon hit the sheen of water on her breasts and made them bright as moons themselves. The little pink stripes on her skin looked like birthday ribbons.

"You're going to go blind," she said.

"I don't make you go naked."

"I didn't make you come down here."

I put my hands in front of me and clasped them together.

She came to me and kissed me lightly on the lips. Her breath smelled of fruit. She took hold of my arms, lifted them over her head and around her neck, said, "You'll have to pull out, you know. I don't have any birth control. And don't make more of this than it is."

I pulled her to me and kissed her. Our tongues made war.

She looked down. "Goodness, Jack. There's something in your blanket."

"You've already seen it. You weren't much impressed."

She took hold of the edges of the blanket and pulled it over my head, knocking my arms off of her. She threw the blanket down on the grass and took hold of me.

"My," she said, "how the little fella's grown."

3

After we made love on my blanket, we stumbled giggling to the camper and smeared fruit on one another and licked it off. Between licking and giggling, we made love again. Every time we moved apart our bodies made a sound like two sheets of flypaper being pulled apart.

When we finished we went down to the lake and rinsed off again and tried to make love again, but neither of us was up to it. We went back to the camper and fell asleep in each other's arms.

I dreamed good for a time. Kind of dreams a man dreams when he's holding a woman in his arms. But the dreams didn't last. I thought about my aliens and I thought about Grace's story about Popalong Cassidy and the Producer and the Great Director. I thought about all that movie junk on down the highway. I tried to make everything add up but nothing would.

It all went away and folded into a cloud the color and texture of Grace's pubic hair.

Next morning Bob woke me by pulling on my foot. I got my head out from between Grace's legs and looked up.

"That's disgusting, you know," Bob said.

I picked up Grace's shirt from the floorboard and draped it over her. I got my clothes and sat out on the tailgate and put them on.

"Well, I hope we enjoyed ourselves," Bob said.

"We did."

Bob went away and I woke Grace up and she got dressed and we helped Crier and Bob load some fruit and bamboo water containers in the camper. Then we were off.

After a few days we came to Shit Town. The post Grace had told us about was gone, and now there was an official sign made of crude lumber. On it was: SHIT TOWN, POPULA-TION: WHO GIVES A FUCK.

Civic pride.

Shit Town wasn't much. Some shacks made of sticks and crooked lumber mostly. It looked like a place the Big Bad Wolf would blow down.

Out next to the road was a line of cars, and people were living in those too. Some of the cars were fixed up with huts connected to them. Snazzy stuff.

We parked on the opposite side of the highway, locked up and walked over to Main Street, which was a dirt track, and went down it.

A few people ogled us, and we ogled them back.

No one offered us the Key to the City.

In spite of Shit Town not looking like much, I suppose by present standards it's pretty prosperous. There were a lot of people moving about and there was an aura of industry in the air.

Down at the end of the street was a well house. Most likely it had been built over an open spring, as I figured that was what had attracted folks to this spot in the first place, as the lake had attracted us to Jungle Home.

Beyond this I could see a lot of stumps leading to the

jungle. In a short time, with only their hands and crude tools, these people had cut a lot of trees.

I figured eventually this kind of industry would lead to Shit Town having burger joints that served dinosaur and rabbit burgers, and eventually the place might move up the evolutionary line to having a kind of thrift store where you could get shower curtains, house shoes, bird feeders and Bermuda shorts.

A lot of women were pregnant, and though I'm not good at guessing things like that, they looked pretty close to domino date to me. Of course, time here is too hard to judge.

There were little huts along the street and some of them had plank counters out front with things to trade on them. There was one that had flat-in-the-middle green bread with flies on it, and behind the counter was this woman leaning on a hut post with her dress hiked up and her butt free to the air. There was a guy with his pants down against her, and he was putting it to her. If the woman liked it, it didn't show, and the fella looked like a man called to duty.

It didn't take long, and when they finished, she let down her dress and took the loaf of bread and went away. The man pulled up his pants and looked at us.

"Ya'll want bread?"

"I don't think so," Bob said.

We went on down the street and came to another stand, and on its counter was a turtle shell turned upside down, and there was a wooden pestle in it. All around the shell were piles of fruit.

A guy with a belly that looked like a bag of rocks under his shirt got off a stump when he saw us coming and came over and smiled at us. All this teeth had gone south except one dead center of his bottom gum. The rest of him didn't look too good either.

"Want me to make you a fruit drink?" he said. "Mashed right here while you wait."

"Nope," Crier said.

Next to the fruit juice place was a hut with a sign out front painted in black mud that read: LIBRARY.

"They're kidding," Bob said.

I went over and pulled the curtain of reeds aside and looked in. There was just enough room for one person in there, and that one person had to sit on a rotting stump because the roof was low. There was one crude shelf of books, and under the shelf was a little sign that said: PLEASE RETURN BOOKS.

I went inside and looked at what they had to offer. There was a Bible covered in red plastic with a zipper on it. I unzipped it and looked inside. Saw that everything Jesus had said was printed in red so you could tell it from ol' So-and-So.

Alongside it was a collection of Rod McKuen's poetry, and a copy of *Jonathan Livingston Seagull* with "This book belongs to David Webb and is his inspiration" written inside.

There were two copies of the *Watchtower*, one concentrating on the dilemmas of dating in the modern world, the other on the deterioration of the family unit.

There was also a pamphlet for raising chinchillas for fun and profit (neither the fun or profit being to the advantage of the chinchillas); a postcard with a gerbil's picture on the front and a note on the back that said they could be seen at some petting zoo; a photo-novel of *Superman* 3; and a souvenir hand fan from Graceland with a picture of the erstwhile King of Rock'n'Roll on one side (prebloat) and the words to "You Ain't Nothing But A

Hound Dog" on the other. There were also a couple of poems that didn't rhyme written on some dirty popcorn bags with eyeliner pencil.

I took the Elvis fan and fanned myself, then put it back and went outside. The others had wandered down the street, not having felt the pull of the arts.

The guy with the one tooth said, "Find anything?"

"I fanned myself a little."

"It's checked out right now, but there's a pretty good Max Brand novel we got, 'cept the last couple of pages are torn out. Some fella wrote an ending for it, though. He wrote on the inside back cover, 'He rode off into the West and everything was okay.' Seems a good enough ending to most anything, don't it?"

"Does at that. I take it you're also the librarian?"

"Yeah, but people want fruit juice more than they want books. Only thing is they don't always have something good to trade. Tell you, I've had all the dry pussy I want. It's making the head of my dick raw. In the long run I get the bad end of the trade. I'd really rather have some kind of meat, fish, maybe some roots that are good to boil."

"Commerce can be a bitch," I said.

4

When I caught up with the others, they were standing beside the street looking out between a couple of shacks made of mud and sticks, staring at a man hanging from the limb of a big oak tree. He was spinning around, kicking his feet and working his elbows as if in a square dance. The elbows were all he could work of his arms, since his hands were tied behind his back.

On a bench near the oak sat two men and a woman. They looked like benched football players waiting for their turn at an inning.

"Suicide tree I told you about," Grace said. "Come on."

"I don't want to see that," I said.

"Me neither," Bob said.

"I'll pass too," Crier said.

"Do what you want," Grace said to me, "but they're going to hang themselves anyway and you fellas need pants."

"Pants?" I said.

"You think those folks are gonna need them later?"

"I got pants," Crier said. "They're ragged, but they're pants. I'll just hang out."

Grace led Bob and me over to the tree. I looked up at the guy. His face was purple as a plum and his neck was swollen out in such a way it was starting to spread over the rope. His tongue was flopping against his chin and he was biting through it. His eyes were crossed and the lid of one was drooped halfway down and the other eye looked like a table tennis ball being pushed out of a hole from behind.

We went over to the bench. The woman was sitting on the end near us and the men were sitting next to each other. She looked at us. The hair on one side of her head had been burned off, and the hair on the other side wasn't anything to be proud of. It was dirty-brown and kinky as wire. I've seen Brillo pads with more class. She had on a filthy T-shirt and her nipples were punching through it. The jeans she had on were thin enough to shit through. Her face wasn't any kind of special. It was covered with pimples and red welts. She was barefoot.

The two guys weren't fashion models either. They had beards full of dirt, bugs and fruit seeds. Their dark coloring wasn't the result of the sun's rays. You could have packed lunches in the pores of their skin.

I hated to think what I looked like.

"Bench is full," the woman said. "Come back tomorrow. Three's about it for a day. Them's the rules."

"We're not here to hang ourselves," Grace said.

"If you're going to watch," she said, "stay back out of the way. This bastard won't never choke. I bet he's been up there an hour."

"He looks about gone to me," I said.

The man beside her, the skinnier of the two, said, "Who can tell how long he's been up there. Time isn't worth a duck fart here. But you should have seen him just a little while ago. He looked worse than this. I think he's gotten him a second wind."

"Maybe he's changed his mind," I said.

At that the hanging man began to kick his legs vigorously.

"I don't think so," the woman said.

"Look at him," I said.

"You can't pay that any mind. It doesn't mean a thing. He wanted to go worse than the rest of us. He bit Clarence there to get first in line."

Clarence was the skinny fella. He held up a sticklike arm and pushed his short sleeve back. There was a crescent of teeth wounds.

"He called me some things I've never heard," said Clarence, "then he pushed me on the ground and bit me. I told him to go ahead. Hell, I wasn't even next in line. Fran was. But look who he bit. That's the way it's always been for me. I tied his hands for him and boosted him into the rope. More than he deserved, I'll tell you. Which reminds me, you folks around when Gene here goes, maybe you could tie his hands for him. It works better that way, otherwise you claw at the rope, no matter how bad you want to go."

"I'll make do," Gene said. He got up and went over to the hanging man and jumped on him and swung back and forth like a kid on a tire swing. The hanging man's neck lengthened.

"We probably won't be around long enough to help Gene," Grace said, "but we wanted to try and talk you out of your pants, just you fellas. Jack and Bob here don't have anything but these dresses."

"Noticed that," Clarence said, "and I'll tell you boys, you haven't got the legs for it."

From the hanging man came a sound like a semi tire blowing out at high speed.

"Goddamn," Clarence said, "there's the signal."

"Yeah," Fran said. "It's nature's way of saying 'Sayo-nara, motherfucker.'"

"It's nature's way of filling your pants with shit, is what it is," Clarence said. "Get off of him, Gene. Let's get him down and get Fran up there. Come on, get off of him, goddamnit."

"About those pants," Grace said.

"Guess you want them before I hang myself," Clarence said.

"Well," Grace said, "you know how it is, nature's sayonara and all."

Clarence nodded and undressed. He didn't have on any underwear. He tossed the clothes at me. "Take all of it. Shoes too, if they fit. Hell, if they don't fit."

I gathered up the clothes and held them. They smelled a little ripe.

"Hey Gene," Clarence said. "Want to help the other fella out?"

Gene had finally got off the dead man, and he came over to the bench and sat down. He took off his clothes, except for some soiled, green boxer shorts, and gave them to Bob.

"Go on, enjoy them," Clarence said. "You want to thank us later, well, we'll be hanging around."

Clarence loved that. He laughed like a drunk hyena.

He was tying Fran's hands for her when we went away.

5

We collected Crier and went out to the camper. He and Grace sat up front and talked, and Bob and I tried the clothes on. I ended up with some pants too tight in the waist, but I zipped them up high as they would go and left them unsnapped and used the belt I had made for my blanket outfit and ran it through the pants loops for extra support. The shirt fit fine and I wore it with the tails hanging out. The socks were thin but not holey. The shoes were an inch too long and they made me look a little like Bozo the Clown.

Bob's pants fit him in the waist, but were too short. They were what my dad used to call high-water pants. The shirt he had was too narrow across the shoulders, and he got a knife out of the toolbox and slit it halfway down the back. He slit the sides of the shoes too because they were too narrow.

Grace and Crier laughed at our outfits, but just a little. I guess thinking about where the clothes came from took some of the humor out of it.

Crier and Bob stayed with the camper, and Grace and I took Bob's gas can and went around begging for gas. The people who were living in cars that had huts attached to them were the quickest to give up their gas; they had made a stand and they were staying. Some wouldn't even talk to us, and one guy told us he'd pour his goddamn gas on the ground and piss on it before he gave it to us. We took this as a no.

By the end of the day we had a full tank of gas, and we went into Shit Town one last time to see if we could talk someone into giving us enough to fill our can. It never hurt to have extra.

We got off Main Street and went down a little side street lined with huts and cars and we came on this tall, hatchet-faced fella wearing a sweat-stained cowboy hat. He was unusual in that he was clean-shaven.

He had the hood up on an old red-and-white Plymouth convertible, and he had a wrench and he was fiddling with something under there. He didn't look like someone that wanted to get rid of his gas, but we asked anyway.

"I got plans for a big trip," he said. "Need all the gas I can get. Y'all want a drink? It's the local poison. Made out of fruit juice and piss. No kidding. It'll put you higher than goddamn Skylab."

We passed.

He took a swig and shivered. "Things a man'll drink. Look here, name's Steve."

He stuck out his hand and we took turns shaking it and giving our names.

"Guess y'all are heading on down the highway too, huh?"

"That's the plan," I said.

"Maybe I'll see you then. Soon as I get this buddy tuned up, have me a damn good drunk, I'll be ready to roll. I figure sometime tomorrow. Can't say that I see much to keep me here."

We wished him luck and went back to the camper without the gas. I didn't look in the direction of the hanging tree.

It was dark by the time we got back there, and the four of us talked and ate some fruit and went to bed. Crier slept in the front seat as usual, and Bob, Grace and I slept in the back.

Grace was between me and Bob, but she didn't try to molest me, and she didn't try and molest Bob. Bob refrained from playing with himself.

I lay there and thought about Grace and told myself I was too mature and philosophical and had been through too much to expect anything of our relationship other than friendship. Besides, hadn't she said not to make too much of the other night?

Some things you just had to take like an adult. What she did was what she did and it didn't matter to me. She was her own person. And a man's got to do what a man's got to do, and look and see if you're right then go ahead, and every dog has his day, and every cloud has a silver lining, and a penny saved is a penny earned, and everything works out for the best, and . . . it was a long night.

It was later than we planned by the time we got up. We had fruit for breakfast because there wasn't any ham and eggs and coffee on the menu, then we got out of there. Crier and Bob up front, me and Grace in the back.

Grace talked about some books I hadn't read and necking didn't come up.

That's how it went for a few days, and finally I quit worrying about IT every second, and cut down to about once an hour.

So when I wasn't thinking about IT, I was thinking

about what in hell had possessed me to agree to go along on this little run. I wasn't any hero. I had tried to be once and I had gotten nailed up for the trouble. What I did best was mind my own business, and here I was barreling down the highway so I could confront Popalong Cassidy, who did not sound like a nice guy. Worse yet, I was the reason Crier and Bob were going too. Or at least part of it. I guess when a fella gets bored he can do some stupid things. And maybe I thought I was being macho going with Grace to the end of the highway to help her out. I was wondering how I had ever arrived at that. Grace could probably beat up all three of us.

Damn, Bob had been right when he said a set of titties made me go all to pieces. And maybe Grace had known exactly what she was doing that night in the camper and down by the lake—sealing a deal.

And maybe I was being a horse's ass. It really hurt to discover I had a bigger streak of male chauvinist pig in me than I thought. It hurt worse to realize that I was stupid and tittie blind and was probably going to get killed for it. I preferred happy endings.

But even this kind of thinking didn't last. You can only focus on your own death and destruction so long before it gets boring. You begin to wonder about more important matters, like do people who wear suspenders wear them because they like the way they look, or because they hold their pants up? Do people who work on garbage trucks see their work as important? Did they grow up wanting to be garbage men? What kind of tools are used to scrape dead animals off the highway? Who was the idiot who invented those Happy Face symbols, or those signs that read BABY ON BOARD or SHIT HAPPENS? Should those folks be slow-tortured by parboiling, or killed outright? What was the true story on green M&M's?

I tell you, I had lots of interesting things to think about.

6

That night we got some dried brush and stuff and used our flint and steel to build a little fire near the camper, and pretty soon it was a big fire because Bob couldn't get warm enough and he kept piling brush on it.

"You're gonna catch the truck on fire," Crier said.

"No, I ain't," Bob said. "We're right here in front of the fire."

"I won't burn up to save the truck," Crier said.

"Count me out too," Grace said.

"It's all right," Bob said. "I'm watching it."

After that we sat there and thought and said a little now and then, but not too much because we had our minds on some things, like the fact the highway was starting to change. The nights were getting darker, as if the air was getting thicker, and there were posters and popcorn bags and soft drink cups and the like lying about, and I figured pretty soon we'd be getting into the stormy part. Already we were seeing things in the truck mirrors, and sometimes things reflected in the windows; things like the face of King Kong, the Frankenstein monster clinging to the side of the truck, Dracula and Daffy Duck with their arms around one another.

It was pretty disconcerting to see stuff like that, then look and not find anything there to reflect it. On second thought, I guess we were glad of that. Still, it was unnerving.

Anyway, we were sitting there, and Crier said, "Got to see a man about a horse."

"Me too," I said.

We walked out behind the truck and stood in the highway to do our business. It was very dark. I looked down the road the way we had come. There was a bend in the road and it went around behind some trees and there was some moonlight on the highway, but when I looked in the other direction it was dark as the inside of a goat.

I finished pissing and put my equipment up and wandered off the highway and started walking along the edge in the direction of the dark part. I didn't go too far. It was really dark.

I turned and looked at Crier. He was still hosing the concrete. He looked at me and said, "You know, after all we've been through, bad as it's been, I think things are about to get better. I feel it."

I was going to say something to that, but around the corner came two headlights and the faintest glint of a grillwork smile.

Crier, dong in hand, swiveled in the direction of the car and then he was a hood ornament.

The car, a convertible, sailed by me with Crier bent over the hood and the driver hit down on the horn, stomped the brakes and yelled, "Motherfucker!"

Crier went under the car and bounced out from beneath it and lay in the highway with the moonlight for a shroud. He still had his dong in his hand, but it wasn't connected to his body anymore. He had jerked it off, no pun intended. Lying on his back, his fist on his chest, his dong clenched there like a frankfurter, he looked as if he were studying the universe while preparing to eat a weenie.

FIFTH REEL

(Tooling With Steve, Crier Gets Some Sunglasses,
Showdown at the Orbit)

1

The convertible fishtailed to a stop, disappearing into the darker part of the highway, and right before it did, I caught the ghostly reflection of something in one of its mirrors, some kind of monster that faded with the car's movement. Then the driver was out of the car and running toward Crier. I knew the moment I saw his cowboy hat that it was Steve from back at Shit Town.

I got my feet out of the glue and started over to Crier. Steve was down on his knees feeling Crier's chest and neck. He looked up at me and said, "Dead as a rock."

I tried to kick Steve in the face, but he caught my foot and pulled me on my butt.

"I didn't do it on purpose," he said.

I tried to get up and swarm him. He jabbed me in the chest with his palm and knocked me on my butt again.

"I didn't see him. He shouldn't have been standing in the highway."

"You sonofabitch. You goddamn sonofabitch."

Bob and Grace came over. As they neared us they slowed down, as if taking small steps would give the reality of the thing time to go away.

When they stood over us and looked down, Bob said, "Damn. One thing after another."

"One of you get his feet," Steve said, "and let's get him out of the road before we get creamed by somebody."

Grace got Crier's feet and Steve got him under the arms and they started him off the highway. Crier's hand fell off his chest and he dropped what he was holding.

"Put him down," Steve said.

They lowered him to the highway and Steve picked up what Crier had dropped and put it in Crier's shirt pocket. It poked out the top like a periscope.

They picked him up again and carried him over to the side of the road, and Steve went and got in his car and pulled it over to our side and walked back to us. I kept thinking I'd find something on the ground to pick up and hit Steve with, but the urge was going away. There didn't seem to be any reason to hit anyone.

Grace didn't feel that way. She kicked Steve flush in the balls. He dropped to his knees and had a facial workout. When that was over and he got his breath back, he said, "Damn, lady."

"It didn't make me feel as good as I hoped," Grace said, "but it still does a little something for me."

Then the camper blew up.

2

Hot, sticky morning with the convertible's tape deck blasting Sleepy LaBeef who's singing something about how he's a boogie-woogie man, jetting along with the top down, doing about ninety plus, me in the front seat, Steve at the wheel, bugs on the windshield, Grace, Bob and Crier in the back. Crier strapped in with a seat belt, leaning to the left, head partly out the window, hair standing up like wire, eyelids blown back by the wind, eyes glassy as cheap beads, pecker in his pocket, the tip of it shriveling and turning brown.

"Oh no," Grace says, "the fire's all right. It isn't too big. Nosir. Just right. I'm in front of it. No problem. It's not too close to the truck. Ol' Bob's got it under control. Ol' Bob's got it by the balls. Ol' Bob—"

"Shut up, will you," Bob says.

Steve sings along with Sleepy LaBeef. New bugs hit the windshield. Outside the scenery is changing. More popcorn bags and garish posters lying about, blowing up as we jet by. The trees are starting to fill with film. Broken TV sets and fragments of antennas clutter the side of the road. Crier's pecker continues to wither.

Steve moves the convertible up to a hundred and it's rocking a little. The sun is glinting off the hood and the tires are whining: I hope no one is standing in the road. All seats are taken.

3

High noon and we ran out of Sleepy LaBeef. Then we got Steve.

"Now the reason I'm here is my wife. Finding out your gal can work a dick better than Tom Mix could work a lariat is all right, but the bad news on a thing like that is finding out the dick she works best don't belong to you. Wrong cow pony, you know. It can deflate a man's ego."

"What about you?" Grace said.

"Oh yeah," Steve said, not catching her tone. "Especially when all I ever got was the old in-and-out and are-you-finished-yet."

"Imagine that," Grace said.

"Worse than that, her man was none other than Fred Trual, and that goddamn got me, I'll tell you. He's a real baboon's ass, all the personality of a snot rag and as loyal as a paid-for date. He also stole my song 'My Baby Done Done Me Wrong,' and that was enough for me to swear I'd kill him.

"How in hell do you figure a woman. This Fred is not only ugly, but he's been in the pen and rumor has it he poisoned his old maiden aunt for what she was gonna leave him, and he knew that wasn't nothing but five hundred dollars. I mean we're talking a greedy sonofabitch here. He even eats until he gets sick. I've known him since grade school. Wasn't worth a damn then either. But the gals always went for him. Must have had some kind of smell that got to them. Had to be that. He wasn't pretty and he wasn't smart and he wasn't nice. He and Tina Sue even stole my car."

"See you got it back," I said. "Are you sure we heard both sides of Sleepy?"

"About three times to a side," Steve said. "I got it back all right, but not because they gave it to me. I'll tell you about it."

"That's all right," Grace said. "No need to bother."

"I don't mind," Steve said, and he made a corner and the tires screeched like startled owls. "I told myself when I caught up with them I was going to kill Fred. I thought I might even kill her too. And I thought when they were both dead I was going to get out my guitar and sing the song I wrote over their dead bodies, then maybe on the back of my guitar I'd write another one in their blood, right then and there. That's how mad I was. Nasty, huh."

"You're not a nice fella, Steve," Bob said.

"Now I didn't mean to run over that ol' boy, I swear it. I'm a sensitive fella, don't think I'm not. I mean I can write the kind of songs that make the whiningest, sorriest-living, beer-drinkingest and gal-losingest sonofabitch cry like a baby with a thermometer up its ass. Kind of song that'll make women's thangs tingle and make fellas call home to make sure their old ladies aren't doing it with the next-door neighbor. Know what I mean?"

"I think you sort of summed it up there," Bob said.

"It'll make me a rich man. Or would if we were back in the real world. I'd be able to buy clothes that aren't on sale at the goddamn K mart. Go to some place to buy stuff that ain't made out of genuine plastic and genuine cheap. I'd be able to get me a new hat made out of real hat stuff and have it be one of those with a fancy band around it with a feather fresh out of a peacock's ass sticking up in it. I'd get me some unchewed toothpicks to stick in the band. I'd move to Nashville and sing my sexy little heart out. I'd wine and dine and chase them honky-tonk angels until my dick needed a wheelchair to get around. Course, that's what I would have done. I reckon Fred's made a mint off it now. It's probably on the radio back home. Go in any joint with a juke and I bet you can hear my song coming out of it, probably sung by George Jones or Randy Travis. And ol' Fred's spending my money. Tell you, I still want to kill him. If I got the chance I'd kill him deader than the ol' boy in the back seat there, then I'd really get rough."

"I take it you don't like Fred," Bob said.

"You're getting it. Let me backtrack on my story here."

"I thought that was all of it," Grace said. "I mean that's enough to hold me. What about you guys?"

"I want to hear it all," Bob said.

I was starting to get interested too, but I didn't say anything. I didn't want Grace to kick me in the balls.

"Well, when I found out Fred and Tina Sue were doing what they were doing from this private detective fella I hired, I couldn't hardly believe it. 'Cept that he had some real clear pictures of them in action and he didn't help matters none by saying stuff like, 'That's her best shot there, the one with the whip and the Mouseketeer hat,' and 'By God, I didn't know human bodies could do them sort of things. Hell, I didn't know snakes could do them sort of things. Look at that, will you. I bet he's got his head halfway in there, whadaya think?'

"I wasn't just hurt that Tina Sue was waxing another man's rope, or that the man was stupid, greedy, and maybe

a murderer. There was the fact that Fred seemed to be
having a hell of a lot better time with Tina Sue than I'd ever
had. I didn't even know she had a Mousketeer hat. To put
it simple, I was charmed by them sweet little eight-by-ten
color glossies. Here I was busting chops and sweating
gravel just to make a living, trying to write songs on the side
so I could be a country-and-western singer, making the
occasional trip to Nashville to try and peddle my songs—
and not having much luck with it—and I find out my
suspicions about my wife are true, and worse, it's old Fred
and he's having a better time than me. Then to put the
goddamn Howdy Doody smile on it, I found out they not
only went off together in my car, but took my song on
account of Fred claimed he wrote it some years back and I
won it from him in a poker game. I only played poker with
Fred and them other boys a few times, and I didn't never
win. Come to think of it, I think Fred cheats.

"Anyway, I got all this from the note."

The wind was picking up and posters and cups and
popcorn bags were tornadoing around the car and beginning to collect on the windshield and flutter into the seats
and slap Crier in the face.

Steve pulled over and put the convertible's roof up and
Bob took the bags off Crier's face and tossed them out. Back
on the road, Steve continued his story.

"The note was stuck in the refrigerator door when I got
home, on account of the bitch took all the fruit magnets
with her. Even the one I bought for myself that was made
like a big strawberry. The note said what she had done and
that she thought the car was as much hers as mine (which
was a hoot) and that the new song I said I wrote and was
bragging about I didn't write, 'cause her boyfriend did, and
she said she and the boyfriend were heading to Nashville to
make the money off of it. She said she thought it was a

better song than she thought before, now that she knew I
didn't write it. She said good-bye and that she had popped
the tops on all the beer in the refrigerator so it would go
flat, and for me to take a water hose and run it up my ass
and turn it on full blast.

"I tell you, there wasn't a cheerful line in that note. I
of course went straight on over to Fred's. I was back a day
earlier than they expected. I had been up to Nashville, see,
and I come back early to check with the private detective
guy, and to see if I could talk some things out if my
suspicions were correct, so I figured I just might get the
jump on them two before they were gone with my song.

"Thinking that I had left my convertible with Tina Sue
and drove her damned old VW up to Nashville didn't make
me no happier, and I tell you when I got up in Fred's yard
and seen my Plymouth sitting there, the sides of it all
muddy and the hubcaps covered over with the stuff, my
eyes filled with murder. I slammed on my brakes hard
enough to throw my hat in the backseat. I got that dude
back on my head and went straight up on Fred's porch. Last
year's Christmas wreath was still hanging on the door; one
of them with the plastic mistletoe and those damned ol'
gold-sprayed pine cones glued on it. I jerked that little
buddy off the door and stomped the cones and kicked the
rest of it out in the yard.

"One of Fred's old two-bit hounds come around from
the back then and stood off the porch growling at me. I got
hold of Fred's sandy old doormat and threw it at the dog
and it ran off under the house where it could collect some
more ticks.

"About the time I turned around, I saw that the curtain
over one of the windows was falling back into place, and I
knew then that Fred was home. The window he'd taken a
peek out of had MERRY CHRISTMAS stenciled on it, and I yelled

out, 'I know goddamn good and well you're in there, shit-bag. Come on out. And it ain't even Christmas, you dumb cocksucker.'

"He didn't come out, so I got off the porch and got hold of the cinder block he was using for a step and put it on the porch, got up there and got hold of it again and shoved it through the window with the stenciling on it.

"He come out of there then with a chair leg in his hand, and he come out swinging. We sort of run together and rolled off the porch and out in the yard. His old hound come out from under the porch then and got hold of my pants leg and started growling and tugging on it. I kicked the mutt off and wrestled up to my feet, and thought I was going to do pretty good, when Fred hit me one on the noggin with that chair leg, and the last thing I remembered was the toes of my K mart boots coming up."

"But it didn't kill you," Grace said.

"No it didn't. I woke up and the first thing I seen when I got up on my elbow was the toes of them boots again."

"And they were still from K mart," Grace said.

"Still from K mart. But the knot on my head was from Fred. Next thing I see is Fred and that hound dog. The dog is sitting on his butt staring at me, his ol' tongue hanging out like he just had him a bitch and was damn proud of it, and Fred he still has his chair leg, and he bends over me and says, 'Hurt much, Steve?'

"I tell him, 'Not at all. Sometimes when I'm home I take a chair leg to my own head.'

"He hit me again, and when I woke up, I was hot and it was dark and crowded and I could smell that perfume Tina Sue always wore."

Steve paused and pointed at the glove box. "I got a last cigar in there. Been saving it. Get it for me, will you?"

I got it out and he bit off the end and spat tobacco out

the window and put the cigar in his mouth and sucked on it. "I don't care what they say, these things taste a hell of a lot better when you know they ain't made by a bunch of Cubans."

He punched in the lighter.

"All right, damnit," Grace said. "What was this dark, cramped place that smelled like Tina Sue?"

"I'm gonna tell you." He took the lighter and lit the cigar, puffed dramatically. "The trunk of this car."

"Uh oh," Bob said.

"Uh oh is right. The greedy sonofabitch had shown his true colors. I figure he decided he wasn't gonna share any song money with Tina Sue, and he killed her. Then I come along and he had to kill me—least he thought he killed me. And he put us in the trunk of the car and drove us out to the Orbit and walked off, probably hitched home. It wasn't such a smart idea, really. I mean someone would have caught up with him. But then whatever happened to the drive-in happened, and I was trapped in there, and I guess back home in Texas there isn't even a drive-in no more. I don't know what would be there in its place, if anything. But there's no body in the trunk for the police to find, in fact there's no car. So I guess Fred did all right by accident. He's probably making money off my song right now."

"Look at it this way," Bob said. "Maybe the song wasn't any good and he couldn't sell it."

Steve sat and thought about that. The fire on his cigar went out. Finally he said, "I'm not sure how I feel about that."

"What I want to know," Grace said, "is how did you get out of the trunk?"

"Oh, that. Wasn't nothing to that. I was hot and pissed and I bent up my legs and kept donkey-kicking the trunk till I busted the lock. When I got out of there didn't nobody care, things being like they were. I ended up using some wire I had back there to fasten the trunk down."

"Is Tina Sue . . . you know?" Grace said.

"Back there? Naw. I left here there a while, but when things got real bad back there, well, I ate her."

4

After a time, even Steve played out. Course, we had gotten most of his life story, and I guess maybe there wasn't much else to tell. The story wasn't exactly exemplary. I couldn't see it as a movie. He sang us a few of the songs he'd written. Nashville wasn't missing anything. Grace said it all sounded like "Home on the Range" to her, no matter what words he sang. He got quiet then, went into one of those artistic funks, no doubt. He made corners faster than ever and he wouldn't play the Sleepy LaBeef tape.

I had a hard time relaxing, way Steve was driving. And I was thinking about Crier and his dead eyeballs getting whipped by the wind. I knew it wasn't a thing to get on Crier's nerves, but it was damn sure giving mine a workout, and I didn't even have to look at him. Still, the thought of those dead eyeballs behind me . . .

When Steve had asked for that cigar, I had seen that there were some sunglasses in the glove box, and I got those out. They were neon yellow and had little bulldogs in the top corners of the frames and the dogs had black BB eyes that rolled around at the slightest movement. It wasn't exactly what I was looking for, but it was something.

I handed them back to Bob and told him what I

321

wanted, and he put them on Crier. It helped. Crier even looked alive. He appeared to be nothing more than an excessively cool dude with his dick in his pocket.

Course, a little later in the day he started to bloat up and stink a little, and I couldn't think of anything to help that. We had to pull over and put him in the trunk, sunglasses and all. Steve fussed about this, because he had to work at unwiring the lid, but he did it. I think he was afraid if he didn't, Grace would kick him in the balls. She had that look.

We got Crier dumped in the back without his dick falling out of his pocket, got him wired in, and we were off. It seemed strange not to have the old boy with us, after all we had been through, but it did smell a mite fresher, especially to Bob and Grace.

It got darker and darker and pretty soon we got to that stuff Grace told us about. Storms whipped posters and popcorn sacks and the like every which way. The moon looked even more false than usual and it shone like a projector light through the trees, hitting the strips of film that twisted and twined there. Film ghosts were no longer reflected in the mirror and the windows. The highway was full of them: cowboys with six-shooters, knights with swords and lances, apes and madmen, giant stalking machines from *War of the Worlds*, the smiling Brady Bunch. We drove through them all as if they were mist.

Film strips crawled onto the highway and made smashed cellophane sounds beneath our tires.

When Steve got tired, we pulled over and I got behind the wheel. I drove until I couldn't, then I swapped with Bob who drove until he had to swap with Grace.

When it got back around to me, the gas gauge showed a quarter tank.

5

Daylight, and things looked a little better. No ghosts melting through the car, and no film crawling. A little storm activity, but nothing special. The sun looked worse than ever, like a pie pan spray-painted gold.

The trees were rubbery-looking and the ground reminded me of Styrofoam. The fruit we found to eat was shriveled and bitter to the taste. Everything around us looked a little cheap and off center, like the way it is when you make a real close examination of what you bought at a thrift sale.

We found a few chocolate almonds lying about and some soft drink puddles, so I knew we were getting close to the highway's end; the place Popalong had told Grace about. It struck me that Steve ought to know what he was in for. All he knew was that he was giving us a ride to the end of the highway. He didn't know we had some idea what was there, and he didn't know what we had in mind.

Steve had a mirror in his glove box, one of those kinds with the props behind it, and he had that and his pocket knife and a little kit with a tiny pair of scissors and a toenail clipper in it, and he was working on his whiskers. It made me hurt to watch him.

"Who you cleaning up for?" Bob asked him.

"Myself. I never could stand whiskers. I still don't look so good when I finish, since I can't get close enough, but it beats looking like you boys."

"I think we ought to explain something to you," I said.

"About what?" Steve said. He finished up and folded the mirror stand and put it and the kit in the glove box.

"About the end of the road," Grace said.

Steve leaned on the car and got what was left of his cigar out of his pocket. When it died out he hadn't relit it. He didn't light it now. He put it in his mouth and rolled it from one side to the other.

"We kind of know what's at the end," Grace said. "We've got an idea what we're going to do there." And she told Steve a condensed version of the story she told us. When she finished Steve quit moving his cigar. He took it out of his mouth and put it in his pocket. I couldn't help but think of Crier's dick.

"Sounds like you folks are going to get killed, is what it sounds like to me," Steve said.

"We don't expect you to go if you don't want," Grace said. "We'd appreciate your carrying us as far as you can, though."

"What if I said this was as far as I was going?" Steve said.

"That would be it then," Grace said.

"You'd walk through this stuff at night?"

"I would," Grace said.

"I'm not crazy about that part," Bob said. "I might even be talked out of it. I might even ride back with you the other way."

"You?" Steve asked me.

"All that matters right now," I said, "is are you going to the end or not. If you go back, you know what you've got."

"Sounds like I have a pretty good idea of what I'm gonna get if I go forward too." He looked hard at me. "Tell you what else, I think if I go back and Bob here goes with me, you'll go too. You don't look like any kind of hero to me. The gal here will keep walking, I can tell that. She doesn't think she needs much of anybody."

"That's not true," Grace said. "I can use all the help I can get. But if I don't get it, I'm going on."

"I'm no knight in white armor, lady," Steve said.

"Never crossed my mind you might be."

Steve smiled and put the cigar back in his mouth. He still didn't light it.

"All right, I'll haul you on, but maybe we ought to come up with a game plan. And first thing to start with is getting rid of the old boy in the trunk. He's starting to stink all the way from the back. It bothers my driving. I don't figure we'll have to eat him, with all this fruit and stuff out there, so let's get shed of him."

6

I got Crier's legs and Bob got him by the shoulders and we lifted him out of the Plymouth's trunk. He had swollen up a bit, and he really did stink.

We carried him over to the side of the road and put him down. I said, "I told him I wouldn't do this. I promised I'd get him to the end of the highway."

"Me too," Bob said, "but a person doesn't always get what they want, and you can't always keep your promise. Besides, if he'd known he was gonna stink like this, maybe he wouldn't have asked it of us."

Crier's dick had come out of his pocket and rolled up next to the spare, and since it was past the handling stage, and looked like a big jalapeño going to rot, Steve got a couple of sticks and scissored it out of there and carried it over and dropped it next to Crier.

"We ought to bury him," I said.

"Something will just dig him up," Steve said. "And this ground isn't any kind of ground for digging. But if you want, there's a worn-down spot over there and we can throw him off in that, maybe find something to cover him up, for all that amounts to."

We carried Crier over to the worn-down spot and put

him in it. He was stiff as a tire iron and lay there in the indentation as if he had fallen sideways out of a chair and frozen. Steve kicked the dick on over and into the hole and we got some brush and limbs and the few rocks we could find, and put them on top of him. We got everything covered but the bottom of his shoes. Our hands sure did smell bad.

We got in the car and drove away. Bob said, "I guess we could have at least put his dick in his pocket."

7

All over the place were these TVs and antennas and papers, and the darker it got the more those papers came and swirled and collected in the trees with the film, which was now thicker than the leaves.

Over to the right, just above the trees, you could see what looked like an inverted tornado dipping down, and all of its swirls were filled with posters and bags and stuff. And on the ground were lots of TV sets. It was like we were getting closer to the garbage dump.

It got darker and we kept driving, but now we had all the windows up because the paper storm had really gotten bad, and it somehow seemed safer from the ghosts that way, even if they weren't really dangerous.

All along the highway were people impaled on antennas, and the headlights would wink at the metal between their legs, and sometimes you could see blood and shit on the antennas. But more often you didn't, and as we looked closer, we saw why. There were few real people impaled. Most of what was there were dummies.

A thing I couldn't put a name to began to move in the back of my mind, but whatever was crawling back there went away when I saw what was in the distance.

The Orbit, its tall tin fence sparkling in the lightning flashes like a woman's wedding band catching the fire from a candlelight dinner.

From that distance, it looked like the crumbled remains of an old castle, way the shadows fell over and moved around on it, way the lightning popped and fizzled overhead, way the paper and posters swirled around and into it like ghosts heading home.

We pulled off the road near one of the impaled dummies, turned off the lights, and talked about it.

"Seems to me," Steve said, "driving on in isn't the answer, not if it's like you say it is, Grace."

"That's how he said it was, though he called it a kind of church."

"This is your show," Bob said. "What do you want to do? Tell us, and then I'll tell you if I'll do it."

"Wait until morning. Let me sleep on it. Turn the car around and pull off near the trees on the other side, and take turns at watch. That way nobody comes up on us. In the morning I'll know what to do."

"In other words," Bob said, "you'll be ready to do something even if it's wrong?"

"Pretty much," Grace said. "One of you guys take first watch." She leaned against her side of the car and closed her eyes and went to sleep, or pretended to.

"Yes, Commandant," Bob said.

"Once they got the right to vote, it's been downhill ever since," Steve said.

"I heard that," Grace said.

We guys tried to talk for a while, but we didn't really have anything to talk about. We knew Steve's life story. I took the first watch and we took turns doing that all night, and the last watch was Grace's, I think, because I'd come awake from time to time and see who was on duty. Anyway, next thing I knew it was morning and Grace had the door open and was dumping some fruit in my lap.

It wasn't good fruit. It was kind of sour, but I ate it anyway, and lots of it. I looked at the morning and thought it looked pretty fresh, more real than usual. The papers had stopped swirling and the film lay in the trees and on the ground like burnt bacon.

Grace, Bob and Steve were over by one of the dummies and Steve had a stick and was poking it. I got out of the car and went over there.

Bob said, "Popalong sure works to make things look scary. Speaking of scary, you look like hell."

"Thanks."

"We sort of got us a game plan," Steve said. "Or rather Grace has one."

"All right," I said, "let me hear it."

It wasn't complicated. It went like this. We'd wait until near dark, then start toward the Orbit, going along the edge of the jungle until we got around on the left-hand side of the place and could work around to the back, then climb up on the fence and have a look over. After that, we could play it by ear. Locate Sue Ellen, go in there and nab her and get out of there. As for Popalong, Grace said, "Don't worry about him none. I'll take care of him, come hell or high water."

Thing was, it was going to be night by the time we did what we wanted to do (provided we were able to do it), and coming back to the car was going to be some kind of dreadful, what with that blood-sucking film and those storms out there, not to mention the shadows and the ghosts which, though harmless, didn't do much for the disposition.

Still, it was the only plan we had, simple as it was.

We whiled away the day eating fruit, then when it

started getting windy and the sun started its plunge, we got to walking.

It turned out to be a longer hike than it looked like, and by the time we were at the edge of the Orbit, it was dark and the film was moving.

Steve had the scissors from his shaving kit, and he used that to do some snipping, but we finally had to get away from the jungle, and more out in the clear, so as to stay ahead of the stuff.

There didn't seem to be anyone on sentry duty, and the closer we got the more dummies and real people there were on the antenna poles. The air was full of the odor of rotting bodies and spoiled candy and stale soft drinks.

We went around the edge of the fence and worked our way toward the back, and as we went, we could hear the sounds of television—laugh tracks and voices—and the thought of actually seeing Popalong began to get to me.

Around back, I got Grace up on my shoulders and she looked over the fence, sat there on my shoulders for a while, taking it in.

"Well," Bob said.

"I'll be goddamned," Grace said.

I put her down then and made Bob let me up on his shoulders. I was goddamned too.

What I saw was this vast circle of people gathering around this throne made of television sets, and on the throne was Popalong, the flickerings of some show or another throbbing on his face. And below him and to the left, on another throne of busted sets, was a young girl with her long hair loose. Sue Ellen, I figured.

At the bottom of the double throne were two men. They sat on televisions, well out in front of those behind them. They had ringside seats. I took them for two of the four thugs that had helped Popalong capture Grace and her friends.

But the thing that got to me were the people. You see, from where I was you could get a good view of that part of the lot, and after my eyes had adjusted and I'd taken in the scene, I began to realize that most of the people were pregnant women. There were a few men, but not many. Most of the crowd was not a crowd at all.

Dummies tied to antennas. Lobby cards of actors. Posters with pictures of men and women on them wrapped around stacked television sets. A skeleton here and there with clothes on, or a skull stuck on top of a speaker.

The truth was, Popalong didn't really have many followers. Perhaps he had exaggerated to Grace to sound impressive, or maybe many of them were decorating the poles along the way, or had been eaten.

Didn't his followers demand constant entertainment? What was *Father Knows Best* compared to a public burning? And even if that burning was filmed and shown again and again, could it suffice? New things needed to be filmed and shown so they could be made real. Then fresh realities had to be created. Time after time after time.

Popalong and his followers seemed to be killing themselves out of an audience. The harder Popalong worked for ratings, the fewer people he had to poll.

I got down and Bob and Steve had looks, then we huddled. Grace went over first and I followed. Then Bob. Bob got on my shoulders and gave Steve a hand over.

We began to work our way through the crowd of posters and dummies and skeletons and lobby cards, and sometimes when we came to a real person, they looked at us without curiosity if they looked at us at all; the real stuff was on the TV set.

Grace moved ahead of us, and came out at the front of the crowd and looked up at Popalong.

I saw that Sue Ellen (it had to be her) was dead. Had been for a while. Her face and hands were the color of pee-stained sheets. Her knucklebones punched out of her papery flesh like volcanic eruptions. Her eyes were holes filled with popcorn. One kernel dangled from her left socket like a booger in a nostril.

A tremor went up Grace's back. She yelled at Popalong, "Remember me?"

"It's like a movie," Popalong said. "You coming into my lair."

There was a surge of wind and a mass of paper and popcorn and soft drink slush blew through the drive-in and passed on.

When the wind was gone and the paper had quit rustling, Grace said, "You and this place look all worn out. Your church is light in the pews. I think you're nothing more than a walking TV set with a line of shit."

"It's good of you to come," Popalong said. "Of course, you know what comes next."

The two toughs got up and turned toward Grace. They didn't look as weak as the others. Better diet. More human flesh maybe.

"Good to see you boys," Grace said. "I think about you lots."

The one on Grace's left got to her first. He had a piece of glass wedged into a short stick and he tried to stab her in the stomach.

Before we could make any kind of move to help her, Grace sidestepped the glass, slapped the thug's hand down and kicked him between the eyes so hard his head went back more than his neck allowed. He folded up like an accordion at her feet.

The other tough bolted.

He was a good runner. We didn't chase him. He headed for the exit. He wouldn't last long out there. Not at night, not with the film crawling.

Popalong's followers seemed uncertain. This was the sort of thing they saw a lot of, but in this case it was short and sweet and not nearly melodramatic enough. They shuffled their feet. Maybe they wanted to see it on film.

If any of them had it in their heads to go for Grace, it was an idea that went away when she turned and glared at them.

Popalong's followers were now no more than a pack of pregnant women and skinny men, their brains no better than straw. They might as well have been the dummies that the sky kept raining.

We pushed to the front. I looked up at Popalong. A Western was playing on his face. Just as a Hollywood Indian took a bullet and fell off his horse, Popalong made the tube go black. "You're just a television set," I said. "We can turn you off anytime we want."

Grace grabbed one of the dummies and pulled at it. It came loose of the antenna that held it. She grabbed the antenna and pulled it out of the asphalt and stepped up on the base of the television throne and poked at Popalong with it.

"Come down so I can change your channels," she said. "Come down so I won't have to bring you down. I want to see you come down, King Popalong. Come on down where you belong."

"Stop it," Popalong said. "You fools are ruining things. I've got anything you want to see. There's not a show so exotic that I don't have it. Anything happens to me and you'll be back in darkness. You'll have to talk to entertain yourselves."

Grace poked him again. He stood up. She poked his knee and his knee buckled and he went down and tried to get up again, but the knee twisted under him and he came tumbling down the sets. As he went, he grabbed out and got hold of Sue Ellen's hand. She came off her throne and tumbled after him.

Popalong hit with a crunch and a smash of glass. Sue Ellen lay on top of him.

Popalong tried to get his hands underneath him. Steve went over and straddled him and pulled Sue Ellen off, then took the guns out of Popalong's holster and stepped back.

Popalong folded his knees under him and lifted his body upright. A chunk of glass fell out of his face. There was a gap dead center of the set and dozens of hairline fractures went out from it. The entire thing pulsed like an asshole straining to shit. Something sparked in the ruined depths, and the sparks jumped about like little red rats trying to abandon ship.

He tried to get up again, but his legs weren't having it. A rope of smoke twisted out of the hole in his face and rose up. The rabbit ears under his hat pushed it back and felt the air, as if searching for signals. But nothing was on that face but wreckage.

The rabbit ears went away and the hat fell back into place.

"It's all over now," Grace said, and started forward.

I grabbed her elbow. "That's enough."

"Not hardly," she said.

"Don't be his high priestess," I said. "You're giving him a TV or movie ending. Kind where the wronged person deals out revenge on the bad guy. He's too messed up to be a bad guy. He's pathetic. He's out of it, through. Don't martyr him for yourself and these people. It won't do a thing for Timothy or Sue Ellen."

"It's not like he's got anything left to hurt anyone with," Bob said.

"Guess you got two cents to put in on this, Steve," Grace said.

"It was me, I'd take him out. Hell, I'll shoot him for you if you like. It won't bother me none. But this is your show. You name the channel."

Grace looked at Popalong's ruptured face, at the scrawny body that held up the massive head, the black cowboy suit that hung off of him like a kid wearing daddy's clothes.

She went over and picked up Sue Ellen and walked away. Popcorn dribbled out of Sue Ellen's eye sockets, sprinkled the ground like snow.

Steve sighed. "This is kind of disappointing. Kind of like a cowboy movie without a final showdown, ain't it?"

"It's exactly like that," I said.

DISSOLVE TO:

Epilogue

We used some of the drier pieces of cardboard and paper we could find and built a mound and put Sue Ellen on it and covered her with some more pieces. Then Steve lit it with a match he'd found in one of the derelict cars, and after a while, most of Sue Ellen was cremated. What was left over we scooped up in Coke cups and took it off in the woods and tossed it around.

Popalong's dead bodyguard was hauled off during all the commotion by one of the drive-in people, and I guess he got eaten.

Next morning, we went to look for Crier's body. It was gone. Something had dug him out. Whatever it was got his dick too.

As for Popalong, in time he crawled back up that stack of TVs and found his place on the throne. He sat there with his tongue of blue and red wires hanging out and the inside of his face popping sparks and fizzling from time to time. But finally that quit.

He grew thin inside that cowboy suit, and when the flesh went away, there were no bones in him, just cable wires and rods of antenna held together with tightly wrapped film.

Steve brought his car into the drive-in, and he and Grace took up together and went to living out of it. I tell you, I never expected that to happen. Maybe all those bangs Grace got on the head had clouded her sense of judgment.

Bob and I built our place out of TV sets. Walls and ceiling. We used antenna pieces and part of an old car to make it work. In the mornings we wake up and watch Grace come out of the Plymouth and do her martial arts exercises. In the nude.

The bending over stuff is dynamite.

She's got a big round tummy now. She says I didn't pull out fast enough and the baby's mine. She says it's pretty far along, but isn't showing much because she's tall. Since I didn't eat the King's popcorn and neither did she, she thinks the baby has a good chance to be healthy. I don't know how I feel about that.

The other women have had their babies and—

Yes, I'm talking about you guys. But hold up, I'm almost through here. Just be polite and let me get through this.

—they look like the Popcorn King. Two bodies welded together, one on the other's shoulders, to make a single unit. Unlike the King, they are covered in eyes. The eyes look like the eyes that were on the corn the King puked up. Each eye blinks at a different time. I feel like I'm constantly receiving Morse code.

They're all sexless. I mean there's no equipment that I can see. Keeps from having to wipe a lot of asses. They came out of the cannon practically walking. They can put simple sentences together already. They're almost as tall as me. They like to listen to me read, and though they understand a lot of the words, a lot of sentences, I don't think they get the gist of it all—

Okay, Leroy. I take it back. You do understand. That's all for today, guys, girls, whatever. Go find a car to tear up. I was kidding about there being a test at the end of this. . . .

What test?

Forget it, Leroy. Bye now.

That was about all I had written. I'm back inside the hut now and I'm sitting here finishing this out as best I can, which is just as well. I'm running out of things to write with. I've looked everywhere, glove boxes, the concession stand over in B lot, you name it. I've written this in pen and pencil, crayon and eyeliner.

But it doesn't matter, I'm also running out of things to say. I guess I can mention that the mothers of those kids, or whatever they are, don't love them. But I'm not sure that's all their fault. How can they be mothers after all they've seen and done?

I see some of the drive-in people looking up at the corpse of Popalong, almost wistfully, I think. At night they wander about in the storms, nothing to do. They've forgotten how to talk to one another. It's a good thing those weird kids were born practically grown.

Sometimes I take the kids hunting with me. They chase down the game on foot. Bob says he thinks he saw one throw a stick without touching it the other day. Kid just willed it up and there it went, hit a rabbit in the back of the head and killed it.

Bob admits he saw this out of the corner of his eye, and it may not be like that, but I wouldn't be surprised.

Well, like I said we hunt a lot. Thought a better diet

might help the people here, help them get a better frame of mind. But all it does is help them get around faster.

Sometimes I think I'll start back down the highway, but I'd have to go on foot and I don't like the idea of those storms or that film out there at night. Still, I think about it. Shit Town might be a better life than this. Hell, getting back to Jungle Home wouldn't be too bad.

Let's see . . . Oh yeah, Grace has a shadow now, and Steve is starting to have one. Bob and I still don't. I'm not sure what this means, but it worries me a little, especially when I see Grace working out and popping the air with her punches, and right behind her, capering like a chimp, making fun of her moves, is her shadow. Maybe I'll stop getting up in the morning to watch her. That shadow takes the joy out of it.

Bob and I have talked about having the kids get some TV sets and start them stacking them, help us rebuild one of those pyramids Popalong had his followers burn down. If what Popalong says is true, we could go up there and have a look around.

But maybe that's not such a good idea. It's only in Hollywood movies that the afflicted are always able to get the nasty aliens and twist their tentacles behind their backs and make them return things to normal.

I figure if we go up there nothing will work out the way we want. We could get done to us what was done to Popalong, or worse. And unlike Popalong, it isn't something we'd like to happen.

It's hard to know what to do next. Life is like that Max Brand book the guy in Shit Town was talking about. There's always a couple of pages torn out, so you don't know how it's going to end.

Still, I'm a sucker for a happy ending. Hell, I used to believe in God and astrology. So I'm going to give myself a happy ending even if I don't get one in real life. The best ending that comes to mind is what that person wrote on the inside back cover of that book. It may not be the truth for any of us, but like the fella said, you can't really think of anything better than that.

So lie or not, here goes:

He rode off into the West and everything was okay.